Favell Lee Mortimer

Far off or Asia Described - With Anecdotes and Numerous

Illustrations

Part I

Favell Lee Mortimer

Far off or Asia Described - With Anecdotes and Numerous Illustrations
Part I

ISBN/EAN: 9783337279172

Printed in Europe, USA, Canada, Australia, Japan

Cover: Foto ©Andreas Hilbeck / pixelio.de

More available books at **www.hansebooks.com**

Esther, the little Jewess, saying "Jesus Christ is OUR Redeemer."

FAR OFF:

OR,

ASIA DESCRIBED.

WITH
ANECDOTES AND NUMEROUS ILLUSTRATIONS.

PART I.

BY
THE AUTHOR OF "THE PEEP OF DAY,"
ETC., ETC.

Thirty-fourth Thousand.

LONDON:
HATCHARDS, 187 PICCADILLY.
1869.

In the Frontispiece may be seen an English lady who went to live upon Mount Sion, to teach little Jewesses and little Mahomedans to know the Saviour. That lady has led three of her young scholars to a plain just beyond the gates of Jerusalem; and while two of them are playing together, she is listening to little Esther, a Jewess of eight years old. The child is fond of sitting by her friend, and of hearing about the Son of David. She has just been singing,

"Glory, honour, praise, and power,
Be unto the Lamb for ever,
Jesus Christ is our Redeemer,
Hallelujah, praise the Lord;"

and now she is saying, "Oh, ma'am, that's "sweet! Jesus Christ is *our* Redeemer, *our* "Redeemer: no *man* can redeem his brother, "no *money*,—nothing,—but only the precious "blood of Christ!"

PREFACE.

THIS little work pleads for the notice of parents and teachers on the same ground as its predecessor, "Near Home."

Its plea is not completeness, nor comprehensiveness, nor depth of research, nor splendour of description; but the very reverse,—its simple, superficial, desultory character, as better adapted to the volatile beings for whom it is designed.

Too long have their immortal minds been captivated by the adventures and achievements of knights and princesses, of fairies and magicians; it is time to excite their interest in real persons, and real events. In childhood that taste is formed which leads the youth to delight in novels and romances; a taste which has become so general, that every town has its circulating library, and every shelf in that library—its works of fiction.

While these fascinating inventions are in course of perusal, many a Bible is unopened, or, if opened, hastily skimmed; many a seat in church is unoccupied, or, if occupied, the service and the sermon disregarded—so intense is the sympathy of the novel reader with his hero, or his heroine.

And what is the effect of the perusal? Many a young mind, inflated with a desire for admiration and adventure, grows tired of home, impatient of restraint, indifferent to simple pleasures, and averse to sacred instructions. How important, therefore, early to endeavour to prevent a taste for FICTION, by cherishing a taste for FACTS!

But this is not the only aim of the present work; it seeks also to excite an interest in *those* facts which ought *most* to interest immortal beings—facts relative to souls, and their eternal happiness—to God, and His infinite glory.

THESE are the facts which engage the attention of the inhabitants of heaven. We know not whether the birth of princes, and the coronations of monarchs are noticed by the angelic hosts; but we do know that the repentance of a sinner, be he Hindoo or Hottentot, is celebrated by their melodious voices in rapturous symphonies.

Therefore "Far Off" desires to interest its little readers in the labours of missionaries,—men despised and maligned by the world, but honoured and beloved by the Saviour of the world. An account of the scenery and natives of various countries is calculated to prepare the young mind for reading with intelligence those little Missionary Magazines, which appear every month, written in so attractive a style, and adorned with such beautiful illustrations.* Parents have no longer reason to complain of the difficulty of finding sacred entertainment for their children on Sunday, for these pleasing messengers,—if carefully dealt out,—one or two on each Sabbath, would afford a never-failing supply.

To form great and good characters, the mind must be trained to delight in TRUTH,—not in comic rhymes, in sentimental tales, and sceptical poetry. The truths revealed in God's Holy Word should constitute the firm basis of education; and the works of Creation and Providence—the superstructure, while the Divine blessing can alone rear and cement the edifice.

Parents, train up your children to serve God, and to enjoy His presence for ever; and if there be amongst them—an EXTRAORDINARY child, train him up with extraordinary care, lest instead of doing extraordinary *good* he should

---

* The titles of some of the principal are,—

"Church Missionary Juvenile Instructor."

"Missionary Repository for Youth."

"Juvenile Missionary Magazine."

"Juvenile Missionary Herald."

"Children's Missionary Newspaper."

"Church Missionary Gleaner" (the last is suitable also for adults.)

"The Book and its Missions" (suitable only for adults, but abounding in anecdotes suitable to relate to children.)

do extraordinary *evil*, and be plunged into extraordinary misery.

> Train up—the child of imagination—not to dazzle, like Byron, but to enlighten, like Cowper:
>
> the child of wit—not to create profane mirth, like Voltaire, but to promote holy joy, like Bunyan:
>
> the child of reflection—not to weave dangerous sophistries, like Hume, but to wield powerful arguments, like Chalmers:
>
> the child of sagacity—not to gain advantages for himself, like Cromwell, but for his country, like Washington:
>
> the child of eloquence—not to astonish the multitude, like Sheridan, but to plead for the miserable, like Wilberforce:
>
> the child of ardour—not to be the herald of delusions, like Swedenborg, but to be the champion of truth, like Luther:
>
> the child of enterprise—not to devastate a Continent, like the Emperor Napoleon, but to scatter blessings over an Ocean, like the missionary Williams:—
>
> and if the child be a prince,—train him up not to reign in pomp and pride, like the fourteenth Louis, but to rule in the fear of God, like our own great ALFRED.

CONTENTS.

₊ *In consequence of the information added to this volume respecting Hindostan, Thibet, and Japan, it has been found needful to transfer the account of Australia to the Second Part of "Far Off."*

LIST OF ILLUSTRATIONS.

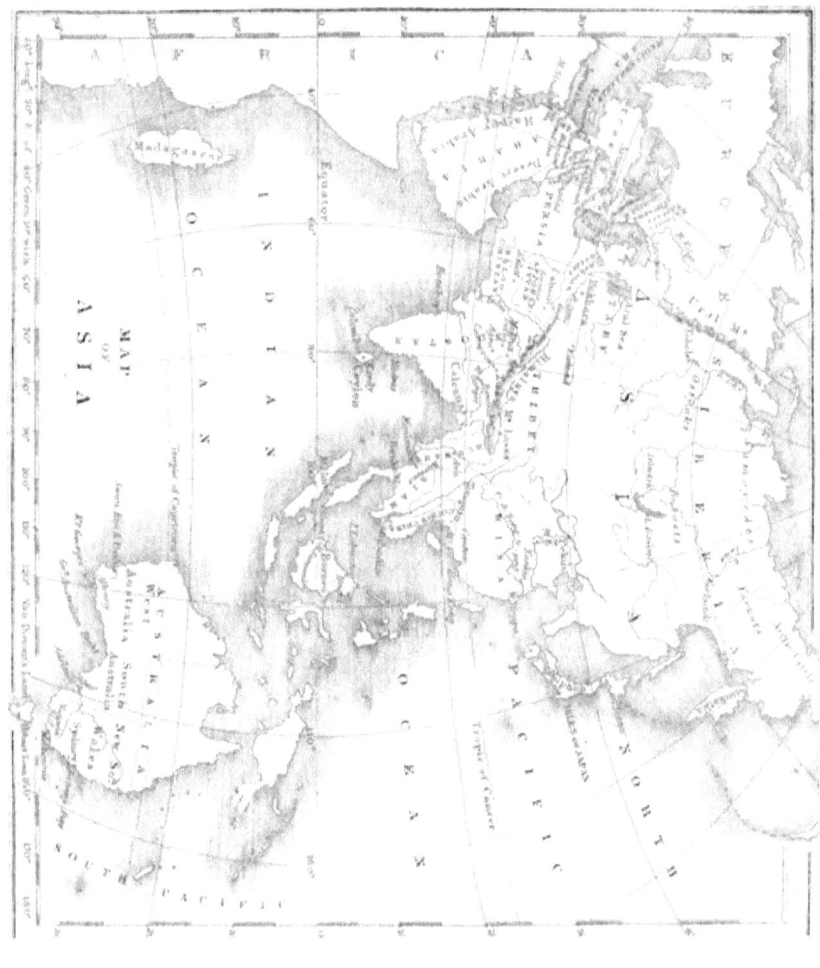

FAR OFF.

PART I.

ASIA.

Of the four quarters of the world—Asia is the most glorious.

There the first man was created.

There the Son of God became a man.

There the apostles first preached.

There nearly the whole Bible was written.

Yet now there are very few Christians in Asia : compared with the number of heathens.

There are more people in Asia than in any other quarter of the globe.

THE HOLY LAND.

Of all the countries in the world which would you rather see ?

Would it not be the land where Jesus lived ?

He was the Son of God : He loved us and died for us.

What is the land called where He lived? Canaan was once its name: but now Palestine, or the Holy Land.

Who lives there now?

Alas! alas! The Jews who once lived there are cast out of it. There are some Jews there still; but the Turks are the lords over the land. You know the Turks believe in Mahomet.

What place in the Holy Land do you wish most to visit?

Some children will reply, Bethlehem, because Jesus was born there: another will answer, Nazareth, because Jesus was brought up there; and another will say "Jerusalem," because He died there.

I will take you first to Bethlehem.

BETHLEHEM.

A good minister visited this place, accompanied by a train of servants, and camels, and asses.

It is not easy to travel in Palestine, for wheels are never seen there, because the paths are too steep, and rough, and narrow for carriages.

Bethlehem is on a steep hill, and a white road of chalk leads up to the gate. The traveller found the streets narrow, dark, and dirty. He lodged in a convent kept by Spanish monks. He was shown into a large room with carpets and cushions on the floor. There he was to sleep. He was led up to the roof of the house to see the prospect. He looked, and beheld the fields below where the shepherds once watched their flocks by night : and far off he saw the rocky mountains where David once hid himself from Saul.

But the monks soon showed him a more curious sight. They took him into their church, and then down some narrow stone steps into a round room beneath. "Here," said they, "Jesus was born." The floor was of white marble, and silver lamps were burning in it. In one corner, close to the wall, was a marble trough, lined with blue satin. "There," said the monks, "is the manger where Jesus was laid." "Ah!" thought the traveller, "it was not in such a manger that my Saviour rested his infant head ; but in a far meaner place."

These monks have an image of a baby, which they call Jesus. On Christmas-day they dress it in swaddling-clothes and lay it in the manger, and then fall down and worship it.

The next day, as the traveller was ready to mount his camel, the people of Bethlehem came with little articles which they had made. But he would not buy them, because they were images of the Virgin Mary and her holy child, and little white crosses of mother-o'-pearl. They were very pretty: but they were idols, and God hates idols.

JERUSALEM.

Here our Lord was crucified.

Is there any child who does not wish to hear about it?

The children of Jerusalem once loved the Lord, and sung His praises in the temple. Their young voices pleased their Saviour, though not half so sweet as angels' songs.

Which is the place where the temple stood?

It is the Mount Moriah. There is a splendid building now on that Mount.

Is it the temple? Oh, no, that was burned many hundreds of years ago. It is the Mosque of Omar; it is the most magnificent mosque in all the world. How sad to think that Mahomedans should worship now in the very spot where once the Son of God taught the people. No Jew, no Christian may go into that mosque. The Turks stand near the gate to keep off both Jews and Christians.

Every Friday evening a very touching scene takes place near this mosque. There are some large old stones there, and the Jews say they are part of their old temple wall: so they come at the beginning of their Sabbath (which is on Friday evening) and sit in a row opposite the stones. There they read their Hebrew Old Testaments, then kneel low in the dust, and repeat their prayers with their mouths *close* to the old stones: because they think that all prayers whispered between the cracks and crevices of these stones will be heard by God. Some Jewesses come, wrapped from head to foot in long white veils, and they gently moan and softly sigh over Jerusalem in ruins.

What Jesus said has come to pass, "Behold, your house is left unto you desolate." The *thought* of this sad day made Jesus weep, and now the *sight* of it makes the Jews weep.

But there is a place still dearer to our hearts than Mount Moriah. It is Calvary. There is a church on Calvary: but such a church! a church full of images and crosses. Roman Catholics worship there—and Greeks too: and they often fight in it, for they hate one another, and have fierce quarrels. That Church is called "The Church of the Holy Sepulchre." It is pretended that Christ's tomb or sepulchre is in it. Turks stand at the door and make Christians pay money before they will let them in.

When they enter, what do they see?

In one corner a stone seat. "There," say the monks, "Jesus sat when He was crowned

with thorns." In another part there is a stone
pillar. "There," say the monks, "He was
scourged." There is a high place in the middle
of the church with stairs leading up to it.

Church of the Holy Sepulchre.

When you stand there the monks say, "This is
the top of Calvary, where the cross stood." But
we know that the monks do not speak the
truth, for the Romans destroyed Jerusalem soon
after Christ's crucifixion, and no one knows the
very place where He suffered.

On Good Friday the monks carry all round
the church an image of the Saviour as large as
life, and they fasten it upon a cross, and take it
down again, and put it in the sepulchre, and
they take it out again on Easter Sunday. How

foolish and how wrong are these customs! It
was not in this way the apostles showed their
love to Christ, but by preaching His word.

Mount Zion is the place where David brought
the ark with songs and music. On that Mount
there is a church where the Gospel is preached
and prayers are offered up in Hebrew (the Jew's
language.) The minister is called the Bishop of
Jerusalem. He is a Protestant. A few Jews
come to the church at Mount Zion, and some
have believed in the Lord Jesus.

And there is a school there where little Jews
and Jewesses, and little Mahomedans sit side by
side, while a Christian lady teaches them about
Jesus. In the evening, after school, she takes
them out to play on the green grass near the
city. A little Jewess once much pleased this
kind teacher, as she was sitting on a stone looking at the children playing. Little Esther
repeated the verse,—

> Glory, honour, praise, and power,
> Be unto the Lamb for ever ;
> Jesus Christ is our Redeemer.
> Hallelujah, praise the Lord !

And then she said very earnestly, " Oh, ma'am,
how sweet to think that Jesus is *our* Redeemer !
No *man* can redeem his brother : no money—
no money can do it—only the precious blood
of Jesus Christ." Little Esther seemed as if

she loved Jesus, as those children did who sang
His praises in the temple so many years ago.

But there is another place—very sad but very
sweet—where you must come. Go down that
valley—cross that small stream—(there is a
narrow bridge)—see those low stone walls—
enter: it is the Garden of Gethsemane. Eight
aged olive-trees are still standing there; but
Jesus comes there no more with His beloved
disciples. What a night was that when He
wept and prayed—when the angel comforted
Him—and Judas betrayed Him!

The mountain just above Gethsemane is the
Mount of Olives. Beautiful olive-trees are
growing there still. There is a winding path
leading to the top. The Saviour trod upon that
Mount just before He was caught up into
heaven. His feet shall stand there again, and
every eye shall see the Saviour in His glory.
But will every eye be glad to see Him ?

O no; there will be bitter tears then flowing
from many eyes.

And what kind of a city is Jerusalem ?

It is a sad and silent city. The houses are dark
and dirty, the streets are narrow, and the pavement rough. There are a great many very old
Jews there. Jews come from all countries when
they are old to Jerusalem, that they may die and
be buried there. Their reason is that they think

Mount of Olives.

that all Jews who are buried in their burial-
ground at Jerusalem will be raised *first* at the
last day, and will be happy for ever. Most of the
old Jews are very poor : though money is sent
to them every year from the Jews in Europe.

There are also a great many sick Jews in Jerusalem, because it is such an unhealthy place.
The water in the wells and pools gets very bad
in summer, and gives the ague and even the
plague. Good English Christians have sent a
doctor to Jerusalem to cure the poor sick people.
One little girl of eleven years old came among
the rest—all in rags and with bare feet : she was
an orphan, and she lived with a Jewish washer-
woman. The doctor went to see the child in
her home. Where was it ? It was near the

mosque, and the way to it was down a narrow,
dark passage, leading to a small close yard.
The old woman lived in one room with her
grandchildren and the orphan : there was a divan
at each end, that is, the floor was raised for
people to sleep on. The orphan was not allowed
to sleep on the divans, but she had a heap of
rags for her bed in another part. The child's
eyes glistened with delight at the sight of her
kind friend the doctor. He asked her whether
she went to school. This question made the
whole family laugh : for no one in Jerusalem
teaches girls to read except the kind Christian
lady I told you of.

THE DEAD SEA.

The most gloomy and horrible place in the
Holy Land is the Dead Sea. In that place there
once stood four wicked cities, and God destroyed
them with fire and brimstone.

You have heard of Sodom and Gomorrah.

A clergyman who went to visit the Dead Sea
rode on horseback, and was accompanied by
men to guard him on the way, as there are
robbers hid among the rocks. He took some of
the water of the Dead Sea in his mouth, that he
might taste it, and he found it salt and bitter ;

but he would not swallow it, nor would he bathe in it.

He went next to look at the river Jordan. How different a place from the dreary, desolate Dead Sea! Beautiful trees grow on the banks, and the ends of the branches dip into the stream. The minister chose a part quite covered with branches and bathed there, and as the waters went over his head he thought, "My Saviour was baptized in this river." But he did not think (as many pilgrims do who come here every year) that his sins were washed away by the water: no, he well knew that Christ's blood alone cleanses from sin. There is a place where the Roman Catholics bathe, and another where the Greeks bathe every year: they would not on any account bathe in the same part, because they disagree so much.

After drinking some of the sweet soft water of Jordan, the minister travelled from Jericho to Jerusalem. He went the very same way that the good Samaritan travelled, who once found a poor Jew lying half killed by thieves. Even to this day thieves often attack travellers in these parts; because the way is so lonely, and so rugged, and so full of places where thieves can hide themselves.

A horse must be a very good climber to carry a traveller along the steep, rough, and narrow paths; and a traveller must be a bold man to venture to go to the edge of the precipices, and near the robbers' caves.

SAMARIA.

In the midst of Palestine is the well where the Lord spoke so kindly to the woman of Samaria. In the midst of a beautiful valley there is a heap of rough stones: underneath is the well. But it is not easy to drink water out of this well. For the stone on the top is so heavy, that it requires many people to remove it; and then the well is deep, and a very long rope is necessary to reach the water. The clergyman (of whom I have spoken so often) had nothing to draw with; therefore, even if he could have removed the stone, he could not have drunk of the water. The water must be very cool and refreshing, because it lies so far away from the heat. That was the reason the Samaritan woman came so far to draw it: for there were other streams nearer the city, but there was no water like the water of Jacob's well.

The city where that woman lived was called Sychar. It is still to be seen, and it is still full of people. You remember that the men of that city listened to the words of Jesus, and perhaps that is the reason it has not been destroyed.

The country around is the most fruitful in all Canaan; there are such gardens of melons and cucumbers, and such groves of mulberry-trees.

GALILEE.

How different from Sychar is Capernaum! That was the city where Jesus lived for a long while, where He preached and did miracles. It was on the borders of the lake of Gennesareth. The traveller inquired of the people near the lake, where Capernaum once stood; but no one knew of such a place: it is utterly destroyed. Jesus once said, " Woe unto Capernaum." Why? Because it repented not.

The lake of Gennesareth looked smooth as glass when the traveller saw it; but he heard that dreadful storms sometimes ruffled those smooth waters. It was a sweet and lovely spot; not gloomy and horrible, like the Dead Sea. The shepherds were there leading their flocks among the green hills, where once the multitude sat down while Jesus fed them.

Not very far off is the city where Jesus lived when He was a boy.

NAZARETH.—All around are rugged, rocky hills. In old times it was considered a wicked city; perhaps it got this bad name from wicked

people coming here to hide themselves: and it
seems just fit for a hiding-place. From the top
of one of the high crags the Nazarenes once
attempted to hurl the blessed Saviour.

There is a Roman Catholic convent there,
where the minister lodged. He was much dis-
turbed all day by the noise in the town; not the
noise of carts and wagons, for there are none
in Canaan, but of screaming children, braying
asses, and grunting camels. One of his servants came to him complaining that he had lost
his purse with all his wages. He had left it in
his cell, and when he came back it was gone.
Who could have taken it? It was clear one of
the servants of the convent must have stolen it,
for one of them had the key of the room. The
travellers went to the judge of the town to complain; but the judge, who was a Turk, was
asleep, and no one was allowed to awake him.
In the evening, when he did awake, he would
not see justice done, because he said he had
nothing to do with the servants at the convent,
as they were Christians. Nazareth, you see, is
still a wicked city, where robbery is committed
and not punished.

There is much to make the traveller sad as he
wanders about the Holy Land.

That land was once *fruitful*, but now it is
barren. It is not surprising that no one plants

and sows in the fields, because the Turks would take away the harvest.

Once it was a *peaceful* land, but now there are so many enemies that every man carries a gun to defend himself.

Once it was a *holy* land, but now Mahomet is honoured, and not the God of Israel.

When shall it again be fruitful, and peaceful, and holy? When the Jews shall repent of their sins and turn to the Lord. Then, says the prophet Ezekiel (xxxvi. 35), "They shall say, This land that was desolate is become like the garden of Eden."*

SYRIA.

THOSE who love the Holy Land will like to hear about Syria also: for Abraham lived there before he came into Canaan. Therefore the Israelites were taught to say, when they offered a basket of fruit to God, "A Syrian was my father." It was a heathen land in old times; and it is now a Mahomedan land; though there are a few Christians there, but very ignorant Christians, who know nothing of the Bible.

* Taken chiefly from "A Pastor's Memorial," by the Rev. George Fisk; a work of the deepest interest, abounding in rich descriptions, striking narratives, and touching reflections.

Syria is a beautiful land, and famous for its grand mountains, called Lebanon. The same clergyman who travelled through the Holy Land went to Lebanon also. He had to climb up very steep places on horseback, and slide down some, as slanting as the roof of a house. But the Syrian horses are very sure-footed. It is the custom for the colts from a month old to follow their mothers; and so when a rider mounts the back of the colt's mother, the young creature follows, and it learns to scramble up steep places, and to slide down: even through the towns the colt trots after its mother, and soon becomes accustomed to all kinds of sights and sounds: so that Syrian horses neither shy nor stumble.

The traveller was much surprised at the dress of the women of Lebanon: for on their heads they wear silver horns sticking out from under their veils, the strangest head-dress that can be imagined.

There are sweet flowers growing on the sides of Lebanon; but at the top there are ice and snow.

The traveller ate some ice, and gave some to the horses; and the poor beasts devoured it eagerly, and seemed quite refreshed by their cold meal.

The snow of Lebanon is spoken of in the Bible as very pure and refreshing. " Will a man leave the snow of Lebanon which cometh from the rock of the field?"—Jer. xviii. 14.

Head-dress of Druse women.

The traveller earnestly desired to behold the cedars of Lebanon: for a great deal is said about them in the Bible; indeed the temple of Solomon was built of those cedars. It was not easy to get close to them; for there were craggy rocks all round: but at last the traveller reached them, and stood beneath their shade. There were twelve very large old trees, and their boughs met at the top, and kept off the heat of the sun. These trees might be compared to holy men, grown old in the service of God: for this is God's promise to his servants,—"The righteous shall flourish like the palm-tree: he

PT. I.   C

shall grow like a cedar in Lebanon."—Ps xcii. 12.

Cedars of Lebanon.

DAMASCUS.

This is the capital of Syria.

It is perhaps the most ancient city in the world. Even in the time of Abraham, Damascus was a city; for his servant Eliezer came from it.

But Damascus is most famous on account of a great event which once happened near it. A man going towards that city suddenly saw in the heavens a light brighter than the sun, and heard a voice from on high, calling him by his name. Beautiful as the city was, he saw not its beauty as he entered it, for he had been struck blind by the great light. That man was the great apostle Paul.

Who can help thinking of him among the gardens of fruit-trees surrounding Damascus?

The damask rose is one of the beauties of Damascus. There is one spot quite covered with this lovely red rose.

I will now give an account of a visit a stranger paid to a rich man in Damascus. He went through dull and narrow streets, with no windows looking into the streets. He stopped before a low door, and was shown into a large court behind the house. There was a fountain in the midst of the court, and flower-pots all round. The visitor was then led into a room with a marble floor, but with no furniture except scarlet cushions. To refresh him after his journey, he was taken to the bath. There a man covered him with a lather of soap and water, then dashed a quantity of hot water over him, and then rubbed him till he was quite dry and warm.

When he came out of the bath, two servants brought him some sherbet. It is a cooling drink, made of lemon-juice and grape-juice mixed with water.

The master of the house received the stranger very politely: he not only shook hands with

him, but afterwards he kissed his own hand, as
a mark of respect to his guest. The servants
often kissed the visitor's hand.

The dinner lasted a long while, for only one
dish was brought up at a time. Of course there
were no ladies at the dinner, for in Mahomedan
countries they are always hidden. There were
two lads there, who were nephews of the master
of the house; and the visitor was much surprised to observe that they did not sit down to
dinner with the company; but that they stood
near their uncle, directing the servants what to
bring him; and now and then presenting a cup
of wine to him or his guests. But it is the custom in Syria for young people to wait upon their
elders; however, they may speak to the company while they are waiting upon them.

Damascus used to be famous for its swords;
but now the principal things made there are
stuffs embroidered with silver, and boxes of
curious woods, as well as red and yellow slippers. The Syrians always wear yellow slippers,
and when they walk out they put on red slippers
over the yellow. If you want to buy any of the
curious works of Damascus, you must go to the
bazaars in the middle of the town; there the
sellers sit as in a market-place, and display their
goods.

SCHOOLS.—It is not the custom in Syria for

girls to learn to read. But a few years ago, a good Syrian, named Assaad, opened a school for little girls as well as for boys.

It was easy to get the little boys to come; but the mothers did not like to send their little girls. They laughed, and said, "Who ever heard of a girl going to school? Girls need not learn to read." The first girl who attended Assaad's school was named Angoul, which means, "Angel." Where is the child that deserves such a name? Nowhere; for "there is none righteous, no, not one." Angoul belonged not to Mahomedan parents, but to those called Christians; yet the Christians in Syria are almost as ignorant as heathens.

Angoul had been taught to spin silk; for her father had a garden of mulberry-trees, and a quantity of silk-worms. She was of so much use in spinning, that her mother did not like to spare her: but the little maid promised, that if she might go to school, she would spin faster than ever when she came home. How happy she was when she obtained leave to go! See her when the sun has just risen, about six o'clock, tripping to school. She is twelve years old. Her eyes are dark, but her hair is light. Angoul has not been scorched by the sun, like many Syrian girls, because she has sat in-doors at her wheel during the heat of the day. She

is dressed in a loose red gown, and scarlet cap
with a yellow handkerchief twisted round it like
a turban.

At school Angoul is very attentive, both while
she is reading in her Testament, and while she
is writing on her tin slate with a reed dipped in
ink.   She returns home at noon through the
burning sun, and comes to school again to stay
till five.   Then it is cool and pleasant, and Angoul spins by her mother's side in the lovely
garden of fruit-trees before the house.   Has she
not learned to sing many a sweet verse about the
garden above, and the heavenly Husbandman ?
As she watches the budding vine, she can think
now of Him who said, " I am the true vine."
As she sits beneath the olive-tree, she can call
to mind the words, "I am like a green olive-
tree in the house of my God."   Angoul is growing like an angel, if she takes delight in medi-
tating on the word of God.*

ARABIA.

THIS is the land in which the Israelites wandered for forty years.   You have heard what a
dry, dreary, desert place the wilderness was.
There is still a wilderness in Arabia ; and there

* Extracted chiefly from the Rev. George Fisk's " Pastor's
Memorial " and Kinnear's Travels.

are still wanderers in it; not Israelites, but Arabs. The men live in tents, and go from place to place with their large flocks of sheep and goats. But there are other Arabs who live in towns as we do.

Do you know who is the father of the Arabs?

The same man who is the father of the Jews.

What, was Abraham their father?

Yes, he was.

Do you remember Abraham's ungodly son Ishmael?

He was cast out of his father's house for mocking his little brother Isaac, and he went into Arabia.

And what sort of people are the Arabs?

Wild and fierce people.

Travellers are afraid of passing through Arabia, lest the Arabs should rob and murder them; and no one has ever been able to conquer the Arabs. The Arabs are very proud, and will not bear the least affront. Sometimes one man says to another, "The wrong side of your turban is out." This speech is considered an affront never to be forgotten. The Arabs are so unforgiving and revengeful that they will seek to kill a man year after year. One man was observed to carry about a small dagger. He said his reason was, he was hoping some day to meet his enemy and kill him.

Of what religion are this revengeful people? The Mahomedan.

Mahomed was an Arab. It is thought a great honour to be descended from him. Those men who say Mahomed is their father wear a green turban, and very proud they are of their green turbans, even though they may only be beggars.

Arab Tent.

THE ARABIAN WOMEN.—They are shut up like the women in Syria when they live in towns, but the women who live in tents are obliged to walk about; therefore they wear a thick veil over their face, with small holes for their eyes to peep out.

The poor women wear a long shirt of white or

blue; but the rich woman wrap themselves in magnificent shawls. To make themselves handsome, they blacken their eyelids, paint their nails red, and wear gold rings in their ears and noses. They delight in fine furniture. A room lined with looking-glasses, and with a ceiling of looking-glasses, is thought charming.

ARAB TENTS.—They are black, being made of the hair of black goats. Some of them are so large that they are divided into three rooms, one for the cattle, one for the men, and one for the women.

ARAB CUSTOMS.—The Arabs sit on the ground, resting on their heels, and for tables they have low stools. A large dish of rice and minced mutton is placed on the table, and immediately every hand is thrust into it; and in a moment it is empty. Then another dish is brought, and another; and sometimes fourteen dishes of rice, one after the other, till all the company are satisfied. They eat very fast and each retires from dinner as soon as he likes, without waiting for the rest. After dinner they drink water, and a small cup of coffee without milk or sugar. Then they smoke for many hours.

The Arabs do not indulge in eating or drinking too much, and this is one of the best parts of their character.

The three Evils of Arabia.

The first evil is want of water. There is no river in Arabia : and the small streams are often dried up by the heat.

The second evil is many locusts, which come in countless swarms and devour every green thing.

The third evil is the burning **winds**. When a traveller feels it coming, he throws himself on the ground, covering his face with his cloak lest the hot sand should be blown up his nostrils. Sometimes the men and horses are choked by this sand.

These are the three great evils ; but there is a still greater—the religion of Mahomed : for this injures the soul ; the other evils only hurt the body.

The three Animals of Arabia.

The animals for which Arabia is famous are animals to ride **upon**.

Two of them are often seen in England ; but the third animal is never used in England. These three animals are the ass, the horse, and the camel. Most English boys have ridden upon an ass. In Arabia the ass is a handsome and spirited creature. The horse is strong and swift and yet obedient and gentle. The camel is just

suited to Arabia. His feet are fit to tread upon
the burning sands ; because the soles are more
like india-rubber than like flesh; his hard mouth,
lined with horn, is not hurt by the prickly plants
of the desert ; and his hump, full of fat, is as
good to him as a bag of provisions : for on a
journey the fat helps to support him and
enables him to do with very little food. Besides
all this, his inside is so made that he can live
without water for three days.

A dromedary is a swifter kind of camel, and
is just as much superior to a camel as a riding-
horse is to a cart-horse.

The three Productions of Arabia.

These are coffee, dates, and gums.

For these Arabia is famous.

The coffee plants are shrubs. The hills are
covered with them ; the white blossoms look
beautiful among the dark green leaves, and so
do the red berries.

The dates grow on the palm-trees ; and they
are the chief food of the Arabs. The Arabs
despise those countries where there are no dates.
They say, "How can people live without dates?"

There are various sweet-smelling gums that
flow from Arabian trees.

The three Parts of Arabia.

You see from what I have just said that there are plants and trees in Arabia. Then it is clear that the whole land is not a desert. No, it is not; there is only a part called Desert Arabia; that is on the north. There is a part in the middle almost as bad called Stony Arabia, yet some sweet plants grow there; but there is a part in the south called Happy Arabia, where grow abundance of fragrant spices, and of well-flavoured coffee.

The three Cities of Arabia.

Arabia has long been famous for three cities, called Mecca, Medina, and Mocha.

Mecca is considered the holiest city in the world. And why? Because the false prophet Mahomed was born there. On that account Mahomedans come from all parts of the world to worship in the great temple there. Sometimes Mecca is as full of people as a hive is full of bees.

Of all the cities in the East, Mecca is the gayest, because the houses have windows looking into the streets. In these houses are lodgings for the pilgrims.

And what is it the pilgrims worship?

A great black stone which they say the angel
Gabriel brought down from heaven as a founda-
tion for Mahomed's house. They kiss it seven
times, and after each kiss they walk round it.

Mahomed.

Then they bathe in a well, which they say is
the well the angel showed to Hagar in the
desert, and they think the water of this well
can wash away all their sins. Alas! they know
not of the blood which can wash away *all* sin.

Medina contains the tomb of Mahomed : yet it
is not thought so much of as Mecca. Perhaps

the Mahomedans do not like to be reminded that Mahomed died like any other man, and never rose again.

Mocha.—This city is in a part whence very fine coffee is sent to Europe.

Travels in the Desert.

Of all places in Arabia, which would you desire most to see: Would it not be Mount Sinai? Our great and glorious God once spoke from the top of that mountain.

The same clergyman who visited Canaan went to Sinai also. As he knew there were many robbers on the way, he hired an Arab sheikh to take care of him. A sheikh is a chief, or captain. Suleiman was a fine-looking man, dressed in a red shirt, with a shawl twisted round his waist, a purple cloak, and a red cap. His feet and legs were bare. His eyes were bright, his skin was brown, and his beard black. To his girdle were fastened a huge knife and pistols, and by his side hung a sword. This man brought a band of Arabs with him to defend the travellers from the robbers in the desert.

One day the whole party set out mounted on camels. After going some distance, a number of children were seen scampering among the rocks, and looking like brown monkeys. These were the children of the Arabs who accompanied the Englishman. The wild little creatures ran to their fathers and saluted them in the respectful manner that Arab children are taught to do.

At last a herd of goats was seen with a fine boy of twelve years old leading them. He was the son of Suleiman. The father seemed to take great delight in this boy, and introduced him to the traveller. The kind gentleman, riding on a camel, put down his hand to the boy. The little fellow, after touching the traveller's hand, kissed his own, according to the Arabian manner.

The way to Mount Sinai was very rough: indeed, the traveller was sometimes obliged to get off his camel, and to climb among the crags on hands and knees. How glad he was when the Arabs pointed to a mountain, and said, "That is Mount Sinai." With what fear and reverence he gazed upon it! Here it was that the voice of the great God was once heard speaking out of the midst of the smoke, and clouds, and darkness.

How strange it must be to see in this lonely, gloomy spot, a great building! Yet there is one at the foot of the mountain. What can it be? A convent. See those high walls around. It is necessary to have high walls, because all

around are bands of fierce robbers. It is even
unsafe to have a door near the ground. There
is a door quite high up in the wall; but what
use can it be of, when there are no steps by
which to reach it? Can you guess how people
get in by this door? A rope is let down from
the door to draw the people up. One by one
they are drawn up. In the inside of the walls

Convent of Mount Sinai.

there are steps by which travellers go down
into the convent below. The monks who live
there belong to the Greek church.

The clergyman was lodged in a small cell
spread with carpets and cushions, and he was
waited upon by the monks.

These monks think that they lead a very holy
life in the desert. They eat no meat, and they

rise in the night to pray in their chapel. But God does not care for such service as this. He never commanded men to shut themselves up in a desert, but rather to do good in the world.

One day the monks told the traveller they would shew him the place where the burning bush once stood. How could they know the place? However, they pretended to know it. They led the way to the chapel, then taking off their shoes, they went down some stone steps till they came to a round room under ground, with three lamps burning in the midst. "There," said the monks, "is the very spot where the burning bush once stood."

There were two things the traveller enjoyed while in the convent, the beautiful garden full of thick trees and sweet flowers, and the cool pure water from the well. Such water and such a garden in the midst of a desert were sweet indeed.

The Arabs, who accompanied the traveller, enjoyed much the plentiful meals provided at the convent; for the monks bought sheep from the shepherds around, to feed their guests. After leaving the convent, Suleiman was taken ill, in consequence of having eaten too much while there. The clergyman gave him medicine, which cured him. The Arabs were very fond of their chief, and were so grateful to the stranger for giving him medicine, that they called him " the good physician." Suleiman himself shewed his gratitude by bringing his own black coffee-pot into the tent of the stranger, and asking him to drink coffee with him; for such is the pride of an Arab chief that he thinks it is a very great honour indeed for a stranger to share his meal.

But the traveller soon found that it is dangerous to pass through a desert. Why? Not on account of wild beasts, but of wild men. There was a tribe of Arabs very angry with Suleiman, because he was conducting the travellers through *their* part of the desert. They wanted to be the guides through that part, in hopes of getting rewarded by a good sum of money. You see how covetous they were. " The love of money is the root of all evil."

These angry Arabs were hidden among the rocks and hills; and every now and then they came suddenly out of their hiding-places, and with a loud voice threatened to punish Sulieman.

How much alarmed the travellers were! but none more than Sulieman himself. He requested the clergyman to travel during the whole night, in order the sooner to get out of the reach of the enemy. The clergyman promised to go as far as he was able. What a journey it was! No one durst speak aloud to his companions, lest the enemies should be hidden among the rocks close by, and should overhear them. At midnight the whole company pitched their tents by the coast of the Red Sea. Early in the morning the minister went alone to bathe in its smooth waters. After he had bathed, and when he was just going to return to the tents, he was startled by hearing the sound of a gun. The sound came from the midst of a small grove of palm-trees close by. Alarmed, he ran back quickly to the tents: again he heard the report of a gun: and again a third time. The travellers, Arabs and all, were gathered together, expecting an enemy to rush out of the grove. But where was Suleiman? He had gone some time before into the grove of palm-trees to talk to the enemies.

Presently the traveller saw about forty Arabs leave the grove and go far away. But Suleiman came not. So the minister went into the grove to search for him, and there he found—not Suleiman—but his dead body !

There it lay on the ground, covered with blood. The minister gazed upon the dark countenance once so joyful, and he thought it looked as if the poor Arab had died in great agony. It was frightful to observe the number of his wounds. Three balls had been shot into his body by the gun which went off three times

Three great cuts had been made in his head; his neck was almost cut off from his body, and his hand from his arm!

How suddenly was the proud Arab laid low in the dust! All his delights were perished for ever. Suleiman had been promised a new dress of gay colours at the end of the journey: but he would never more gird a shawl round his active frame, or fold a turban round his swarthy brow.

The Arabs wrapped their beloved master in a loose garment, and placing him on his beautiful camel, they went in deep grief to a hill at a little distance. There they buried him. They dug no grave; but they made a square tomb of large loose stones, and laid the dead body in the midst, and then covered it with more stones.

There Suleiman sleeps in the desert. But the day shall come when "the earth shall disclose her blood, and shall no more cover her slain:" and then shall the blood of Suleiman and his slain body be uncovered, and his murderer brought to judgment.*

Extracted chiefly from "The Pastor's Memorial," by the Rev. G. Fisk.

TURKEY IN ASIA.

Is there a Turkey in Asia as well as a Turkey in Europe?

Yes, there is; and it is governed by the same Sultan, and filled by the same sort of persons. All the Turks are Mahomedans.

You may know a Mahomedan city at a distance. When we look at a Christian city we see the steeples and spires of churches; but when we look at a Mahomedan city we see, rising above the houses and trees, the domes and minarets of mosques. What are domes and minarets? A dome is the round top of a mosque: and the minarets are the tall slender towers. A minaret is of great use to the Mahomedans.

Do you see the little narrow gallery outside the minaret? There is a man standing there. He is calling people to say their prayers. He calls so loud that all the people below can hear, and the sounds he utters are like sweet music. But would it not make you sad to hear them when you remembered what he was telling people to do? To pray to the God of Mahomet. Not to the God and Father of the Lord Jesus Christ, but to a FALSE god: to NO god. This man goes up the dark narrow stairs winding inside the minaret five times a-day; first he goes as soon as the sun rises, then at noon, next in the afternoon, then at sunset, and last of all in the night. Ascending and descending those steep stairs is all his business, and it is hard work, and fatigues him very much.

In the court of the mosque there is a fountain. There every one washes before he goes into the mosque to repeat his prayers, thinking to please God by clean hands instead of a clean heart. Inside the mosque there are no pews or benches, but only mats and carpets spread on the floor. There the worshippers kneel and touch the ground with their foreheads. The minister of the mosque is called the Imam. He stands in a niche in the wall, with his back to the people, and repeats prayers.

But he is not the preacher. The sheikh, or chief man of the town, preaches: not on Sunday, but on Friday. He sits on a high place and talks to the people—not about pardon and peace, and heaven and holiness—but about the duty of washing their hands before prayers, and of bowing down to the ground, and such vain services.

In the mosque there are two rows of very large wax candles, much higher than a man, and as thick as his arm, and they are lighted at night.

It is considered right to go to the mosque for prayers five times a-day; but very few Mahomedans go so often. Wherever people may be they are expected to kneel down and repeat their

prayers, whether in the house or in the street.
But very few do so. While they pray, Mahomedans look about all the time, and in the midst
speak to any one, and then go on again; for
their hearts are not in their prayers; they do
not worship in spirit and in truth.

There are no images or pictures in the mosques,
because Mahomet forbid his followers to worship idols. There are Korans on reading-stands
in various parts of the mosque, for any one to
read who pleases.

The people leave their red slippers at the door,
keeping on their yellow boots only; but they do
not uncover their heads as Christians do.

Was Christ ever known in this Mahomedan
land? Yes, long before he was known in England. Turkey in Asia used to be called Asia
Minor (or Asia the less), and there it was that
Paul the Apostle was born, and there he preached
and turned many to Christ. But at last the
Christians began to worship images, and the
fierce Turks came and turned the churches into
mosques. This was the punishment God sent
the Christians for breaking His law. In some of
the mosques you may see the marks of the pictures which the Christians painted on the walls,
and which the Turks *nearly* scraped off.

How dreadful it would be if our churches
should ever be turned into mosques! May God
never send us this heavy punishment!

ARMENIA.

One corner of Turkey in Asia is called Armenia. There are many high mountains in Armenia, and one of them you would like to see very much. It is the mountain on which Noah's Ark rested after the flood. I mean Ararat.*

It is a very high mountain with two peaks; and its highest peak is always covered with snow. People say that no one ever climbed to the top of that peak. I should think Noah's ark rested on a lower part of the mountain between the two peaks, for it would have been very cold for Noah's family on the snow-covered peak, and it would have been very difficult for them to get down. How pleasant it must be to stand on the side of Ararat, and to think, "Here my great father Noah stood, and my great mother, Noah's wife; here they saw the earth in all its greenness, just washed with the waters of the flood; and here they rejoiced and praised God!"

I am glad to say that all the Armenians are not Mahomedans. Many are Christians; but, alas! they know very little about Christ except His name. I will tell you a short anecdote to shew how ignorant they are.

Once a traveller went to see an old church in

* It is remarkable that this mountain lies at the point where three great empires meet, namely, Russia, Persia, and Turkey.

Armenia, called the Church of Forty Steps, because there are forty steps to reach it : for it is built on the steep banks of a river.

The traveller found the churchyard full of boys. The churchyard was their school-room. And what were their books ? The grave-stones that lay flat upon the ground. Four priests were teaching the boys. These priests wore *black* turbans; while Turkish Imams wear *white* turbans.) One of these Armenian priests led the traveller to an upper room, telling him he had something very wonderful to show him. What could it be ? The priest went to a niche in the wall and took out of it a bundle ; then untied a silk handkerchief, and then another, and then another—till he had untied twenty-five silk handkerchiefs. What was the precious thing so carefully wrapped up ? It was a New Testament.

It is a precious book indeed : but it ought to be read, and not wrapped up. The priest praised it, saying, "This is a wonderful book ; it has often been laid upon sick persons, and has cured them." Then a poor old man, bent and tottering, pressed forward to kiss the book, and to rub his hoary head. This was worshipping the *book*, instead of Him who wrote it.

An Armenian village looks like a number of mole-hills : for the dwellings are holes dug in the ground with low stone walls round the holes ;

the roof is made of branches of trees and heaps
of earth. There are generally two rooms in the
hole—one for the family, and one for the cattle.

A traveller arrived one evening at such a village ; and he was pleased to see fruit-trees overshadowing the hovels, and women, without veils,
spinning cotton under their shadow. But he
was not pleased with the room where he was to
sleep. The way lay through a long dark passage under ground ; and the room was filled
with cattle : there was no window nor chimney.
How dark and hot it was! Yet the air was too
damp for him to sleep out of doors, because a
large lake was near; therefore he wrapped his
cloak around him, and lay upon the ground ; but
he could not sleep because of the stinging of insects, and the trampling of cattle : and glad he
was in the morning to breathe again the fresh air.

Rich Armenians have fine houses. Once a
traveller dined with a rich Armenian. The
dinner was served up in a tray, and placed on a
low stool, while the company sat on the ground.
One dish after another was served up till the
traveller was tired of tasting them. But there
was not only too much to *eat ;* there was also too
much to *drink.* Rakee, a kind of brandy, was
handed about; and afterwards a musician came in
and played and sang to amuse the company. In
Turkey there is neither playing, nor singing, nor

drinking spirits. The Turks think themselves much better than Christians. "For," say they, "we drink less and pray more." They do not know that real Christians are not fond of drinking, and are fond of praying; only *they* pray more in *secret*, and the Turks more in *public*.

KURDISTAN.

The fiercest of all the people in Asia are the Kurds.

They are the terror of all who live near them.

Their dwellings are in the mountains; there some live in villages, and some in black tents, and some in strong castles. At night they rush down from the mountains upon the people in the valleys, uttering a wild yell, and brandishing their swords. They enter the houses, and begin to pack up the things they find, and to place them on the backs of their mules and asses, while they drive away the cattle of the poor people; and if any one attempts to resist them, they kill him. You may suppose in what terror the poor villagers live in the valleys. They keep a man to watch all night, as well as large dogs; and they build a strong tower in the midst of the village, where they run to hide themselves when they are afraid.

The reason why the Armenians live in holes

in the ground is because they hope the Kurds may not find out where they are.

Those Kurds who live in tents often move from place to place. The black tents are folded up and placed on the backs of mules; and a large kettle is slung upon the end of the tent-pole. The men and women drive the herds and flocks, while the children and the chickens ride upon the cows.

The Kurds have thin, dark faces, hooked noses, and black eyes, with a fierce and malicious look.

They are of the Mahomedan religion, and the call to prayers may be heard in the villages of these robbers and murderers.

MESOPOTAMIA.

This country is part of Turkey in Asia. It lies between two very famous rivers, the Tigris and the Euphrates, often spoken of in the Bible. The word Mesopotamia means "between rivers." It was between these rivers that faithful Abraham lived when God first called him to be His friend. Should you not like to see that country? It is now full of ruins. The two most ancient cities in the world were built on the Tigris and Euphrates.

Nineveh was on the Tigris.

What a city that was at the time Jonah preached there! Its walls were so thick that three chariots could go on the top all abreast.

But what is Nineveh now? Look at those green mounds. Under those heaps of rubbish lies Nineveh. A traveller has been digging among those mounds, and has found the very throne of the kings of Nineveh, and the images of winged bulls and lions which adorned the palace. God overthrew Nineveh because it was wicked. So the prophet Nahum declared He would. (iii. 8.)

There is another ancient city lying in ruins on the Euphrates—it is Babylon the Great.

There is nothing but heaps of bricks to be seen where once proud Babylon stood. Where are now the streets fifteen miles long? Where are the hanging gardens?—gardens one above the other, the wonder of the world. Where is now the temple of Belus (or of Babel, as some think), with its golden statue? All, all are now crumbled into rubbish. God has destroyed Babylon, as He said by the prophet Jeremiah, chap. l. 40.

There are dens of wild beasts among the ruins. A traveller saw some bones of a sheep in one,— the remains, he supposed, of a lion's dinner; but he did not like to go further into the den to see

who dwelt there. Owls and bats fill all the
dark places. But no *men* live there, though
human bones are often found scattered about, and
they turn into dust as soon as they are touched.

There is now a great city in Mesopotamia,
called Bagdad. In Babylon no sound is heard
but the howlings of wild *beasts;* in Bagdad *men*
may be heard screaming and hallooing from
morning to night. The drivers of the camels
and the mules shout as they press through the
narrow, crooked streets, and even the ladies
riding on white donkeys, and attended by black
slaves, scream and halloo.

In summer it is so hot in Bagdad that people
during the day live in rooms under ground, and
sleep on their flat roofs at night.

It is curious to see the people who have been
sleeping on the roof get up in the morning.
First, they roll up their mattresses, their cover-
lids, and pillows, and put them in the house.
The children cannot fold up theirs, but their
mothers or black slaves do it for them. The
men repeat their prayers, and then drink a cup
of coffee, which their wives present to them.
The wives kneel as they offer the cup to their
lords, and they stand with their hands crossed
while their lords are drinking, then kneel down
again to receive the cup, and to kiss their lord's
hand. Then the men take their pipes, and lounge

on their cushions, while the women say their
prayers. And when do the children say their
prayers? Never. They know only of Mahomet; they know not the Saviour who said
"Suffer little children to come unto me."

PERSIA.

Is this country mentioned in the Bible? Yes;
we read of Cyrus, **the king of** Persia. Isaiah
spoke of him before he was born, and called
him by his name. See chap. xlv.

Persia **is** now a Mahomedan country. The
Turks you remember, **are** Mahomedans too.
Perhaps you think these two nations, the Turks
and the Persians, must agree well together, as
they are of the same religion. Far from it. No
nations hate one another more than Turks and
Persians do; and the reason is, that though
they both believe in Mahomet, they disagree
about his son-in-law, Ali. The Persians are
very fond of *him*, and keep a day of mourning
in memory of his death: whereas the Turks do
not care for Ali at all.

But is this a reason why they should hate
one another so much?

Even in their common customs the Persians
differ from the Turks. The Turks sit cross-

legged on the ground; the Persians sit upon their heels. Which way of sitting should you prefer? I think you would find it more comfortable to sit like a Turk.

The Turks sit on sofas and lean against cushions; the Persians sit on carpets and lean against the wall. I know you would prefer the Turkish fashion. The Turks drink coffee without either milk or sugar; the Persians drink tea with sugar, though without milk. The Turks wear turbans! the Persians wear high caps of black lamb's-wool.

Not only are their *customs* different, but their *characters*. The Turks are grave, and the Persians lively. The Turks are silent, the Persians talkative. The Turks are rude, the Persians polite. Now I am sure you like the Persians better than the Turks. But wait a little—the Turks are very proud; the Persians are very deceitful. An old Persian was heard to say, "We all tell lies whenever we can." The Persians are not even ashamed when their falsehoods are found out. When they sell they ask too much; when they make promises they break them. In short, it is impossible to trust a Persian.

The Turks obey Mahomet's laws; they pray five times a-day, and drink no wine. But the Persians seldom repeat their prayers, and they do drink wine; though Mahomet has forbidden it. In short the Persians seem to have no idea of right and wrong. The judges do not give right judgment, but take bribes. The soldiers live by robbing the poor people, for the king pays them no wages, but leaves them to get food as they can; and so the poor people often build their cottages in little nooks in the valleys, where they hope the soldiers will not see them.

THE COUNTRY.—Persia is a high country and a dry country. There are high mountains and wide plains; but there are very few rivers and running brooks, because there is so little rain. However, in some places the Persians have cut canals, and planted willow-trees by their side. Rice will not grow well in such a dry country, but sheep find it very pleasant and wholesome. The hills are covered over with flocks, and the shepherds may be seen leading their sheep and carrying the very young lambs in their arms. This is a sight which reminds us of the good Shepherd: for it is written of Jesus, "He gathereth the lambs in His arms."

The sweetest of all flowers grows abundantly in Persia—I mean the rose. The air is filled with its fragrance. The people pluck the rose-leaves and dry them in the sun, as we dry hay. how pleasant it must be for children in the spring to play among the heaps of rose-leaves! Once a traveller went to breakfast with a Persian prince, and he found the company seated upon a heap of rose-leaves with a carpet spread over it. Afterwards the rose-leaves were sent to the distillers to be made into rose-water.

Persian cats are beautiful creatures, with fur as soft as silk.

The best melons in the world grow in Persia.

The three chief materials for making clothes are all to be found there in abundance. I mean wool, cotton, and silk. You have heard already of the Persian sheep; so you see there is wool. Cotton-trees also abound. Women and children may be seen picking the nuts which contain the little pieces of cotton. There are mulberry-trees also, to feed the numerous silk-worms.

POOR PEOPLE.—The villages where the poor live are miserable places. The houses are of mud, not placed in rows, but straggling, with dirty narrow paths winding between them.

In summer the poor people sleep on the roofs; for the roofs are flat, and covered with earth, with low walls on every side to prevent the sleepers falling off. Here the Persians spread their carpets to lie upon at night.

Winter does not last long in Persia, yet while it lasts it is cold. Then the poor, instead of sleeping on their roofs, sleep in a very curious warm bed. In the middle of each cottage there is a round hole in the floor, where the fire burns.

In the evening the fire goes out, but the hot cinders remain. The Persians place over it a low round table, and then throw a large coverlid over the table, and all round about. Under this coverlid the family lie at night, their heads peeping out, and their feet almost touching the warm fireplace underneath. This the Persians call sleeping in a comfortable bed.

The poor wear dirty and ragged clothes, and the children may be seen crawling about in the dust, and looking like little pigs. Yet in one respect the Persians are very clean; they bathe often. In every village there is a large bath.

The poor people have animals of various kinds—a few sheep, or goats, or cows. In the day one man takes them all out to feed. In the evening he brings them back to the village, and the animals of their own accord go home to their own stables. Each cow and each sheep knows where she will get food and a place to sleep in. The prophet Isaiah said truly, "The ass knoweth his owner, and the ox his master's crib; but Israel doth not know, my people doth not consider."

The Persian Ladies.—They wrap themselves up in a large dark-blue wrapper, and in this dress they walk out where they please. No one who meets them can tell who they are.

And where do these women go? Chiefly to

the bath, where they spend much of their time
drinking coffee and smoking. There, too, they
try to make themselves handsome by blackening
their eyebrows and dyeing their hair. Sometimes the ladies walk to the burial-grounds,
and wander about for hours among the graves.
When they are at home they employ themselves
in making pillau and sherbet. Pillau is made of
rice and butter; sherbet is made of juice mixed
with water.

The ladies have a sitting-room to themselves.
One side of it is all lattice-work, and this makes
it cool. At night they spread their carpets on
the floor to sleep upon, and in the day they
keep them in a lumber room.

PERSIAN INNS.—They are very uncomfortable
places. There are a great many small cells
made of mud, built all round a large court.
These cells are quite empty, and paved with
stone. The only comfortable room is over the
doorway of the court, and the first travellers
who arrive are sure to settle in the room over
the doorway.

Once an English traveller arrived at a Persian
inn with his two servants. All three were very
ill and in great pain, from having travelled far
over burning plains and steep mountains.

But as the room over the doorway was occupied, they were forced to go into a little cold

damp cell. As there was no door to the cell, they hung up a rug to keep out the chilling night air and they placed a pan of coals in the midst. Many Persians came and peeped into the cell; and seeing the sick men looking miserable as they lay on their carpets, the unfeeling creatures laughed at them, and no one would help them or give them anything to eat. The travellers brought some bread and grapes at the bazaar, but these were not fit food for sick men, yet it was all they could get. At last a Persian merchant heard of their distress; and he came to see them every day, bringing them warm milk and wholesome food: when they were well enough to be moved, he took them to his house, and nursed them with the greatest care.

Who was this kind merchant? Not a Mahomedan, but of the religion of the fire-worshippers, or Parsees. Was he not like the good Samaritan of whom we read in the New Testament? O that Bahram, the merchant, might know the true God!

PILGRIMS AND BEGGARS.—Very often you may see a large company of pilgrims, some on foot and some mounted on camels, horses, and asses. They are returning from Mecca, the birth-place of Mahomed. What good have they got by their pilgrimage? None at all. They think they are grown very holy, but they make such an uproar at the inns by quarrelling and fighting when they are travelling home, that no one can bear to be near them.

There is a set of beggars called dervishes. They call themselves very holy, and think people are bound to give money to such holy men. They are so bold that sometimes they refuse to leave a place till some money has been given.

Once a dervish stopped a long while before the house of the English ambassador, and refused to go away. But a plan was thought of to *make* him go away.

The dervish was sitting in a little niche in the wall. The ambassador ordered his servants to build up bricks to shut the dervish in. The men began to build, yet the dervish would not stir, till the bricks came up as high as his chin : then he began to be frightened, and he said he would rather go away.

THE KING OF PERSIA.—He is called King of kings. What a name for a man ! It is the title of God alone. But in the Bible you will find that the kings of Persia called themselves by that title more than two thousand years ago. (Ezra vii. 12.) The king sits on a marble throne, and his garments sparkle with jewels of dazzling brightness. The walls of his state-chamber are covered with looking-glasses. One side of the room opens into a court adorned with flowers and fountains. Great part of his time is spent in amusements, such as hunting and shooting, writing verses, and hearing stories. He keeps a man called a story-teller, and he

King of Persia sitting on his heels.

will never hear the same story repeated twice. It gives the men a great deal of trouble to find new stories every day. The king keeps jesters, who make jokes; and he has mimics, who play antics to make him laugh. He dines at eight in the evening from dishes of pure gold. No one is allowed to dine with him; but two of his little boys wait upon him, and his physician stands by to advise him not to eat too much.

Do you think he is happy in all his grandeur? Judge for yourself.

All his golden dishes come up covered and sealed. Why? For fear of poison. There is a chief officer in the kitchen who watches the cook, to see that he puts no poison into the food: and he seals up the dishes before they are taken to the king, in order that the servants may not put in poison as they are carrying them along. In what fear this great king lives. He cannot trust his own servants.

TEHERAN.—This the royal city. It is built in a barren plain, and is exceedingly hot, as the hills around keep off the air. It is a mean city, for it is chiefly built of mud huts.

The king's palace is called the "Ark," and is a very strong as well as a grand place.*

CHINA.

THERE is no country in the world like China.

How different it is from Persia, where there are so few people: whereas China is crowded with inhabitants.

How different it is from England where the

* Extracted chiefly from Southgate's "Travels."

people are instructed in the Bible: whereas China is full of idols.

China is a heathen country; yet it is not a savage country, for the people are quiet, and orderly, and industrious.

It would be hard for a child to imagine what a great multitude of people there are in China.

If you were to sit by a clock, and if all the Chinese were to pass before you one at a time, and if you were to count one at each tick of the clock, and if you were never to leave off counting day or night—how long do you think it would be before you had counted all the Chinese?

Twelve years. O what a vast number of people there must be in China! In all, there are about three hundred and sixty millions!

If all the people in the world were collected together, out of every THREE—ONE would be a Chinese. How sad it is to think that this immense nation (except a few) knows not God, nor His glorious Son!

There are too many people in China, for there is not food enough for them all; and many are half-starved.

FOOD.—The poor can get nothing but rice to eat and water to drink; except now and then they mix a little pork or salt fish with their rice. Any sort of meat is thought good; even a hash of rats and snakes, or a mince of earthworms. Cats' flesh and dogs' flesh are considered as nice as pork, and cost as much.

An Englishman was once dining with a Chinaman, and he wished to know what sort of meat was on his plate. But he was not able to speak Chinese. How then could he ask? He thought of a way. Looking first at his plate, and then at the Chinaman, he said, "Ba-a-a," meaning to ask, "Is this mutton?" The Chinaman understood the question, and immediately replied, "Bow-wow," meaning to say, "It is puppy-dog." You will wish to know whether the Englishman went on eating; but I cannot tell you this.

While the poor are in want of food, the rich eat a great deal too much. A Chinese feast in a rich man's house lasts for hours. The servants bring in one course after another, till a stranger wonders when the last course will come. The food is served up in a curious way; not on dishes, but in small basins—for all the meats are swimming in broth. Instead of a knife and fork, each person has a pair of chop-sticks, which are something like knitting-needles; and with these he cleverly fishes up the floating morsels, and pops them into his mouth. There are spoons for drinking the broth.

You will be surprised to hear that the Chinese are very fond of eating birds' nests. Do not suppose that they eat magpies' nests, which are made of clay and sticks, or even little nests of moss and clay: the nests they eat are made of a sort of gum. This gum comes out of the birds' mouths, and is shining and transparent, and the nests stick fast to the rock. These nests are something like our jelly, and must be very nourishing.

The Chinese like nothing cold; they warm all their food, even their wine. For they have wine not made of grapes, but of rice, and they drink it not in glasses, but in cups. Tea, however, is the most common drink; for China is the country where tea grows.

Tha hills are covered with shrubs bearing a white flower, a little like a wild white rose. They are tea-plants. The leaves are picked; each leaf is rolled up with the finger and dried on a hot iron plate.

The Chinese do not keep all the tea-leaves; they pack up a great many in boxes, and send them to distant lands. In England and in Russia there is a tea-kettle in every cottage. Some of the Chinese are so very poor that they cannot buy new tea-leaves, but only old tea-leaves which are sold in shops. I do not think poor people in England would buy old tea-leaves. Some very poor Chinese use fern-leaves instead of tea-leaves.

The Chinese do not make tea in the same way that we do. They have no tea-pot, nor milk-jug, nor sugar-basin. They put a few tea-leaves in a cup, pour hot water on them, and then place a cover on the cup till tea is ready. Whenever you pay a visit in China a cup of tea is offered.

APPEARANCE.—The Chinese are not at all like the other natives of Asia. The Turks and Arabs are fine-looking men, but the Chinese are poor-looking creatures. You have seen their pictures on their boxes of tea, for they are fond of drawing pictures of themselves.

Their complexion is rather yellow, but many of the ladies who keep in-doors, are rather fair. They have black hair, small dark eyes, broad faces, flat noses, and high cheek-bones. In general they are short. The men like to be stout; and the rich men are stout: the fatter they are the more they are admired: but the women like to be slender.

A Chinaman does not take off his cap in company, and he has a good reason for it; his head is close shaven: only a long piece behind is allowed to grow, and this grows down to his heel, and is plaited. He wears a long dark-blue gown, with loose hanging sleeves. His shoes are clumsy, turned up at the toes in an ugly manner, and the soles are white. The Chinese have more trouble in whitening their shoes than we have in blacking ours.

A Chinese lady wears a loose gown like a Chinaman's; but she may be known by her head-dress, her baby feet, and her long nails. Her hair is tied up, and decked with artificial flowers; and sometimes a little golden bird, sparkling with jewels, adorns her forehead. Her feet are not bigger than those of a child of five years old; because, when she was five, they were cruelly bound up to prevent them from growing. She suffered much pain all her childhood, and now she trips about as if she were walking on tip-toes. A little push would throw her down. As she walks, she moves from side to side like a ship in the water, for she cannot walk firmly with such small feet. The Chinese are so foolish as to admire these small feet, and to call them the "golden lilies." As for her finger-nails, they are seldom seen, for a Chinese lady hides her hands in her long sleeves; but the nails on the left hand are very long, and are like birds' claws. The nails on the right hand are not so long, in order that the lady may be able to tinkle on her music, to embroider, and to weave silk.

The gentlemen are proud of having one long nail on the little finger, to show that they do not labour like the poor, for if they did, the nail would break. Men in China wear necklaces and use fans.

What foolish customs I have described! Surely you will not think the Chinese a wise people, though very *clever*, as you will soon find.

Men and women dress in black, or in dark colours, such as blue and purple; the women sometimes dress in pink or green. Great people dress in red, and the royal family in yellow. When you see a person all in white, you 'may know he is in mourning. A son dresses in white for three years after he has lost one of his parents.

HOUSES.—See that lantern hanging over the gate. The light is rather dim, because the sides are made of silk instead of glass. What is written upon the lantern? The master's name. The gateway leads into a court into which many rooms open. There are not doors to all the rooms, to some there are only curtains. Curtains are used instead of doors in many hot countries, because of their coolness; but the furniture of the Chinese rooms is quite different from the furniture of Turkish and Persian rooms. The Chinese sit on chairs as we do, and have high tables like ours: and they sleep on bedsteads, yet their beds are not like ours, for instead of a mattress there is nothing but a mat.

Instead of pictures the Chinese adorn their

rooms with painted lanterns, and with pieces of white satin on which sentences are written; they have also book-cases and china jars. But they have no fire-places, for they never need a fire to keep themselves warm : the sun shining in at the south windows makes the room tolerably warm in winter; and in summer the weather is very hot. The Chinese in winter put on one coat over the other till they feel warm enough. In the north of China it is so cold in winter that the place where the bed stands (which is a recess in the wall) is heated by a furnace underneath, and the whole family sit there all day crowded together.

The Chinese houses have not so many stories as ours; in the towns there is one floor above the ground-floor, but in the country there are no rooms up-stairs.

It would amuse you to see a Chinese country house. There is not one large house, but a number of small buildings like summer-houses, and long galleries running from one to another. One of these summer-houses is in the middle of a pond with a bridge leading to it. In the pond there are gold and silver fish; for these beautiful fishes often kept in glass bowls in England, came first from China. By the sides of the garden-walks large cages are placed; in one may be seen some gold and silver pheasants, in another a splendid peacock, in another a gentle stork, and in another an elegant little deer. There is often a grove of mulberry-trees in the garden, and in the midst of the grove there are houses made of bamboo, for rearing silk-worms. It is the delight of the ladies to feed these curious worms. None but very quiet people are fit to take care of them, for a loud noise would kill them. Gold and silver fish also cannot bear much noise.

In every large house in China there is a room called the Hall of Ancestors. There the family worship their dead parents, and grand-parents, and great-grand-parents, and those who lived still further back. There are no images to be seen in the Hall of Ancestors, but there are tablets with names written upon them. The family bow down before the tablets, and burn incense and gold paper! What a foolish service! What good can incense and paper do the dead? And what good can the dead do to their children? How is it that such clever people as the Chinese are so foolish?

RELIGION.—You have heard already that the Chinese worship the dead.

Who taught them this worship?

It was a man named Confucius, who lived a long while ago. This Confucius was a very wise man. From his childhood he was very fond of sitting alone, thinking, instead of playing with other children. When he was fourteen he began to read some old books that had been written not long after the time of Noah. In these books he found very many wise sentences, such as Noah may have taught his children. The Chinese had left off reading these wise books, and were growing more and more foolish.* Confucius, when he was grown up, tried to persuade his countrymen to attend to the old books. There were a few men who became his scholars, and who followed him about from place to place. They might be seen sitting under a tree, listening to the words of Confucius.

Confucius was a very tall man, with a long black beard and a very fine high forehead.

Had he known the true God, how much good

---

* These are some of the sentences written in the old books:—

"Never say, There is no one who sees me, for there is a wise Spirit who sees all."

"Man no longer has what he had before the fall, and he has brought his children into his misery. Oh Heaven! you only can help us. Wipe away the stains of the father, and save his children.

"Never speak but with great care. Do not say, It is only a single word. Remember that no one has the keeping of your heart and tongue but you."

These sentences are like some verses in the Psalms and Proverbs; and it may be, they were spoken first by some holy men of old.

Here is one more remarkable than all:—

"God hates the proud, and is kind to the humble."

he might have done to the Chinese : but as it was, he only tried to make them happy in *this* world. He himself confessed that he knew nothing about the *other* world. He gave very good advice about respect due to parents ; but he gave very bad advice about worship due to them after they were dead.

Was he a good man ? Not truly good ; for he did not love God ; neither did he act right ; for he was very unkind to his wife, and quite cast her off. Yet he used to talk of going to other countries to teach the people. It would have been a happy thing for him, if he had gone as far as Babylon ; for a truly wise man lived there, even Daniel the prophet. From him he might have learned about the promised Saviour and life everlasting. But Confucius never left China.

He was ill-treated by many of the rich and great, and he was so poor that rice was generally his only food. When he was dying he felt very unhappy, as well he might, when he knew not where he was going. He said to his followers just before his death, "The kings refuse to follow my advice ; and since I am of no use on earth, it is best that I should leave it." As soon as he was dead, people began to respect him highly, and even to worship him. At this day, though Confucius died more than two thousand years ago, there is a temple to his honour in every large city, and numbers of beasts are offered up to him in sacrifice. There are thousands of people descended from him, and they are treated with great honour as the children of Confucius, and one of them is called kong, or duke.

There is another religion in China besides the religion of Confucius, and a much worse religion. About the same time that Confucius lived, there was a man called La-on-tzee. He was a great deceiver, as you will see. He pretended that he could make people completely happy. There were three things, he said, he would

Treading the fire.

do for them: first he would make them rich

by turning stone into gold; next, he would prevent their being hurt by swords or by fire, through charms he could give them; and, last of all, he could save them from death by a drink he knew how to prepare.

What an awful liar this man must have been! Yet many people believed in him, and STILL believe in him. There are now priests of La-on-tzee, and once a year they rush through hot cinders and pretend they are not hurt. You will wonder their tricks are not found out, seeing they cannot give any one the drink to keep him from dying. It is indeed wonderful that any one can believe these deceitful priests.

Buddha.

Their religion is called the *"Taou"* sect. Taou means reason. The name of folly would be a better title for such a religion.

There is a *third* religion in China. It is the sect of Buddha.* This Buddha was a man who once pretended to be turned into a god called Fo. You see he was even worse than La-on-tzee.

Buddha pretended that he could make people happy; and his way of doing so was very strange. He told them to think of nothing, and then they would be happy. It is said that one man fixed his eyes for nine years upon a wall without looking off, hoping to grow happy at last. You can guess whether he did. There are many priests of Buddha, always busy in telling lies to the people. They recommend

---

* The means by which the Buddhist religion entered China are remarkable. A certain Chinese emperor once read in the book of Confucius this sentence, "The true saint will be found in the West." He thought a great deal about it: at last he dreamed about it. He was so much struck by his dream that he sent two of his great lords to look for the true religion in the West. When they reached India, they found multitudes worshipping Buddha. This Buddha was a wicked man who had been born in India a thousand years before. The Chinese messengers believed all the absurd histories they heard about Buddha, and they returned to China with a book which had been written about him. Ah! had they gone as far as Canaan they might have heard Paul and Peter preaching the Gospel. Alas! why did they go no further—and why did they go so far, only to return to fill China with idols?

them to repeat the name of Buddha thousands and thousands of times, and some people are so foolish as to do this; but no one ever found any comfort from the plan.

The priests of Buddha say that men's souls, when they leave their bodies, go into other bodies. This idea is enough to make a dying person very miserable. One poor man, when he was dying, was in terror because he had been told his soul would go into one of the Emperor's horses. Whenever he was dropping off to sleep, he started up in a fright, fancying that he felt the blows of a cruel driver hurrying him along: for he knew how very fast the Emperor's horses were made to go. How different are the feelings of a dying man who knows he is going to Jesus. He can say with joy;—

> " For me my elder brethren stay,
> And angels beckon me away,
> And Jesus bids me come."

The Buddhists are full of tricks by which to get presents out of the people.

Once a-year they cause a great feast to be made, and for whom? For the poor? No. For beasts? No. For children? No. For themselves? No. You will never guess. For ghosts! The priests declare that the souls of the dead are very hungry, and that it is right to give them a feast. A number of tables are set out, spread with all kinds of dishes. No one is seen to eat, nor is any of the food eaten; but the priests *say* the ghosts eat the *spirit* of the food. When it is supposed the ghosts have finished dinner, the people scramble for the food, and take it home; —and no doubt the priests get their share.

The dead are supplied with money as well as with food, and that is done by burning gilt paper; clothes are sent to them by cutting out paper in the shape of clothes (only much

Chinese family worshipping.

smaller), and by burning the articles; and even houses are conveyed to the dead by making baby-houses and burning them.

As an instance of the deceits of the priests, I

will tell you of two priests who once stood crying over a poor woman's gate. "What is the matter," inquired the woman. "Do you see those ducks?" the priests replied; "our parents' souls are in them, and we are afraid lest you should eat them for supper." The foolish woman out of pity gave the ducks to the cunning priests, who promised to take great care of the precious birds; but in fact, they ate them for their own supper.

The Buddhist priests may be known by their heads close shaven, and their black dress. The priests of Taou have their hair in a knot at the top of their heads, and they wear scarlet robes. There are no priests of Confucius; and this is a good thing.

All the religions of China are bad, but of the three, the religion of Confucius is the least foolish.

The religion of Taou teaches men to act like madmen.

The religion of Buddha teaches them to act like idiots.

The religion of Confucius teaches them to act like wise men, but without souls.

THE EMPEROR.—There is no Emperor in the world who has as many subjects as the Emperor of China: he has six times as many as the Emperor of Russia.

Neither is it possible for any man to be more

honoured than this Emperor; for he is worshipped by his people like a god. He is called "The Son of Heaven," and "Ten Thousand Years;" yet he dies like every other child of earth. His sign is the dragon, and this is painted on his flags—a fit sign for one who, like Satan, makes himself a god.

Chinese dragon.

Yet the Emperor is also styled "Father of his people;" and to show that he feels like a father, when there is a famine or plague in the land, he shuts himself up in his palace to grieve for his people; and by this means he gets the love of his subjects.

Once a-year, too, this great Emperor tries to encourage his people to be industrious by ploughing a part of a field and sowing a little corn; and the Empress sets an example to the women, by going once a-year to feed silk-worms and to wind the balls of silk.

The Emperor wears a yellow dress, and all his relations wear yellow girdles.

But the relations of the Emperor are not the most honourable people in the land: the most learned are the most honourable. Every one in China who wishes to be a great lord studies day and night. One man, that he might not fall asleep over his books, tied his long plaited tail of hair to the ceiling, and when his head nodded, his hair was pulled tight, and that woke him.

But what is it the Chinese learn with so much pains?

Chiefly the books of Confucius, and a few more: but in none of them is God made known: so that, with all his wisdom, the Chinaman is foolish still. The words of the Bible are true, " The world by wisdom knew not God." Yet to know God is better than to know all beside.

There is a great hall in every town, where all the men who wish to be counted learned meet together once a-year. They are desired to write, and then to show what they have written ; and then those who have written well and without a mistake, have an honourable title given to them ; and they are allowed to write another year in another greater hall; and at last the most learned are made mandarins.

What is a mandarin? He is a ruler over a town, and is counted a great man. The most learned of the mandarins are made the Emperor's counsellors. There are only three of them, and they are the greatest men in all China, next to the Emperor.

There are many poor men who study hard in hopes to be one of these three.

This is the greatest honour a Chinaman can obtain. But a Christian can obtain a far greater, even the honour of a crown and a throne in the presence of the Lord Jesus Christ at His coming.

The mandarins are all of the religion of Confucius, and despise the poor who worship Buddha.

ANIMALS AND TREES.—Once there were lions in China, but they have all been killed; there are still bears and tigers in the mountains and forests on the borders of the land.

There are small wild cats, which are caught and kept in cages, and then killed and cooked. There are tame cats, too, with soft hair and hanging ears, which are kept by ladies as pets.

There are dogs to guard the house, and they too are eaten; but as they are fed on rice only, their flesh is better than the flesh of our dogs. The dogs are so sensible, that they know when the butcher is carrying away a dog that he is going to kill him, and the poor creatures come round him howling, as if begging for their brother's life.

The pig is the Chinaman's chief dish; for it can be fed on all the refuse food, and there is very little food to spare in China.

There are not many birds in China, because there is not room for many trees. Only one bird sings, and she builds her nest on the ground; it is a bird often heard singing in England floating in the air,—I mean the lark.

In most parts of China men carry all the burdens, instead of horses and asses carrying them.

A gentleman is carried in a chair by *two* men, and a mandarin by *four*; yet the Emperor rides on horseback.

The three Great Cities.

Pekin on the north.
Nankin in the middle.
Canton on the south.

Pekin is the grandest.
Nankin is the most learned.
Canton is the richest.

At Pekin is the Emperor's palace. The gardens are exceedingly large, and contain hills, and lakes, and groves within the walls, besides houses for the Emperor's relations.

At Nankin is the China tower. It is made of china bricks, and contains nine rooms one over another. It is two hundred feet high, a wonderful height.

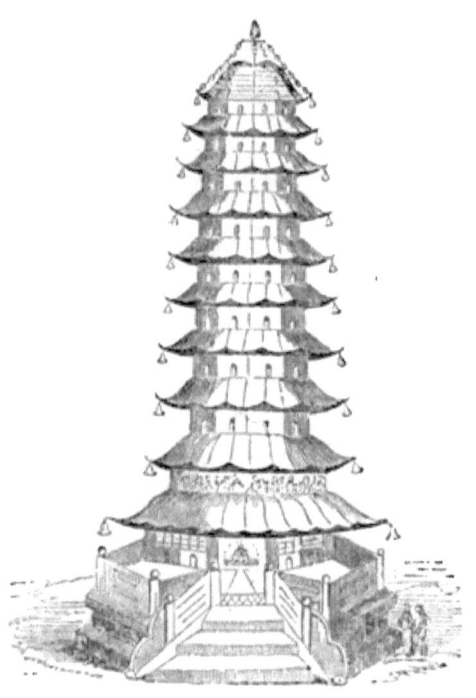

Tower of Nankin.

Of what use is it? Of none—of worse than none. It is a temple for Buddha, and is full of his images.

At Canton there are so many people that there is not room for all in the land; so thousands live on the water in boats. Many have never slept a single night on the shore. The children often **fall** overboard, but as a hollow gourd is tied round each child's neck, they float, and are soon picked up.

For a long while the Chinese would not allow foreigners to come into their cities. A great many foreign ships came to Canton to buy tea and silk ; but the traders were forbidden to enter the town, and they lived in a little island near, and built a town there called Macao.

But lately the Chinese Emperor agreed to permit strangers to come into his country.

He has given one island to the English. It is an island near Canton, called Hong-Kong, and the English have built a city there and called it Victoria.

THE TWO RIVERS.—There is one called Yeang-te-sang, or " the Son of the Ocean." It is the largest in all Asia.

The other is called the Yellow River, for the soft clay mixed with the water gives it a yellow colour.

LAKES.—There are immense lakes, covered with boats and fishermen.

But the best fishers are the tame cormorants, who catch fish for their masters.

THE TWO GREAT WONDERS.—The great CANAL is a wonder. It joins the two rivers ; so that a Chinese can go by water from Canton to Pekin

The great WALL is a greater wonder, but not nearly as useful as the canal.

This wall was built at the north of China to keep the Tartars out. It is fifteen hundred miles long, twenty feet high, and twenty-five broad. But there were not soldiers enough in China to keep the enemies out, and the Tartars came over the wall.

The Emperor of China is a Tartar.

The Empress has not small feet, like the Chinese.

It is the Tartars who forced the Chinese to shave their heads, for they used to tie up their hair in a knot at the top of their heads. Many of the Chinese preferred losing their *heads* to their hair. Was it not cruel to cut off their heads, merely because they would not shave them? But the Tartars were very cruel to the Chinese.

KNOWLEDGE AND INVENTIONS.—We must allow that the Chinese are very clever. They found out how to print, and they found out how to make gunpowder, and they found out the use of the loadstone. What is that? A piece of steel rubbed against the loadstone will always point to the north. The Chinese found out these three things, printing, gunpowder, and the use of the loadstone, *before* we in Europe found them out. But they did not teach them to us; we found them out ourselves.

But there are two arts that the Chinese did teach us: how to make silk, and how to make china or porcelain. And yet I should not say they taught us; for they tried to prevent our learning their arts; but we saw their silk and their porcelain, and by degrees we learned to make them ourselves. A sly monk brought some silkworms' eggs from China hidden in a hollow walking-stick.

LANGUAGE.—There is no other language at all like the Chinese. Instead of letters making words, there is a picture for each word. I call it a picture, but it is more like a figure than a picture.

The Chinese use brushes for writing instead of pens; and they rub cakes of ink on a little marble dish, first dipping them in a little water, as we dip cakes of paint. There is a hollow place in the marble dish to hold the water. What do you think the Chinese mean by " the four precious things ?" They mean the ink, the brush, the marble dish, and the water. They call them precious because they are so fond of writing. Schoolmasters are held in great honour in China, as, indeed, they *ought* to be *everywhere.* Yet schools in China are much like those in Turkey, more fit for parrots than children; only Chinese boys sit in chairs with desks before them, instead of sitting cross-legged on the ground as in Turkey. They learn first to paint the words, and next to repeat lessons by heart. This they do in a loud scream; always turning their backs to their master while they are saying their lessons to him.

The first book which children read is full of stories, with a picture on each page. Would you like to hear one of these stories?

"There was a boy of eight years old, named Un-wen. His parents were so poor that they could not afford to buy a gauze curtain for their bed, to keep off the flies in summer. This boy could not bear that his parents should be bitten by the flies; so he stood by their bed-side, and uncovered his little bosom and his back that the flies might bite him, instead of his parents. 'For,' said he, 'if they fill themselves with my blood, they will let my parents rest.'"

Would it be right for a little boy to behave in this way? Certainly not; for it would grieve kind parents that their little boy should be bitten. Poor little Chinese boys! They do not know about Him who was bitten by the old serpent, that we might not be devoured and destroyed.

PUNISHMEMT.—The Chinese are very quiet and orderly; and no wonder, because they are afraid of the great bamboo stick.

The mandarins (or rulers of towns) often sen-

tence offenders to lie upon the ground, and to
have thirty strokes of the bamboo. But the
wooden collar is worse than the bamboo stick.
It is a great piece of wood with a hole for a man
to put his head through. The men in wooden
collars are brought out of their prisons every

Criminal in a Collar.

morning, and chained to a wall, where everybody passing by can see them. They cannot
feed themselves in their wooden collars, because
they cannot bring their hands to their mouths ;
but sometimes a son may be seen feeding his
father, as he stands chained to the wall. There
are men also whose business it is to feed the
prisoners. For great crimes men are strangled
or beheaded.

CHARACTER.—A Chinaman's character cannot

be known at first. You might suppose from his way of speaking, that a Chinaman was very humble; because he calls himself "the worthless fellow," or "the stupid one," and he calls his son "the son of a dog;" but if you were to tell him he had an evil heart, he would be very much offended: for he only gives himself these names that he may *seem* humble. He calls his acquaintance "venerable uncle," or "honourable brother." This he does to please them. The Chinese are very proud of their country, and think there is none like it. They have given it the name of the "Heavenly or Celestial Empire." They look upon foreigners as monkeys and devils. Often a woman may be heard in the streets saying to her little child "There is a foreign devil" (or a Fan Quei). The Chinese think the English very ugly, and call them the "red-haired nation."

It must be owned that the Chinese are industrious: indeed if they were not they would be starved. A poor man often has to work all day up to the knees in water in the rice-field, and yet gets nothing for supper but a little rice and a few potatoes.

The ladies who can live without working are very idle, and in the winter rise very late in the morning. Why should they rise early when they have nothing to do?

They do not ever keep their rooms neat. They never work with their needles, but hire tailors to make their clothes. They cannot read. They like to stand about talking. How unhappy they must be!

Men, too, play, as children do here: flying kites is a favourite game. Dancing, however, is quite unknown.

The Chinese are **very** selfish and unfeeling. Beggars may be seen in the middle of the town dying, and no one caring for them, but people gambling close by.

The Chinese have an idea that after a man is dead the house must be cleansed from ghosts: so, to save themselves this trouble, poor people often cast their dying relations out of their hovels into the street to die!

But in general sons treat their parents with great respect. They often keep their father's coffin in the house for three months, and a son has been known to sleep by it for three years. Relations are usually kind to each other, because they meet together in the "Hall of Ancestors" to worship the same person. To save money they often eat together, and a hundred often eat every day at the same table.

The Chinese used to be temperate, preferring tea to wine. There are tea-taverns in the towns. How much better than our beer-shops. But lately they have begun to smoke opium. This is the juice of the white poppy, made up into dark balls. The Chinese are not allowed to have it ; but the English (sad to say) sell it to them secretly. There are many opium-taverns in China, where men may be seen lying on cushions snuffing up the hot opium, and puffing it out of their mouths. Those who smoke opium have sunken cheeks and trembling hands, and soon become old, foolish, and sick. Why, then, do they take opium ? Many of them say they wish to leave it off, but cannot.

MISSIONARIES.—Are there any in China ? Yes, many ; and more are going there. But

Missionary Travelling.

how many are wanted for so many people ! Missionaries travel about China to distribute

Bibles and tracts. See one who hired a rough
kind of chair with two bearers. In this he went
to villages among the mountains, where a white
man had never been seen. The children screaming with terror ran to their mothers. The men
came round him to look at his clothes and his
white skin. They were much surprised at the
whitness of his hands, and they put their
yellow ones close to his—to see the difference.
These mountaineers were kind, and brought tea
and cakes to refresh the stranger.

Christian Girls' School.

An English lady went to China to teach little
girls; for no one teaches *them*. She has several
little creatures in her school that she saved from
perishing, because the Chinese are so cruel as
to leave many girl-babies to die in the streets :

they say that girls are not worth the trouble of bringing up.

One cold rainy evening, Miss Aldersey heard a low wailing outside the street-door, and looking out she saw a poor babe, wrapped in coarse matting, lying on the stone pavement. She could not bear to leave it there to be devoured by famished dogs; so she kindly took it in, and brought it up.

It is a common thing to stumble over the bodies of dead babies in the streets. In England it is counted murder to kill a babe, but it is thought no harm in China. Yet the Chinese call themselves good. But when you ask a poor man where he expects to go when he dies, he replies "To hell, of course;" and he says this with a loud laugh. His reason for thinking he shall go to hell is, because he has not money enough to give to the gods; for rich people all expect to go to heaven. Mandarins especially expect to go there. If they were to read the Bible, they would see that God will punish kings, and mighty men, and great captains, and *all* who are wicked.*

---

* Taken from Du Halde, Bishop of Victoria, Rev. Walter Midhurst, and Davies.

COCHIN-CHINA.

Any one on hearing this name would guess that the country was like China; and so it is. If you were to go there you would be reminded of China by many of the customs. You would see at dinner small basins instead of plates, chop-sticks instead of knives and forks: you would have rice to eat instead of bread; and rice-wine to drink instead of grape-wine.

But you would not find *all* the Chinese customs in Cochin-China; for you would see the women walking about at liberty, and with large feet, that is, with feet of the natural size, and not cramped up like the "golden lilies" of China. Neither would you see the people treated as strictly in Cochin-China as in China. Beatings are not nearly as common there, and behaviour is not nearly as good as in China.

The people are very different from the Chinese, for they are gay and talkative, and open and sociable, while the Chinese are just the contrary. However, they resemble the Chinese in fondness for eating. They are very fond of giving grand dinners, and sometimes provide a hundred dishes, and invite a hundred guests. A man is thought very generous who gives such grand dinners. No one in Cochin-China would think of eating his morsel alone, but every one asks those around to partake ; and if any one were not to do so, he would be counted very mean. Yet the people of Cochin-China are always begging for gifts ; and if they cannot get the things they ask for, they steal them. Are they generous ? No, because they are covetous. It is impossible to be at the same time generous and covetous; for what goodness is there in giving away our *own* things, if we are wishing for other people's things ?

And now let us leave the *people* and look at the *land.* It is fruitful and beautiful, being watered abundantly by fine rivers : but these rivers, flowing amongst lofty mountains, often overflow, and drown men and cattle. The grass of such a country must be very rich : and there are cows feeding on it ; yet there is no milk or butter to be had. Why ? Because the people have a foolish idea that it is wrong to milk cows.

In no country are there stronger and larger elephants ; so strong and so large that one can carry thirteen persons on his back at once.

The land is full of idols: for Buddha, or Fo, is worshipped in Cochin-China, as he is in China.

The idols are sometimes kept in high trees, and priests may be seen mounting ladders to present offerings.

But the people are not satisfied with idols in trees ; they have pocket idols, which they carry about with them everywhere.

TONQUIN.—CAMBODIA.

These two kingdoms belong to the king of
Cochin-China : yet all three, Tonquin, Cambo-
dia, and Cochin-China, pay tribute to China,
and therefore they must be considered as conquered countries.

They are all very much like China in their
customs.　There are large cities in them all, and
multitudes of people, but very little is known
about them in England.*

HINDOSTAN.

This word, Hindostan, means "black place," for
in the Persian language "hind" is "black," and
" stan " is "place."　You may guess, therefore,
that the people in Hindostan are very dark ; yet
they are not quite black, and some of the ladies
are only of a light brown complexion.

What a large country Hindostan is!　Has it an
emperor of its own as China has ?　No ; large
as it is, it belongs to the little country called
England.

How did the England get it ?

They conquered it by little and little.　When

* Taken from Murray's "Discoveries in Asia."

first they came there, they found a Mahomedan people, called the Moguls. These Moguls had conquered Hindostan : but by degrees the English conquered them, and became masters of all the land.

There is only one small country among the mountains which has not been conquered by the English, and that place is Nepaul. It is near the Himalaya mountains. See that great, great chain of mountains in the north : they are the Himalaya—the highest mountains in the world.

The word "him," or "hem," means snow—and

Sheep laden with Goods.

snowy indeed are those mountains. Among the Himalaya mountains lies the valley of Cashmere, where beautiful shawls are woven. The wool is taken from beneath the hair of goats that feed in a country beyond the mountains, called Thibet. This fine wool is made into packs, and tied to the backs of sheep that are taught to climb the narrow and slippery paths. These little animals are the wool-carriers to Cashmere.

There is a great river that flows from the Himalaya called the Ganges. It flows by many mouths into the ocean; yet of all these mouths only one is deep enough for large ships to sail in; the other mouths are all choked up with sand. The deep mouth of the Ganges is called the Hooghly.

It was on the banks of the Hooghly that the first English city was built. It was built by some English merchants, and it is called Calcutta. That name comes from the name of a horrible idol called Kalee, of which more will be said hereafter.

Calcutta is now a very grand city; there is the governor's palace, and there are the mansions of many rich Englishmen. It has been called "the city of palaces."

There is another great river on the other side of Hindostan called the Indus. It was from that river that Hindostan got the name of India, or the East Indies.

VILLAGES.—Calcutta is built on a large plain called Bengal. Dotted about this plain are

many villages. At a distance they look prettier
than English villages, for they are overshadowed
with thick trees; but they are wretched places
to live in. The huts are scarcely big enough
to hold human creatures, nor strong enough to
bear the pelting of the storm. When you enter
them you will find neither floor nor window, and
very little furniture; neither chair nor table,
nor bed—nothing but a large earthen bottle for
fetching water, a smaller one for drinking, a
basket for clothes, a few earthen pans, a few
brass plates, and a mat.

A Hindoo is counted very rich who has procured a wooden bedstead to place his mat upon,
and a wooden trunk, with a lock and key, to
contain his clothes; such a man is considered to
have a well-furnished house.

As you pass through the villages, you may
see groups of men sitting under the trees smoking
their pipes, while children without clothes are
rolling in the dust, and sporting with the kids.
Prowling about the villages are hungry dogs and
whining jackals, seeking for bones and offal;
but the children are too much used to these
creatures to be afraid of them. Hovering in
the air are crows and kites ready to secure any
morsel they can see, or even to snatch the food,
if they can, out of the children's little hands.

What a confused noise do you hear as you

pass along! barking, whining, and squalling, loud laughing, and incessant chattering. It is a heathen village, and the sweet notes of praise to God are never sung there.

Yet in every village there is a little temple

Hindoo family going to sacrifice.

with an idol, and a priest to take care of the idol, to lay it down to sleep, and to offer it food, which he eats himself.

The poor people bring the food for the idol with flowers, and place it at the door of the temple.

Appearance.—The Hindoos are pleasing in

their appearance, for their features are well-
formed, their teeth are white, and their eyes
have a soft expression. The women take much
pains to dress their long black hair, which is
soft as silk : they gather it up in a knot at the
top of their heads, and crown it with flowers.
They have no occasion for a needle to make
their dresses, as they are all in one piece. They
wind a long strip of white muslin (called a saree)
round their bodies, and fold it over their heads
like a veil, and then they are full dressed, except
their ornaments, and with these they load themselves ; glass rings of different colours on their
arms, silver rings on their fingers and toes, and
gold rings in their ears and their nose.

The men wear a long strip of calico twisted
closely round their bodies, and another drawn
loosely over their shoulders ; but this last they
cast off when they are at work : it is their upper
garment. On their heads they wear turbans,
and on their feet sandals. The clothes of both
men and women are generally white or pink, or
white bordered with red.

Food.—The most common food is rice ; and
with this curry is often mixed to give it a relish.
What is curry ? It is a mixture of herbs, spices,
and oil.

Very poor people cannot afford to eat either
rice or curry ; and they eat some coarse grain

instead. A lady who made a feast for the poor provided nothing but rice, and she found that it was thought as good as roast beef and plum-pudding are thought in England. The day after the feast some of the poor creatures came to pick up the grains of rice that were fallen upon the ground.

The rich Hindoos eat mutton and venison, but not beef: this they think it wicked to eat, because they worship bulls and cows.

A favourite food is clarified butter, called "ghee;" white, rancid stuff, kept in skin bottles to mix with curry.

Water is the general drink, and there could not be a better. Yet there are intoxicating drinks, and some of the Hindoos have learned to love them, from seeing the English drink too much. What a sad thing that Christians should set a bad example to heathens!

PRODUCTIONS.—There are many beautiful trees in India never seen in England, and many nice fruits never tasted here.

The palm-tree, with its immense leaves, is the glory of India. These leaves are very useful; they form the roof, the umbrella, the bed, the plate, and the writing-paper of the Hindoo.

The most curious tree in India is the banyan, because one tree grows into a hundred. How is that? The branches hang down, touch the ground, strike root there, and spring up into new trees—joined to the old. Under an aged banyan there is shade for a large congregation. Seventy thousand men might sit beneath its boughs.

There is a sort of grass which grows a hundred feet high, and becomes hard like wood. It is called the bamboo. The stem is hollow like a pipe, and is often used as a water-pipe. It serves also for posts for houses, and for poles for carriages.

There is abundance of nice fruits in India; and of these the mangoe is the best. You might mistake it for a pear when you saw it, but not when you tasted it. Pears cannot grow in India; the sun is too hot even for grapes and oranges, excepting on the hills.

The chief productions of India are rice and cotton: rice is the food, and cotton is the clothing of the Hindoo, and quantities of these are sent to England; for though we have wheat for food, we want rice too; and though we have wool for clothing, we want cotton too.

RELIGION.—There is no nation that has so many gods as the Hindoos. What do you think of three hundred and thirty millions? There are not so many people in Hindostan as that. No one person can know the names of all these gods; and who would wish to know them? Some of them are snakes, and some are monkeys!

The chief god of all is called Brahm. But, strange to say, no one worships him. There is not an image of him in all India.

And why not? Because he is too great, the Hindoos say, to think of men on earth. He is always in a kind of sleep. What would be the use of worshipping him?

Next to him are three gods, and they are part of Brahm.

Their names are—

I. Brahma, the Creator.
II. Vishnoo, the Preserver.
III. Sheeva, the Destroyer.

Which of these should you think men ought to worship the most? Not the destroyer. Yet it is *him* they do worship the most. Very few worship Brahm the creator. And why not? Because the Hindoos think he can do no more for them than he has done; and they do not care about thanking him.

Vishnoo, the preserver, is a great favourite; because it is supposed that he bestows all manner of gifts. The Hindoos say he has been *nine* times upon the earth; first as a fish, then as a tortoise, a man, a lion, a boar, a dwarf, a giant; *twice* as a warrior named Ram, and once as a thief, named Krishna. They say he will come again as a conquering king riding on a white horse. Is it not wonderful they should say that?

It reminds one of the prophecy in Rev. xix, about Christ's second coming. Did the Hindoos hear that prophecy in old time? They may have heard it, for the apostle Thomas once preached in India,—at least we believe he did.

Why do the people worship Sheeva the destroyer? Because they hope that if they gain his favour, they shall not be destroyed by him. They do not know that none can save from the destroyer but God.

The Hindoos make images of their gods. Brahma is represented as riding on a goose; Vishnoo on a creature half-bird and half-man; and Sheeva on a bull.

Sheeva's image looks horribly ferocious, with the tiger-skin and the necklace of skulls and snakes; but Sheeva's *wife* is far fiercer than himself. Her name is Kalee. Her whole delight is said to be in blood. Those who wish to please her, offer up the blood of beasts; but those who wish to please her still more, offer up their own blood.

Her great temple, called Kalee Ghaut, is near Calcutta. There is a great feast in her honour once-a-year at that temple. Early in the morning crowds assemble there with the noise of trumpets and kettle-drums. See those wild, fierce men adorned with flowers. They go towards the temple. A blacksmith is ready.

Lo! one puts out his tongue, and the blacksmith cuts it: this is to please Kalee: another chooses rather to have an iron bar run through his tongue. Some thrust iron bars and burning coals into their sides. The boldest mount a wooden

Temple of Kalee.

scaffold and throw themselves down upon iron spikes beneath, stuck in bags of sand. It is very painful to fall upon these spikes; but there is another way of torture quite as painful—it is the swing. Those who determine to swing allow the blacksmith to drive hooks into the flesh upon their backs, and hanging by these hooks they swing in the air for ten minutes, or even for half-an-hour. And why all these cruel tortures? To please Kalee, and to make the people wonder and admire, for the multitude around shout with joy as they behold these horrible deeds.

Would you think it? even little girls enjoy these horrible sights! This shows how wicked the human heart is by nature.

A Christian lady taught heathen children near Calcutta. One day she missed one of her little scholars. Next day the child was in her class as usual.

"Why, my dear, did you stay away yesterday?" inquired the kind teacher.

"My mother took me to see the great goddess Kalee."

"Did Kalee speak to you?

"No," replied the child.

"Do you think she heard you?"

The little girl hesitated. At last she said,—

"No, I fear not. Other stone things cannot generally hear."

"Did she look at you lovingly, as if she were pleased with your offering?"

The child laughed and said,—

"Oh! ma'am you have never seen Kalee, or you would not ask such a question; she is a great frightful, black, stone woman, with a necklace of human skulls round her; and she has a large red tongue, and she is dancing on the dead body of a man."

"Yes," the lady replied, in a sorrowful voice,

"I know all that. And you can tell me who that dead man was."

"Yes; it was Kalee's own husband. You must not blame her; she killed him by *mistake*."

"My little girl, a *goddess* do a thing by *mistake!* How can that ever be? Do you know what is written in your Catechism about God ?"

"Oh, yes. 'We can hide nothing from God, and He knows all things.'"

The child did not know what more to say in favour of Kalee; but instead of owning she was wrong, she replied,—

"But it did me good to see the idol : it does every one good : mother says it does, and I am sure I felt it."

Poor little girl ! Brought up to worship the horrid Kalee, instead of

"Gentle Jesus, meek and mild."

THE CASTES.—The Hindoos pretend, that when Brahma created men he made some out of his mouth, some out of his arms, some out of his breast, and some out of his foot. They say the priests came out of Brahma's mouth, the soldiers came out of his arm, the merchants came out of his breast, the labourers came out of his foot. You may easily guess who invented this history. It was the priests themselves : it was they who wrote the sacred books where this history is found.

The priests are very proud of their high birth, and they call themselves Brahmins.

The labourers, who are told they come out of Brahma's foot, are much ashamed of their low birth. They are called sudras.

You would be astonished to hear the great respect the sudras pay to the high and haughty Brahmins. When a sudra meets a Brahmin in the street, he touches the ground three times with his forehead, then, taking the priest's foot in his hand, kisses his toe.

The water in which a Brahmin has washed his feet is thought very holy. It is even believed that such water can cure diseases.

A Hindoo prince, who was very ill of a fever, was advised to try this remedy. He invited the Brahmins from all parts of the country to assemble at his palace. Many thousands came. Each, as he arrived, was requested to wash his feet in a basin. This was the medicine given to the sick prince to drink. It cost a great deal of money to procure it; for several shillings were given to each Brahmin to pay him for his trouble, and a good dinner was provided for all. It is said that the prince recovered immediately, but we are quite certain that it was not the water which cured him.

In the holy books, or shasters, great blessings are promised to those who are kind to a Brahmin.

Any one who gives him an umbrella will never
more be scorched by the sun; any one who gives
him a pair of shoes will never have blistered
feet; any one who gives him sweet spices will
never more be annoyed by ill smells; and any
one who gives him a cow will go to heaven.

You may be sure that, after such promises,
the Brahmins get plenty of presents; indeed,
they may generally be known by their well-fed
appearance, as well as by their proud manner of
walking. They always wear a white cord hung
round their necks.

But we must not suppose that all Brahmins
are rich, and all sudras poor; for it is not so.
There are so many Brahmins that some can find
no employment as priests, and they are obliged
to learn trades. Many of them become cooks.

There are sudras as rich as princes; but still
a sudra can never be as honourable as a Brahmin,
though the Brahmin be the cook and the sudra
the master.

But the sudras are not the *most* despised
people. Far from it. It is those who have no
caste at all who are the most despised. They
are called pariahs. These are people who have
lost their caste. It is a very easy thing to lose
caste, and once lost it can never be regained.

A Brahmin would lose his caste by eating with
a sudra; a sudra would lose his by eating with

a pariah, and by eating with *you*—yes, with *you* ; for the Hindoos think that no one is holy but themselves. It often makes a missionary smile, when he enters a cottage, to see the people putting away their food with haste, lest he should defile it by his touch.

Once an English officer, walking along the road, passed very near a Hindoo just going to eat his dinner ; suddenly he saw the man take up the dish and dash it angrily to the ground. Why ? The officer's shadow had passed over the food and polluted it.

If you were to invite poor Hindoos to come to a feast, they would not eat if you sat down with them : nor would they eat unless they knew a Hindoo had cooked their food. Even children at school will not eat with children of a lower caste,—or with their teachers, if the teachers are not Hindoos.

There was once a little Hindoo girl named Rajee. She went to a missionary's school, but she would not eat with her schoolfellows, because she belonged to a higher caste than they did. As she lived at the school, her mother brought her food every day, and Rajee sat under a tree to eat it. At the end of two years she told her mother that she wished to turn from idols, and serve the living God. Her mother was much troubled at hearing this, and begged her child not to bring disgrace on the family by becoming a Christian. But Rajee was anxious to save her precious soul. She cared no longer for her caste, for she knew that all she had been taught about it was deceit and folly; therefore one day she sat down and ate with her schoolfellows. When her mother heard of Rajee's conduct, she ran to the school in a rage, and seizing her little daughter by the hair of her head, began to beat her severely. Then she hastened to the priests to ask them whether the child had lost her caste for ever. The priests replied, "Has the child got her new teeth?" "No," said the mother. "Then we can cleanse her, and when her new teeth come she will be as pure as ever. But you must pay a good deal of money for the cleansing." Were they not *cunning* priests? and *covetous* priests, too?

The money was paid, and Rajee was brought home against her will. Dreadful sufferings awaited the poor child. The cleansing was a cruel business. The priests burned the child's tongue. This was one of their cruelties. When little Rajee was entirely cleansed, she was suffered to go back to school, but her barbarous tormentors had made her so ill that she was obliged to keep her bed at school.

The poor deceived mother came to see her. "I am going to Jesus," said the young martyr.

The mother began to weep, "O Rajee, we will not let you die!"

"But I am glad," the little sufferer replied, "because I shall go to Jesus. If you, mother, would love Him, and give up your idols, we should meet again in heaven."

An hour afterwards Rajee went to heaven; but I have never heard whether her mother gave up her idols.*

THE GANGES.—This beautiful river waters the sultry plain of Bengal. God made this river to be a blessing, but man has turned it into a curse. The Hindoos say the river Ganges is the goddess Gunga; and they flock from all parts of India to worship her. When they reach the river they bathe in it, and fancy they have washed away all their sins. They carry away large bottles of the sacred water for their friends at home.

But this is not all; very cruel deeds are committed by the side of the river. It is supposed that all who die there will go to the Hindoo heaven. It is therefore the custom to drag dying people out of their beds, and to lay them in the mud, exposed to the heat of the broiling sun, and then pour pails of water over their heads.

One sick man, who was being carried to the water, covered up as if he were dead, suddenly threw off the covering, and called out, "I am

* Church Missionary Juvenile Instructor, 1849.

not dead, I am only very ill." He knew that the cruel people who were carrying him were going to cast him into the water while he was still alive: but nothing he could say, could save him : the cruel creatures answered, " You may as well die *now* as at another time ;" and so they drowned him, pretending all the while to be very kind.

It is thought a good thing to be thrown into the river after death. The Ganges is the great burying-place ; and dead bodies may be seen floating on its waters, while crows and vultures are tearing the flesh from the bones. There would be many more of these horrible sights were it not that many bodies are burned, and their ashes only cast into the river.

Some foolish deceived creatures drown themselves in the Ganges, hoping to be very happy hereafter as a reward. The Brahmins are ready to accompany such people into the water. Some men were once seen going into the river with a large empty jar fastened to the back of each. The empty jar prevented them from sinking ; but there was a cup in the hands of each of the poor men, and with these cups they filled the jars, and then they began to sink. One of them grew frightened, and tried to get to shore ; but the wicked Brahmins in their boats hunted him, and tried to keep him in the water ; however they could not catch him, and the miserable man escaped. There are villages near the river whither such poor creatures flee, and where they end their days together; for their old friends would not speak to them if they were to return to their homes.

BEGGARS.—As you walk about Hindostan, you will sometimes meet a horrible object, with no other covering than a tiger's skin, or else an orange scarf; his body is besmeared with ashes, his hair matted like the shaggy coat of a wild beast, and his nails like birds' claws. The man is a beggar, and a very bold one, because he is considered as one of the holiest of men. Who is he?

A sunyasse. Who is *he?*

A Brahmin, who wishing to be more holy than other Brahmins (holy as they are), has left all and become a beggar. As a reward, he expects when he dies, to go straight to heaven, without being first born again in the world. It is wonderful to see the tortures which a sunyasse will endure. He will stand for years on one leg, till it is full of wounds, or if he prefer it, he will clench his fist till the nails grow through the hands.

These holy beggars are found in all parts of India, but they are particularly fond of the most desolate spots. Near the mouth of the Ganges there are some desert places, the resort of tigers, and there many of the sunyasses live in huts.

They pretend not to be afraid of the tigers, and the Hindoos think that tigers will not touch such holy men; but it is certain that tigers have been seen dragging some of these proud men into the woods.

There is another kind of beggars called fakirs; they are just as wicked and foolish as the sunyasses; but they are Mahomedans, and not Brahmins.

ANIMALS.—Some of the fiercest and most disagreeable animals are highly honoured in India.

Serpent Worship.

The monkey is counted as a god; the consequence is, that the monkeys, finding they are treated with respect, grow very bold, and are continually scrambling upon the roofs of the houses. In one place there is a garden where monkeys riot about at their pleasure; for all in that garden is for them alone,—the delicious fruits, the cool fountains, the shady bowers—all are for the worthless, mischievous monkeys.

But if it be strange for men to worship *monkeys*, is it not stranger still to worship *snakes* and *serpents?* Yet there is a temple in India where serpents crawl about at their pleasure, where they are waited upon by priests, and fed with fruits and every dainty. How much delighted must the OLD SERPENT be with this worship!

Feeding Kites.

Kites, also, those fierce birds, are worshipped. There is meat sold in shops on purpose for them; and it is bought and thrown up in the air for the greedy creatures to catch.

There are splendid peacocks flying about in the woods, but the Hindoos do not worship them; they shoot and eat them.

Of all the animals in India, there is none which terrifies man so much as the tiger. The Bengal tiger is a fine and fierce beast. Woe to the man or woman on whom he springs? What then, do you think, must become of the man who falls into his DEN? Tigers' dens are generally hid in jungles, which are places covered with trees, and overgrown with shrubs and tall grass.

A gentleman was once walking through a jungle, when he felt himself sinking into the ground, while a cloud of dust blinded his eyes. Soon he heard a low growling noise. He fancied that he had sunk into a den, and—so he had. Beside him lay some little tigers—too young indeed to hurt him; but these tigers had a mother, and she could not be far off, though she was not in the den when the stranger fell in. The terrified man felt there was no time to be lost, for the tigress, he knew, would *soon* return to her cubs. How could he prepare to meet her? He had neither gun nor sword, nor even stick in his hand. But a thought came into his head.

Snatching a silk handkerchief from his neck, and taking another from his pocket, he bound them tightly round his arm up to his elbow ; and thus prepared to meet his enemy. She soon appeared, crouching on the ground, and then with a spring leaped upon the stranger. At the same moment the brave man thrust his arm between her open jaws, and seizing hold of her rough tongue, twisted it backwards and forwards with all his might. The beast was now unable to close her mouth, and to bite with her sharp fangs ; but she could scratch with her sharp claws : and scratch she did, till the clothes were torn off the man's body, and the flesh from his bones. But the brave man would not loose his hold ; and the tigress was tired out first : becoming alarmed, she made a sudden start backward, and in so doing she jerked her tongue out of the man's hand—then rushed out of the den, and out of the jungle.*

How glad was the man to escape from a horrible fate ! his body was faint and bleeding ; but his life was preserved, and his heart overflowed with gratitude to God for his wonderful deliverance. He who delivered Daniel from the lion's den delivered him from the tiger's den. The tiger's mouth indeed had not been *shut ;*

* Taken from " The Juvenile Missionary Magazine," April, 1849. The story is well authenticated.

but his *open* mouth had not been suffered to devour the Lord's servant.

THE THUGS.

There is a set of people in India more dangerous than wild beasts. They are called Thugs, that is, *deceivers;* and well do they deserve the name, for their whole employment is to *deceive,* that they may *destroy.* Yet they are not ashamed of their wickedness; for they worship the goddess Kalee, and they know that she delights in blood. Before they set out on one of their cruel journeys they bow down before the image of Kalee, and they ask her to bless the shovel and the cloth that they hold in their hands.

What are *they* for?

The cloth is to strangle poor travellers, and the shovel to dig their graves.

A Hindoo family were once travelling, when they overtook three men on the way. These men seemed very civil and obliging; and they soon got acquainted with the family, and accompanied them on their journey. Who were these men? Alas! they were Thugs. It was very foolish of the family to be so ready to go with strangers. At last they came up to three other men, who were sitting under the shade of a tree, eating sugared rice. These men also were

Thugs; and they had agreed with the other
Thugs to help them in their wicked plans. But
the family thought they were kind and friendly
men, and consented to sit down with them in the
shade, and to partake of their food. They did
not know that with the rice was mixed a sort of
drug to cause people to fall asleep. The family
ate and fell asleep; and when they were asleep,
the Thugs, with their cloths, strangled them all
—the father, the mother, and the five young
people,—and then with their shovels they dug
their graves. But before they buried them they
stripped them of their garments and their jewels;
for it was to get these precious spoils they had
committed these dreadful murders. The Thugs
went afterwards to the priests of Kalee to receive
a blessing, and they rewarded the priests by
giving them some of their stolen treasures.

But, after all, these wicked men did not escape
punishment; for the English governors heard of
their crimes, and caught them, and brought
them to justice. Then these murderers confessed the wicked deed just related: but this was
not their only crime; for it had been the business of their lives to rob and to destroy.

Do not these Thugs resemble him who is
always walking about seeking whom he may
devour? Only he destroys the *soul* as well
as the *body*. He is the great Deceiver, and the

great Destroyer. None but God can keep us
from falling into his power: therefore we pray,
"Deliver us from evil," or from the evil one.

THE HINDOO WOMEN.

It is a miserable thing to be a Hindoo lady.
While she is a very little girl, she is allowed to
play about, but when she comes to be ten or
twelve years, she is shut up in the back rooms of
the house till she is married; and when she is
married she is still shut up. She may, indeed,
walk in the garden at the back of the house,
but nowhere else.

Hindoo ladies are not taught even those trifling
accomplishments which Chinese ladies learn;
they can neither paint, nor play music; much
less can they read and write. They amuse
themselves by putting on their ornaments, or by
making curries and sweetmeats to please their
husbands; but most of their time they spend in
idleness,—sauntering about and chattering non-
sense. As rich Hindoos have several wives, the
ladies are not alone: and being so much
together, they quarrel a great deal.

Some English ladies once visited the house of a
rich Hindoo. They were led into the court at the
back of the house, and shown into a little chamber.
One by one some women came in, all looking

very shy and afraid to speak; yet they were dressed very fine in muslin *sarees*, worked with gold and silver flowers, and they were adorned with pearls and diamonds. At last they ventured to admire the clothes of their visitors, and even to touch them. Then they asked the English ladies to come and see their jewels; and they took them into a little dark chamber, with gratings for windows, and displayed their treasures. They talked very loud, and all together and so foolishly, that the ladies reproved them. The poor creatures replied, "We should like to learn to read and work like the English ladies; but we have nothing to do, and so we are accustomed to be idle, and to talk foolishly. Do come again, and bring us books, and pictures, and dolls.

You see what useless, wearisome lives the Hindoo *ladies* lead. Now, hear what hard and wretched lives the *poor* women lead. The wife of a poor man rises from her mat before it is day, and by the light of a lamp spins cotton for the family clothing. Next she feeds the children, and sweeps the house and yard, and cleans the brass and stone vessels. Then she washes the rice, bruises, and boils it. By this time it is ten o'clock, when she goes with some other women to bathe in the river, or if there be no river near in a great tank of rain-water. While there, she often makes a clay image of her god, and worships it with prayers, and bowings, and offerings of fruit and flowers, for nearly an hour. On her return home she prepares the curry for dinner : her kitchen is a clay furnace in the yard, and there she boils the rice. When dinner is ready, she dares not sit down with her husband to eat it : no, she places it respectfully before his mat, and then retires to the yard. Her little boys eat with their father ; but her little girls dine with her upon the food that is left.

It is not the busy life she leads that makes her unhappy : it is the ill-treatment she endures. A kind word is seldom spoken to her : but a hard blow is often given. Her own boys are encouraged to insult her, because she is only a woman. She is taught to worship her husband as a god, however bad he may be. There is a proverb which shows how much women are despised in India. "How can you place the black rice-pot beside the golden spice-box !" By the rice-pot a woman is meant ; by the spice-box a man : and the meaning of the proverb is, that a wife is unworthy to sit at the same table with her husband.

In this manner a *wife* is treated : a *widow* is still more despised. She is obliged to live in her father's house, or (if she have no father) in her brother's house, and to do the hardest work, and never to eat more than one meal a day, and that meal of the coarsest food. Once she was not allowed to marry again, but a law has lately been made by the English government allowing widows to marry again. Widows used to burn themselves in a great fire with their husbands' dead bodies: but the English government has forbidden them to do so any more; yet their hard-hearted relations still make them as miserable as possible.

MISSIONARIES.—There are hundreds of missionaries in India; but not nearly enough for so many millions of people. The Hindoos call them Padri-Sahibs, which means "Father-Gentlemen," and they give them this name to show their love, as well as respect.

Once a missionary who had been long in India, was going back to England for a little while. It was from Calcutta that he set sail. The Christian Hindoos stood in crowds by the river-side to bid him farewell. Among the rest was a little girl with her parents. She was a Christian child, who had turned from idols to serve the living God. The missionary said to her, "Well, my child, you know I am going to England. What shall I bring you from that country?"

"I do not want anything," she modestly replied. "I have my parents, and my brother, and the Padri-Sahibs, and my books: what can I want more?"

"But," said the missionary, "you are only a little girl, and surely you would like something from England. Shall I bring you some playthings?"

"No thank you," said the child; "I do not want playthings—I am learning to read."

Picture of children on the Ganges.

"Come, come," said the missionary, "shall I bring you a playfellow, a white child from England?"

"No, no," answered the little girl; "it would be taking her from her parents."

"Well, then," said her friend, "is there nothing I can bring you?"

"Well, if you are so kind as to insist on bringing me something, ask the Christians in England to send me a Bible-book and more PADRI-SAHIBS."

This was a good request indeed, but to get Padri-Sahibs is a hard thing to do. Who can tell how much good they have done already? There are many Christian villages in India, and they are as different from heathen villages as a dove's nest is different from a tiger's den.

Some very wicked men have been converted. You have heard of those proud and hateful beggars, the Sunyasees and the Fakirs.

One day a missionary, who had gone for his

Picture of Fakir and teacher.

health to the Himalaya mountains, was walking in the verandah of his house, when he was surprised by a man suddenly throwing himself down at his feet and embracing his knees. The missionary could not tell who he was, for a dark blanket covered the man's head and face. But soon the covering was lifted up, and a swarthy and withered countenance was shown : the missionary knew it to be that of an old Fakir he once had known, as the chief priest of a gang of robbers, but now the Mahomedan was become a Christian ; and he had travelled six hundred miles, hoping to see once more the face of his teacher; and lo ! he had seen it at last.*

SCHOOLS.—The Hindoos have schools of their own, but only for boys. The scholars sit in a shed, cross-legged upon mats, and learn to scratch letters with iron pins upon large leaves. But what can they learn from Brahmin teachers except foolish tales about false gods ?

Missionaries have far better schools, where the Bible is taught; the missionaries' wives have schools for girls; and sometimes they take pity on poor orphans, and receive them into their houses.

One evening as a Christian lady was returning home, she saw a Hindoo woman lying on the ground, and a little boy sitting by her side. The

* See " Church Missionary Juvenile Magazine," March, 1849.

lady spoke kindly to the sick woman, and then
the little boy looked up and said, with tears in
his eyes, "My mother is sick and has nothing to
eat; I fear she will die." The lady had com-
passion on the mother and the child, and hastening home, she sent her servant to fetch them both.
They were soon put to rest on a nice clean mat,
with a blanket to cover them; but the mother
died next morning. The little boy was left an
orphan, but not forlorn, nor friendless, for the
Christian lady took care of him. He was five
years old, thin and delicate, and much fairer than
most Hindoo children. He had many winning
ways; but he had a proud heart. He was proud
of his name, "Ramchunda," because it was the
name of a great false god: but when he had
learned about the true God, he asked for a new
name, and was called "John." His wishing to
change his name was a good sign: and there were
other good signs in this little orphan; and before
he died,—for he died soon,—he showed plainly
that he had not a new *name* only, but a new
*nature.**

Little Phebe was another child received by a
missionary's wife. She was not an orphan, yet
she was as much to be pitied as an orphan; for

* This interesting history is related more fully in "the
Pilgrim Boy of Monghyr," one of the series of Missionary
Stories, published by Snow, 35 Paternoster Row.

her mother told the missionaries that if they did
not take the child, she would throw her to the
jackals.   It was a happy exchange for the infant
to leave so cruel a mother to be reared by a
Christian lady, who instead of throwing her to
jackals, brought her to Jesus.

She died when only five years old by an
accident: when washing her hands in the great
tank, she fell in and was drowned.*

But some Hindoo children, though carefully
instructed, do not grow gentle and loving, like
John and Phebe.

The tents of some English soldiers were
pitched in a lonely part of India; and the
night was dark, when an officer's lady thought
she heard the sound of a child crying.   The
lady sent her servants out to look, and at last
they brought in a little girl of four years old.
And where do you think they found her?
Buried up to her throat in a bog, her little
head alone peeping out.   And who do you think
had put her there?   Her cruel mother.   Yes,
she had left her there to die.

This child gave a great deal of trouble to the
kind lady who had saved her, nor did she show
her any love in return for her kindness; and

* Related by Mrs. Weitbrecht in the "Children's Missionary
Magazine."

after keeping her about two years, the lady sent her to a missionary's school.*

You see how cruelly mothers in India sometimes treat their children. Their religion teaches them to be cruel. A mother is taught to believe that if her babe is sick, an evil spirit is angry. To please this evil spirit, she will put her babe in a basket, and hang it up in a tree for three days.

Mother deserting her infant.

She goes then to look at it, and if it be alive she takes it home. But how seldom does she find it alive! either the ants or the vultures have eaten it, or it has been starved to death.

When there is a famine in the land, many mothers will sell their children for sixpence each;

* "Church Missionary Juvenile Instructor," March, 1850.

and if they cannot sell them, they will leave them to perish.

One missionary received fifty-one poor starving children into his house: they were always crying, "Sahib, roti, roti;" that is, "Master, bread, bread." But the bread came too late to save their lives for all died except one.

Missionary school.

Yet these sick children were very wicked.

One of them stole a brass basin, and sold it for sweetmeats. Though very kindly treated, some of them wished to escape; and to prevent it, the missionary tied them together in strings of fifteen.

There is a tribe in India called Khunds; and they sprinkle their fields with children's blood, and they say this is the way to make the corn grow. The English government once rescued eighty poor children from the Khunds, and sent them to a Christian school. What miserable little creatures they were when they arrived! but they were soon clothed and comforted; and taught to hold a needle, and to know their letters; and, better still, to pronounce the name of Jesus. Like these poor little captives, we were all condemned to die, till Jesus rescued us, and promised everlasting life to those who believe.

THE ENGLISH IN INDIA.

There are many rich English gentlemen living in India: some are judges, and some are merchants, and some are officers in the army. They dwell in large and grand houses, with many windows down to the ground, and a wide verandah to keep off the sun. Instead of *glass*, there is *grass* in the windows; the blinds are made of sweet-scented grass, and servants outside continually pour water on the grass to make the air cool. Instead of *fires* they have *fans*. These fans are like large screens hanging from the ceiling, and waving to and fro to refresh the company. Instead of carpets there are mats on the floor; and round the bed gauze curtains are drawn to keep out the insects.

The servants are all Hindoos, and a great number are kept; and this is necessary, because each servant will do only one kind of work.

Each horse has two servants, one to take care of it, and the other to cut grass: even the dog has a boy to look after it alone. The servants do not live in their master's house, but in small huts near. The place where they live is called "the compound."

When English people travel they do not go in carriages, but in palanquins. A palanquin is like a child's cot, only larger; and there a traveller can sleep at his ease.

The men who carry the palanquins are called "bearers." Babies are carried out of doors by their nurses, but children of three or four are taken out by the bearers.

There was once a little girl of three years old who taught her bearer to fear God.

Little Mary was walking out in a grove with her heathen bearer. She observed him stop at a small Hindoo temple, and bow down to the stone image before the door.

The lisping child inquired,—"Saamy, what for—you do that?"

"O missy," said he, "that is my god!"

"Your god!" exclaimed the child; "your god, Saamy! Why your god can no see, no can hear, no can walk—your god stone! My

God make you, make me, make everything!"
Yet Saamy still, whenever he passed the temple
bowed down to his idol : and still the child reproved him. Though the old man would not
mind, yet he loved his baby-teacher. Once,
when he thought she was going to England, he
said to her,—"What will poor Saamy do when
missy go to England? Saamy no father, no
mother."

"O Saamy!" replied the child, "if you love
God He will be your father, and mother too."

The poor bearer promised with tears in his
eyes that he would love God. "Then, " said
she, "you must learn my prayers;" and she
began to teach him the Lord's Prayer. Soon
afterwards Mary's papa was surprised to see the
bearer enter the room at the time of family
prayers, and still more surprised to see him
take off his turban, kneel down, and repeat the
Lord's Prayer after his master. The lispings
of the babe had brought the old man to God :
Saamy did not only bow the knee, he worshipped in spirit and in truth, and lived like
a true Christian.*

* "The Little Missionary." Published by Groom, Soho
Square Bazaar, and Paternoster Row.

Chief Cities.

There are three great cities which may be called English cities, though in India: because Englishmen built them, and live in them, and rule over them. Their names are Calcutta, Madras, and Bombay.

The capital city is Calcutta. There the chief governor resides. Part of Calcutta is called the Black Town. It is only a heap of mud huts crowded with Hindoos. The other part of Calcutta is called the English Town: and it consists of beautiful houses by the river-side, each house surrounded by a charming garden, and a thick grove.

Madras is built on a plain by the sea, and is adorned by fine avenues of trees, amongst which the English live in elegant villas and gardens. Here also there is a Black Town. It is very hard to land at Madras, because there is no harbour.

Bombay has one of the best harbours in the world. It is built on a small island covered with cocoa-nut groves.

Now let us compare these places with each other.

Calcutta boasts of her fine river; but then the ground is flat and marshy, and therefore the air is damp and unhealthy, and there are no grand prospects.

Madras is very dry, and sandy, and dusty; but then there is the sea to enliven and refresh it.

Bombay has the sea also, besides the groves, and at a little distance, high mountains, which look beautiful, and which it is delightful to visit. There are no such mountains near Calcutta or Madras.

These are the chief English cities. I must now speak of the favorite city of the Hindoos.

It is Benares, on the Ganges.

You might go from Calcutta in a boat, and after sailing four hundred miles, you would reach Benares. The Hindoos say that it was built by their god Sheeva, of gold and precious stones; but that, as we are living in a bad time, it *appears* to be made of bricks and mud, though really very different. They say that Benares is eighty thousand steps nearer heaven than any other city, and that whoever dies there (even though he eat BEEF!) will go to heaven.

A missionary once reproved a Hindoo for telling lies. The answer was, "Why, what of that? do I not live at Benares?" The man thought he was quite safe, however wicked he might be.

In walking about Benares a stranger might be surprised to meet every now and then a white bull, with a hump on its back, without a driver or a rider, or any one to keep it in order.

You must know that a white bull is said to belong to the chief god of Benares, and it is considered a sacred animal, and is allowed to do as it pleases.

And how does it behave?

It behaves much in the same manner as a child would behave who had its own way. The white bull helps itself to the fruit and vegetables sold in the streets, and even to the sweetmeats. It has a great taste for flowers; and it cunningly hides itself near the doors of the temples, to watch for the people coming out with their garlands of marigolds round their necks. At these the bull eagerly snatches with its tongue, and swallows them in a moment. Finding it is petted by every one, it grows so bold, as to walk into the houses, and even to go up the stone stairs on to the roof, where it seems to enjoy the cool air, as it quietly chews the cud.

In the spring the white bulls like to wander out in the fields to eat the tender green grass. A farmer finding one of these bulls in his fields made him get into a boat, and sent him by a man across the river Ganges. But the cunning creature came back in the evening; for he watched till he saw some people setting out in a boat, and then jumped in; and though the passengers tried to turn him out, he would stay there. In this way he got back to the corn-fields.

So much respected are these bulls that a Hindoo would sooner lose his own life than suffer one of them to be killed. An English gentleman was just going to shoot one that had broken into his garden, when his Hindoo servant rushed between him and the bull, saying, "shoot me, sir, shoot me, but let him go!" You may be sure that the gentleman did not shoot the servant; and I think it probable he spared the bull's life.

There is one more city to be noticed.

DELHI was once the grandest city in India, and the seat of the great Moguls, those Mahomedans who conquered India before the British came. The ancient palace was built of red stone; it had a room lined with crystal, a golden palm-tree with diamond fruits, and a golden peacock with emerald wings, overshadowing the monarch's throne?

The Persians stripped the palace of all this gorgeous splendour.

We have now described the two most numerous nations in the world, China and Hindostan. They contain together more than half the world. In some respects they are alike, and in some respects they are different.

In these respects they are different:—

IN CHINA.	IN HINDOSTAN.
There is one emperor.	There is no emperor, and the English govern the country.
There is one language.	There are many languages.
They use chairs, and tables, and beds.	They sit and sleep on mats.
They eat with chopsticks.	They eat with their fingers.
They wear shoes.	They go bare-foot, and wear sandals.
The men shave their heads, except one lock.	The men twist up their hair with a comb.
They seldom wash themselves.	They bathe often.
They eat pigs more than any other meat.	They abhor pigs.
They are grave and silent.	They are merry and talkative.
They are industrious.	They are idle.
The most learned rise to be great men.	Every one is high or low according to caste.
The land is well cultivated.	There is much waste land, and many jungles.

Now let us consider in what respects they are *alike.*

China and Hindostan are alike in these respects. They are both very *populous,* though China has twice as many inhabitants as Hindostan.

In both—rice is the chief food.

In both—large grown-up families live together.

In both—the women are shut up.

In both—foreigners are hated.

In both—conjurors are admired.

In both—many idols are worshipped.

In both—there are ancient sacred books.

In both the people are in the habit of destroying their own little girls when babies.

In both it is believed that the soul after death goes into another body, and is born over and over again into this world.

Is it not mournful to think that more than half the people in the world have no bright hope to cheer a dying bed? One poor Hindoo was heard to exclaim as he was dying, " Where shall I go *last* of all ?" He asked a wise question. He wanted to know where, after having been born ever so many times, he should be put for *ever* and *ever.* This is the great point we *all* want to know. *This* the Bible tells us.*

* Extracted from Weitbrecht's "Protestant Missions," Leupolt's "Recollections," "South Indian Sketches," "Hindoo Female Education," "Hindostan," in Library of Entertaining Knowledge.

THE SEPOYS.

WHAT is a Sepoy? He is a soldier; *not* a British soldier, but a native of India.

Did Indian soldiers ever fight for the British? Yes, they did, for the British could not bring

Sepoys.

enough soldiers of their own to India (they did bring *some*, but not *enough*); so they determined long ago to employ the natives to fight for them. They did not allow them to be captains and generals in the army, only private soldiers. For a great many years the plan succeeded. The Sepoys seemed happy; they had good pay and good treatment; they behaved well, and minded their English captains.

There were thousands and thousands of these dark soldiers. It was strange to see them in the same red coats and white trousers that English soldiers wear, but with faces as dark as the earth on which they trod.

It was the great desire of the British to keep these men in good humour, and care was taken to say nothing that could offend them. It was a rule that no officer should teach his soldiers about Christ. Some of these soldiers believed in Mahomed, and some believed in Brahma, but none believed in Jesus. If any one *did* turn to Jesus through what a missionary might say, he ran the risk of being turned out of the army; but it was very, very seldom that any Sepoy did turn.

So these Sepoys continued year after year in heathen darkness, without hope and without God in the world,—but *not* without SATAN.

And you shall hear what awful wickedness Satan put into the hearts of these ignorant Sepoys —to rise up suddenly and kill all their English officers. How horrible a thought! But that was not all; the Sepoys determined to kill *every* English person, whether man, woman, or little child.

And what was the reason of this determination?

You shall hear. It was the king of Oude who first proposed the plan.

There are many kingdoms in India. The

English had conquered all these kingdoms, except one.* Still they had not taken away *all* his power from the king of Oude. At last they took his kingdom right away and sent him to another place, promising to give him money to make up for the loss of his kingdom.

The king of Oude was very angry,—*so* angry that he made up his mind to destroy the British. But *how* could he do it? He sent to ask the king of Delhi to help him; this king also was displeased with the British; so he readily consented to do them harm.

The two kings agreed to get the Sepoys to rise up on a certain day and shoot their officers. How could they let the Sepoys know their plans? They sent men to go cunningly about from place to place and tell them *secretly.* The British officers never found out what was going on; they still thought the Sepoys were faithful. Had they known their wicked plans, they would have taken away the guns and swords of those wicked men.

It was arranged that the Sepoys in every place should rise up on the *same* day; but happily, before that day arrived, *one* regiment of Sepoys rose up. This was well for the British, for many of them had time to escape. God in His mercy

* Nepaul.

made it happen thus, that **He** might spare the lives of many of his people.

THE REBELS OF MEERUT.

IT was at Meerut that the Sepoys first broke out in open rebellion. Meerut is a town about forty miles from Delhi.

On the 10th day of May, 1857, the people of Meerut rise in the morning, dreading no evil. It is Sunday. The English soldiers attend the English church, as usual, in the morning. As for the Sepoys, it is no Sunday to them. Some of them know no God but Brahma, others—no Saviour but Mahomed. The kings had put it in their heads that the British wanted to make them Christians. Alas! the British were too selfish to care what the Sepoys were, so that they were good soldiers and servants.

At five o'clock the English soldiers are again marching to church. Carriages are standing before the doors of the English bungalows to take the ladies out, either to church, or for a drive in the cool air.

O Sepoys, now is the time for you to begin your bloody work! The English soldiers are saying their prayers. They have left their arms

at home.   Now rise and slay, burn and destroy,
and please your heathen gods.

Suddenly a great noise is heard, a cry of fire,
the sound of guns, loud yells, and clattering
hoofs.

The English officers, who are just mounting
their horses, rush wildly forward.

The commanding officer, Colonel Finnis, is trying to persuade the rebels to be quiet.   A Sepoy
fires and kills the Colonel's horse,—more muskets
are pointed at him, and ball after ball enters his
body.

The darkness has come on, but the streets are
lighted up by the flames of thatched roofs.   The
dark nurses rush out of the burning houses,
clasping fair children in their arms,—the babes
are torn from them and cut in pieces by the Sepoys' swords.   Ladies are driving away in their
carriages, and the Sepoys are galloping after
them, and dragging them out, and slaying them
on the ground.

Who can tell the horrors of that night!

Every white person trembled for his life.
Some hid themselves among the bushes in the
garden.   One dark nurse hid two little children
in a safe place, and saved their lives, but their
parents were killed.

The Sepoys were soon hunted out of the town
by the English soldiers.   Then the people of

the town rose up, and continued the bloody work the Sepoys had begun.

These wretched townsmen spent the whole night in searching for white men, women, and children, and all they found,—they murdered,—but they did not find the two little creatures the kind nurse had hid.

The next morning many white people crept out of their hiding-places, for they heard the voice of the English soldiers, who had returned from pursuing the Sepoys. Now the native townsmen could harm the poor creatures no more: for they were afraid of the English soldiers. Thirty-one persons had been murdered.

Where were the murderous Sepoys gone? to Delhi—only forty miles off.

THE MARTYR OF DELHI.

THOUGH English officers were not allowed to teach the *Sepoys*, yet they could if they pleased, preach to the *townsmen*. There was one officer who chose to preach in the great bazaar, or market-place. His name was Colonel Wheeler. He used to preach in the bazaar of the great city of Agra.

Amongst the crowd came a Mahomedan named Wilayat Ali. None listened with so much atten tion as he did; yet it was a long while before he was persuaded to give up the false prophet, and to believe in the true Saviour. At last he believed and was baptized. What sufferings he had then to endure from his Mahomedan neighbours! But in spite of all he became a preacher in the bazaars.

At last he came to live at DELHI. There he often preached. Thousands flocked to hear him. A great prince named Mirza Hajee heard of him. Like Nicodemus of old—this prince sometimes crept in the dark evenings to Wilayat's house, that he might hear in secret about Jesus.

On Monday morning Wilayat rose as usual, and breakfasted in his humble dwelling with his wife and children. He then prepared to go out and preach in the bazaar.

He was at the door, when a friend rushed into the house, with terror in his looks. It was Thakoor, a Christian native. "The Sepoys! the Sepoys!" he exclaimed; "they have risen up, and are murdering the Christians. Flee—flee—for your life!"

It was true that during the night the Sepoys from Meerut had arrived at Delhi, and were now helping the Sepoys of Delhi—to kill and to destroy.

Wilayat heard the terrible roar of the great guns. He looked out and saw fifty Sepoys on horseback coming that way. They held drawn swords and burning torches in their hands. As they went they set on fire the houses around.

Street in Delhi.

"Run—run!" cried Thakoor to his friend. Thakoor himself began to run—but the horsemen saw him—pursued him, and killed him in the streets.

Wilayat thought it better not to flee yet. He called Fatima his wife and his seven children around him in his house, and kneeling down offered up this prayer: "O Lord, many of Thy

people have been slain by the sword, and burned
in the fire for Thy sake. Thou didst help *them*
to hold fast the faith. Now, O Lord, *we* have
fallen into the fiery trial. O help us to confess
our dear Lord, that if we die we may obtain a
crown of glory."

Wilayat then kissed his wife and children and
said, "whatever comes—don't deny Christ. If
you confess Him you will have a crown of
glory."

His wife began to weep bitterly. Wilayat
said all he could to comfort her. "O remember,
my dear wife, if you die you will go to Jesus,
and if you live, Jesus will be with you. If any
of our good missionaries are alive, they will
take care of you after my death; but if the missionaries should all die, Christ lives for ever.
Even if the children are killed before your eyes,
do not deny Christ."

While Wilayat was speaking thus to his wife,
a number of Sepoys on horseback rode up to his
house. Seeing that he was a native, they were
not going to hurt him, till some malicious Mahomedans standing near cried out, "He is a Christian!" Then the Sepoys said, "Repeat the
Mahomedan creed, or we will shoot you."

How easy it would have been just to say, "I
believe in God, and Mahomed his prophet!"
but Wilayat would not deny his Lord. Then a

Sepoy fired at him. The bullet passed close by him and went into the wall behind.

The children filled with terror, ran out by the back door. Where did they flee ? To the house of the prince who sometimes came by night to hear about Jesus.

Mirza Hajee received them kindly. "Come in, my children," said he, "and I will protect you from the enemies."

But Fatima did not go with her children. She still remained by her husband's side, among the fierce soldiers at the door. These continued to torment poor Wilayat.

"Tell us what you are ?" said one.

"I am a Christian, and a Christian I will live and die."

"Kill him," said another Sepoy ; "he does not believe in Mahomed."

Several soldiers then pointed their guns at his heart, saying "If you will become a Mahomedan, again we will spare your life, and your wife's too."

In another moment they would have shot him dead, had they not seen two English gentlemen running by. Much as they hated *dark* Christians, they hated *white* Christians more. "Let us run after the Ferringhees," cried the Sepoys ; "we can return to shoot the unbelievers afterwards."

Then the troop of horsemen galloped off.

"Now let us flee," cried Wilayat to his wife; "but first I must go to see whether *my* missionary is safe."

Poor Fatima now ran along the streets alone, crying for her children.

Whom should she meet but Mizra Hajee himself.

"Do not cry," said he; "all your children are safe at my house."

How much rejoiced Fatima was at hearing this! She might have gone at first to the Prince's house, but she loved her husband too well to forsake him in the hour of trouble. She determined *now* to go to the missionary's house, where Wilayat had intended to go.

As she was going along, she saw a great crowd in the streets. It was a number of townsmen all gathered round one poor man. And who was he? Wilayat—the faithful Wilayat.

What were Fatima's feelings when she saw her own dear husband dragged along the ground, while his cruel tormentors were beating him about the head and face with their shoes!

Not being soldiers they had no swords.

"Now preach Christ to us!" some cried out in mocking tones. Others said, "Turn to Mahomed, and we will let you go. Only repeat the creed."

"No; I never, never will!" the faithful

martyr cried. "My Saviour took up His cross and went to God; and I will lay down my life and go to Him."

It was now the heat of the day, and the scorching rays of the sun were beating on the poor sufferers's head.

With a laugh one of the wretches exclaimed, "I suppose you would like some water."

"I do not want water," replied the martyr. "When my Saviour was dying he had nothing but vinegar mingled with gall. But do not keep me in this pain. If you mean to kill me, do so at once.

At this moment a Sepoy on horseback came up. He asked what was the matter.

"Oh," replied the mob, "we have got a devil of a Christian here, and he will not turn! Will you not kill him?"

Gladly the cruel Sepoy granted the request. He lifted up his sword—the martyr called out, "Jesus, receive my spirit!" and with one stroke his head was nearly cut off.

Fatima, standing under a tree, beheld the stroke,—she shrieked with agony, and ran back to her own house. But she found it on fire, and surrounded by people who were plundering it. Then she fled to the Prince's house, where she found her fatherless children. Oh, what sad tidings did she bring to those little ones!

Yet *glorious* tidings also; for their father had died, like Stephen, calling upon God.   Like John the Baptist, he had been beheaded; and he would live and reign with Christ, and with all his brethren who had been beheaded for the witness of Jesus, and for the word of God.   (Rev. xx, 4.)

The widow and her children remained hidden in the Prince's palace for three days.   All this time they heard the shouts, and the shrieks, and the shooting of guns in the streets, while they felt themselves to be in a safe refuge.

At the end of three days Mirza Hajee came to Fatima and said, with a sad countenance, " I dare not keep you any longer.   If I do I shall be killed myself.   Orders have been given that any one who conceals Christians shall die.   But if you will only become a Mahomedan, you may be safe and happy.   I will give you a house, with three pounds a-month for your support."

Fatima thanked the Prince for all his past kindness, but declared that she would not give up her Saviour.   " No," she said; " I will work while I live to support my children; and if I must be killed, God's will be done."

Then one of the Prince's porters let Fatima and her seven children out of the Prince's houses.

For ten days the widow and her fatherless family wandered about the city without a place where to lay their heads.   Fatima had a little money of her own, and with it she bought a little food. She could not leave the city, for the gates were shut and **no** woman was allowed to go out.

No one attempted to kill her, for very few knew she was a Christain. Her husband had been well known as he had been a preacher; but Fatima had been accustomed to keep at home, and was not known.

One day the widow observed a great troop of Sepoys going out of the gates of Delhi.

"Now," thought she, "is the time for us to escape."

She mingled with the crowd, and slipped out without being observed, and her children got out also.

The mother and children felt like prisoners restored to liberty. Now they could wander about the country, and settle where they pleased. They were, indeed, very poor. Twelve shillings was all the money they possessed. They went to a village very near Delhi, and hired a room for threepence a-week. But they soon found this village was unsafe. A number of English soldiers had arrived and were trying to get into Delhi. Cannon-balls were flying about night and day. Every one's life was in danger. Once a bullet was shot into the room where the widow lodged, but it did her no harm, nor her children.

The family left this village, and went to

another forty miles off. Here the widow tried to get work; but the only work she could get was grinding corn: and she earned so little, though she worked night and day, that she could hardly keep her children from starving. For grinding eighteen pounds of corn she only got three-half-pence.

After living three months in this village, she heard the joyful news that the English had taken Delhi out of the hands of the Sepoys. She was not afraid now to return to the village close to Delhi, where she had lodged before.

It was in the month of September she returned. While living here her children fell very ill. No doubt they had been weakened by want of food. The little baby died. Fatima wept abundantly. But her tears flowed still faster when she found that no one would bury the little body. The people had found out she was a Christian, and the Mahomedans would not touch the body of a Christian baby. Had Fatima met an English soldier she would have asked him to bury it; but as it was, she was obliged to bury it herself. She wrapped the little corpse in a cloth, and carried it in her arms out of the village. Then she began to dig the grave.

Two men passing by saw her digging, and asked her what made her weep. When they knew that she was digging her own baby's grave, they kindly said they would dig it for her. When the men had dug the grave, they said they could do no more. They were not Christians, and they would not put the little body in the ground. So they went away.

Fatima's dead baby.

Fatima then put her darling in, and covered it with earth. She knew that though men had refused to touch its *body*, that her Saviour had not refused to receive its *soul*. Now, indeed, she felt the comfort of being a Christian.

Fatima remembered her husband had told her, that if he died the missionaries would take care of her. She inquired in Delhi whether any of them still lived: She heard that they had *all* been killed, and her own dear minister with the rest. He was a young man named Mackay. He had hid himself in a cellar, and several friends with him. But the Sepoys had found out their hiding place, and had tried to get in, but had not been able, till at last they had brought mattocks and broken through the ceiling. Then they had rushed down upon the poor men, and slaughtered them all. Five other missionaries had been slain in various parts of the city.

What could poor Fatina do now? She remembered the missionaries in Agra, her native town. But though she could read, she could not write. A native Christian named Heera Lal, wrote a letter for her to one of the missionaries at Agra! Oh what was Fatima's joy when an answer arrived, inviting her to go to Agra! She cried for joy, thanked God, and went to her native city with all her children.*

THE CAPTIVES OF LUCKNOW.

I HAVE related the sufferings of a poor Hindoo family during the rebellion. I will now relate the sufferings of an English family. I do not

* Taken from Sherring's "Indian Church during the great Rebellion."

call them martyrs, because they were not perse-
cuted on account of their *religion*, but on account
of their *country*. They were not tempted to
deny the Lord, for they could not have saved
their lives by denying Him. It was only Christian
Hindoos who were killed for Christ's sake.

The little family of whom I am going to speak
lived in the province of Oude. It was a very
small family, consisting of a father and mother,
and little baby-boy. They dwelt in a village
named Gonda, far away from any great town.
Not more than six or seven English people lived
in that place. There were many Sepoys, but
no one was afraid of their doing any harm,—
they were so obedient and respectful.

The little family led a quiet and peaceful life
in their bungalow, overshadowed by the trees
of the compound, and surrounded by the huts of
their Hindoo servants. The baby was now old
enough to walk and to speak a few words. He
was a merry little fellow of sixteen months, and
was growing more amusing every day.

About the middle of May, 1857—news arrived
of the slaughter at Meerut, on that dreadful
Sunday night, and of the slaughter at Delhi on
the following day.

Though the village where they dwelt was
many miles from Meerut and Delhi, yet the
parents were much alarmed. They feared lest

the Sepoys of Gonda should suddenly change their behaviour, as other Sepoys had done.

Every day they heard accounts of slaughters in different places, and every day they grew more uneasy. The poor lady felt so much terrified, that she could neither sleep, nor eat, nor talk, but only sit and cry over her baby. When the little fellow laughed in the glee of his little heart, the fond parents looked at each other, not able to utter their thoughts. If they could have spoken, they would have said,—"Ah! sweet babe, you know not how soon you may be snatched from our arms and murdered before our eyes!"

At night the mother kept a sword under her pillow, and the father a loaded pistol under his; and they both listened to every sound, ready to start up at the least alarm. At the same time, they looked up to the Lord in their hearts, as to their shield and their high tower.

After passing three weeks in this state of terror, a letter arrived from Sir Henry Lawrence, the general of the army. When the affectionate wife heard what was written in the letter, she was filled with grief. Her husband was commanded to send her and the babe to the great city of Lucknow, eighty miles off. This city is the capital of Oude. "Must I part from my beloved husband?—I would rather stay and die here," exclaimed the sorrowful lady.

Dr. Bartrum (for this was her husband's name) explained to his wife how necessary it was to place her in a strong city, with towers and walls —as no one could tell how soon the Sepoys might rise up and murder both mother and babe. With an aching heart Mrs. Bartrum put up a few clothes in a bundle, and took a last look at the rooms where she had spent so many happy hours. She was to begin her journey that very evening. Another mother was to go with her—Mrs. Clark, and also her baby.

Dr. Bartrum promised to go with his wife for some miles, and Mr. Clark was to go also ; but soon they would be obliged to return home.

No one can travel in India during the heat of the day. It was six o'clock in the evening when the two mothers, holding their babes in their arms, mounted their elephants.

They did not venture along the road lest they should meet bands of rebels ; but they went by a secret path, and a native walked before them to show the way.

After travelling sixteen miles they stopped to rest, and refresh themselves at a friend's house. There they drank tea, and fed their weary babes with milk in the middle of the night.

Now came the painful hour of parting. The husbands must now return to their miserable homes. Oh, what did they feel that night as they put their wives upon the elephants, and kissed once more their darling babes, with many a fear of never seeing them again!

Dr. Bartrum uttered his last farewell in a cheerful tone, though with a bleeding heart.

"Good-bye, dear **Kate**, keep up your spirits; we shall soon meet again. Take care of my little darling."

How could poor Kate take care of the darling when she could not even take care of herself?

Great were the dangers of that journey. There was a guard of Sepoys to protect the ladies; but it was a guard that seemed more disposed to murder than to protect. How did the mothers tremble when they heard their guards talking loudly and fiercely throughout that dark night,—when they saw them rolling on the ground, laughing and jesting: and most of all, when they observed them loading their guns!

"What are you going to do?" exclaimed the terrified women.

"Oh," replied the boisterous Sepoys, "there are so many bad men about, we are going to fight for you."

The poor mothers could do nothing but look up to Him who never slumbers nor sleeps. They prayed Him to soften those hard hearts, and their prayers were answered; for when they asked for water to refresh the thirsty babes, the cruel Sepoys gave them some.

At last the night of fear passed away, and the morning came. The travellers were now going by the side of a river. On the other side they observed a party of English people mounted on elephants, going, like themselves, towards Lucknow. How glad they were to see this party! They found some boats, and they went across the river.

The travelling party now consisted in all of seven ladies, twelve children, and five officers. All were very weary, having travelled the whole night.

As it was now nine o'clock in the morning, the heat was getting insupportable, and it was quite necessary that the travellers should rest during the day. They stopped at a village by the river-side. There they procured some food, and bathed the children.

At four o'clock they set out again, and travelled all night. It was a night more terrible than the last. The little band often met troops of enemies, and were afraid of being murdered.

It was on Tuesday morning, June 9th, they entered the beautiful city of Lucknow, having gone eighty miles in two nights.

On a rising ground in the midst of the city there is a large place, enclosed by walls, and

containing seventeen buildings. This court is
called the Residency.   One of the houses in the
court was the palace of the Governor, Sir Henry
Lawrence.   Within the strong walls of this court
the English had taken up their abode ; for though
the Sepoys had been hunted out of the city, no
one knew when they might return, or what the
townsmen of Lucknow might intend to do.

The Residency.

All the houses in the Residency were crowded
with English people, especially with ladies and
children.   Mrs. Bartrum went into a house
called Begum Kotie, which means "Palace of
the Princess ;" but it more resembled a prison
than a palace, and was more fit for beggars than

princesses. It was impossible for any lady to have a room to herself; it was enough to have a corner. There were seven beds in the large room where Mrs. Bartrum lodged, yet there was only one table and three chairs. There were fifteen persons in this room : some were mothers, and some were children. They were all most uncomfortable in this hot and crowded place. They had no servants of their own ; but they got a little help from native women. They asked these women to buy a few things for them in the town. Mrs. Bartrum laid up a store of what she most wanted, not knowing how soon the enemies might surround the place, and prevent her getting anything; she sent for candles and soap, and other articles that would not be spoiled by keeping. She was a lady who could not bear to see her room in disorder, and her child untidy, and she took great pains in washing and scrubbing ; nor did she mind being called servant-of-all-work by her companions, but thought it an honour to be industrious. Many ladies who had always been waited upon by servants. had now to exert themselves. Having so much to do made them bear their troubles better than if they had been idle.

This was the way in which they passed their miserable days.

As soon as it was light they got up, and washed and dressed themselves and their little children.

Then they set the breakfast things on the table ; though they could not have breakfast till the native women thought fit to bring it. At last a woman came in with hot water, and plates of food ; no one could tell what food it was, for it was so thickly covered with flies, that it seemed only a black and living mass.

The heat of the day was spent in fanning away the flies, and in trying to make the room a little cooler. After the babies had been hushed to sleep, the ladies tried to cheer their spirits by a little friendly talk. Seating themselves on the side of a bed they placed their cups on a chair, and drank tea together by the light of a candle stuck in a bottle. Then they spoke of the happy days of childhood,—when they played with their brothers and sisters in their fathers' gardens, far away in England. Then they talked of their dear husbands, exposed to the bullets of the enemy, and they wept to think they might never see them more.

Three weeks of misery had passed away,— when suddenly one afternoon a lady was seized with an agonizing pain. The doctors came, but could not cure poor Mrs. Hale. After suffering for three hours, she ceased to feel any pain ; her forehead was covered with cold moisture, and her reason left her. While the clergyman was reading prayers, her breath stopped and her spirit passed away. This was the first time Mrs. Bartrum had ever seen *death*, and she felt much agitated at the sight.

There was a little Katie left without a mother when Mrs. Hale died. Mrs. Bartrum put the child to sleep that night in her own bed. Just at the same time the mother was laid in her coffin. Next day a kind officer and his wife sent for little Katie, and took care of her; but they had the grief to see her pine away, and die in a few months, for scarcely any babies lived through the troubles of Lucknow.

The day after Mrs. Hale died—a great calamity occurred. Hitherto there had been no enemies surrounding the Residency; but on June 30th a battle was fought about ten miles off, and the English were driven back, and the rebels rushed into the city, and surrounded the walls of the fortress, where the ladies had taken refuge.

On this day the siege began. Now there were bullets and shells constantly flying about, and sometimes piercing the walls. No one could venture out of doors without running the risk of being shot. No fresh food could be bought, and what had been stored up was given out in smaller portions than before. Wretched food it was, consisting of flour, peas, rice, hard biscuits, and hard—very hard—beef. This wretched food was more wretchedly cooked. A native woman boiled it in a saucepan of copper lined with tin, and the tin having been worn out in places—the copper turned the food green, and made it almost poisonous. The woman would not be at the trouble of cooking the peas, and flour, and rice, and meat separately. She put them all together in the saucepan, and sent them up in one disgusting mess. Mrs. Bartrum tried to improve the beef by cutting it up with scissors into little bits before it was boiled; but her pains could not make it really soft and wholesome. Such food soon began to make a great change in the looks of her fat and bonnie boy. His mother now looked at his pale face with grief, and said in her heart, "If papa could see you now, how his heart would ache!"

The little children suffered much from the heat at night, and the mothers often sat up at night fanning and soothing them. There was a large fan or punkah, in the room, but it was hard to get a native to work it up and down; if one was hired, he soon fell asleep, as he cared not about pleasing the poor captives. During these restless nights Mrs. Bartrum thought of the prayer in the Psalm: "Let the sorrowful sighing of the prisoners come before Thee." She remembered also the prayer in the Church-service for all prisoners and captives, and she hoped that God would hear and answer it.

An event happened in July which made every heart sad. The good and great general, Sir Henry Lawrence, was sitting in his room in the Residency when a shell, or ball of fire, was shot into it, and burst close beside him. He was so much hurt that he was obliged to keep his bed: while lying there—another shell wounded him so dreadfully that he was filled with agony, and in two days he expired. He died believing in Jesus, and looking for eternal life. But his death was a terrible calamity, for he was one of the best of men and greatest of generals. A very good clergyman attended him on his death-bed. His name was Polehampton. He intended to write a full account of all that Sir Henry Lawrence said while dying, but he never did; for one morning very soon afterwards, as he was rolling up his bed, he felt a stunning pain pierce his body. He knew he had been shot, and he feared that the ball might still be in him; however, it was soon found lying on the floor. He walked to the hospital leaning on two men, and after lying there a fortnight he was seized with cholera, and died. His death was deeply mourned, for he had spoken of Jesus beside many a dying pillow.

Dreadful accidents happened every day.

Once, as Mrs. Bartrum was standing at the door of her house looking into the courtyard, she observed a little girl playing with a round shot that had fallen upon the ground. Suddenly a bullet struck the child in the temple, and killed her on the spot. This awful sight alarmed the lady so much that she feared to take her baby for one moment in the court.

A sad event happened in her own room. A sweet baby, loved and petted by all, pined away and died. No one now was left of all who once dwelt in that crowded room but the mother of the dead baby, and Mrs. Bartrum and her own baby. The mothers felt so sorrowful that they begged to be put into another room, and so they were allowed to share the room of a lady named Green.

Mrs. Bartrum's baby was no longer a laughing, amusing creature, but a little coaxing, tender pet, clinging so closely to his mother that she could scarcely get through her daily work. There was no servant now to help her even to cook. She got up about five, and went into the court to look for wood, well knowing all the time that she might be shot at any moment. But she was obliged to run the risk, for she could not do without wood to boil the water for breakfast. After she had lighted the fire she made the baby's food. She felt very thankful to a kind friend who gave her a little milk every day for her baby. After breakfast she dressed the baby, and set the room to rights.

Then she washed the clothes, though interrupted much by her darling wanting to be in her arms. When she had done her washing, she tried to make the poor baby go to sleep, and she sat beside him fanning away the flies and mosquitoes, and at the same time reading her Bible. When the little fellow awoke she amused him, and talked to him of papa. Whenever she said, " Where is papa ?" the child pointed to heaven. The mother felt uneasy whenever the babe did this, for she was always fearing lest her dear husband should be dead. Many weeks had passed without a letter; as the enemies around the fortress prevented any letters being brought in.

At last news came that an English regiment was coming into Lucknow. How earnestly Mrs. Bartrum hoped that her husband would come with this regiment! It was nearly four months since she had seen him.

On September 25th there was the sound of great guns all day. At six o'clock in the evening there was the sound of shouts and of cheering. THE ENGLISH SOLDIERS HAD FOUGHT THEIR WAY INTO THE CITY !!—Mrs. Bartrum was waiting in the fortress, longing to know whether her dear Robert was come. An officer entered, and told her HE WAS COME! Oh, what joy! She thanked God, and, with her child in her arms, she ran out amongst the crowd to watch at the gate of the

court for the face of her beloved. One of the
soldiers told her that Dr. Bartrum would not
come into the city till the morning, as he was
staying behind with the great guns.

The English entering Lucknow.

"One night more," thought the fond wife, "and
I shall see him." She felt very happy as she returned to her room, and she hushed her child to
sleep with such gladness as she had not felt for
a long, long while ; but she could not sleep herself for the joy of thinking of the meeting in the
morning. As soon as it was light she rose and

dressed her babe in a clean white dress, that she had long kept ready for him to wear on the day of his papa's return.

With her sweet boy in her arms, she went out to meet her husband. Soon she saw a friend, who told her that her husband was just coming into the city, and was very happy at the thought of seeing her and the child so soon. What delightful news! But the mother could not wait long at the gate, for her baby had not had its breakfast. So she went back,—her heart still overflowing with gladness. After breakfast, she sat at the door of her house to watch for the return of the loved one.

All day she watched, but he came not. And now she began to fear some evil. In the evening she went, with her babe in her arms, to the top of the tallest house in the Residency, and looked down the road; but she could not see the form she knew so well. And now her heart sank within her, and she returned to her room disappointed.

Next day she rose and watched again; but when no one came, her heart grew sick with anxiety. In the afternoon as she was sitting, full of sorrow, in her room, she saw a friend enter. He was a doctor, who had often been kind to her babe, and given it sago and arrowroot. He looked kindly and sadly in her face.

She said,—

" How strange it is my husband is not come in!"

" Yes," he replied, " *it is strange*," and then he turned round and went out of the room.

And now the thought struck the poor lady, "Something has happened they do not like to tell me."

It was too true. Something had happened. Her husband had been struck down at the very gates. When the poor lady heard this terrible news she was more unhappy than words can tell.

The widow of that good clergyman, Mr. Pole-hampton, came to see her. She had felt the same sorrow a little while before. She sat down beside the unhappy lady, and did not speak a word, for she knew that none but God can comfort in such sorrow.

The baby wondered what made mamma cry so bitterly. He clasped his tiny arms round her neck, and kissed away her tears.

How often had she said to him, " Papa is come, and baby will be quite well !" Now she said, "My poor little fatherless boy, who will take care of us now ?

Next day she saw two native servants coming into the court leading a black horse. She knew that horse; it was her own, on which she had taken many happy rides with her husband. On that horse her husband had escaped from Gonda, and had come to Lucknow.

How much the widow longed to know *how* her husband had been killed. An officer came to relate the sad history. He said, "Your husband asked me to come and help him to perform an operation upon a wounded soldier, as we were walking along—the bullets were flying fast; and I said, ' Oh, Bartrum, you are exposing yourself too much,' but he answered, 'There is no danger.' The words were no sooner spoken than a bullet struck the brave doctor on the temple, and he fell upon me, exclaiming, 'It's all up with me!' and so died. It was a comfort to think he suffered no pain. Just before he was struck he had been talking of his delight at the thought of seeing his wife and child.

Such was the officer's account.

Those last words in parting " We shall soon meet again," had not come to pass in this world; but they will come to pass, it is hoped, in another world ; for the doctor had prayed for a new heart when the troubles first came, and had looked to Jesus to save him.

How dark and gloomy were the days of the poor widow, now she could no longer look forward to meeting her husband in this world !

Was she now released from the fortress ? Had the English soldiers delivered the poor captives of Lucknow ? No. There were too few soldiers to *drive out* the enemies, though they had fought their way into the fortress, and were able to keep the enemies from *getting in.* There was firing going on night and day. It was dangerous to walk in the court, but the babe looked so ill that it seemed necessary for him to have fresh air. The two servants who had brought in the black horse waited upon Mrs. Bartrum and the babe. One of them was the child's bearer, and he carried his little master out walking, and he was a great help to the sorrowful lady. All that poor lady cared for now on earth was the babe. While the bearer was nursing him, she sat down and made warm clothes for him against the winter : for it was October, and the cold weather was soon coming.

The poor captives knew not when they should get out of their prison. Every day their distress increased, as their stores grew less and less. The lady knew not what to do for soap to wash her clothes. Her plan was—to grind some of her dried peas between two stones, and to use the peas instead of soap. Yet she could not well spare the peas, for she had not enough to eat. It often cheered her to see her babe calling the monkeys from the roofs of the houses to come and share his little portion of food ; but the child had little appetite, and liked play better than his meals.

As last the HOUR OF DELIVERANCE came.

On November 16th a tremendous firing was heard at a distance. Sir Colin Campbell and General Havelock* had come with a large number of English soldiers, and had fought their way into Lucknow.

The captives had been five months in the fortress, and more than four months besieged by the enemy.

It was at six on the evening of November 19, that the widow and her babe left their horrible prison. They were carried out in a doolie (which is a covered chair, like a palanquin, borne on men's shoulders). The doolie bearers ran as fast as they could to avoid the enemy's guns, and they brought the lady in safety to the English camp, five miles off. In a tent the captives were feasted on tea, and bread, and butter. It was a feast such as they had not tasted for many months. Mrs. Bartrum's baby enjoyed it much. It did his mother's heart good to see him eat his supper with so much relish.

It was not safe to continue in the camp. All that night the captives travelled through the midst of their enemies. The widow was so much frightened on the way by finding herself in her doolie with no other doolies near her, that she fancied that her bearers were taking her to the Sepoys, so she sprang out and walked in the

* A few days afterwards he died from fatigue.

wet grass for three hours with her baby in her arms. Happily she met some English soldiers, who protected her and brought her to a tent.

There she fed her baby with milk, and refreshed herself with tea.

Day after day the captives travelled. The widow did not continue to go in a doolie, she was obliged to get into a bullock-cart. She did not like this, because her baby could hardly bear the jolting of so rough a conveyance. Sometimes she had no other place to sleep in at night than her bullock cart.

The baby's bearer was very kind, and ran into the villages on the way to get milk for the sick child. The noise and dust were intolerable, for the road was crowded with carts, waggons, and camels, forming a train seven miles long. In the day the heat was great, and at night the cold. Distant guns were often heard, and every moment there was danger of an attack from the Sepoys.

After a journey of seventeen days, the travellers reached a railway, and arrived quickly at Allahabad. This great city is built where two great rivers meet, the Ganges and the Jumna. Many English were there, who welcomed with pity the poor captives from Lucknow. The widow was lodged in a comfortable house, and had a room to herself. It seemed strange to enjoy comfort again, after six months of bitter sufferings. The weather was so lovely in this cool season, that she sat in the garden all day with her babe. There she thought of the happy days she had enjoyed with her husband in her bungalow at Gonda, and she sighed to think that no papa was coming to admire the pretty ways of her darling. Yet she knew that she was not the *only* sorrowful mother. All around were the ruins of houses that Sepoys had crushed to the ground, and where happy families had once dwelt.

After spending a quiet month at Allahabad, the widow set out in a steam-boat to go down the river Ganges, five hundred miles—to Calcutta. She shared her little cabin with Mrs. Polehampton. These two widows felt the more for each other's sorrows, as they had both lost such affectionate husbands so lately.

After a voyage of nearly three weeks, they arrived at the great and beautiful city of Calcutta. It was on January 30th that they landed.

A house of refuge for the released captives had been provided by kind friends. Each lady had a bed-room and bath-room to herself, and took her meals with the rest in the large dining-room. Clothes were offered to those ladies who had lost their own, and every kindness was shown to them all. Mrs. Bartrum's heart overflowed with gratitude, though it was pressed down with sorrow on account of her drooping babe. She hoped a voyage to England might do him good, and she determined not to go overland, but round by the Cape. She was in great haste to set out, and occupied herself very diligently in making preparations.

The health of her babe was her chief care. Every evening she took the little, pale, quiet, darling out for a drive ; but still he grew weaker and weaker, and everybody remarked how ill he looked. He had long lost all his spirits, and now he had even ceased to cry, and he sat quiet as a lamb on his mother's lap.

The day for setting sail was fixed for the 12th of February. The mother took the baby to look at the little cabin, where she hoped he would pass four months at sea, and get back his health and his bonnie looks.

But before the day for sailing came the darling grew much weaker. He could scarcely eat any-thing, but slept almost the whole day. Mrs. Polehampton took great interest in the child. She had once lost a baby of her own. She told Mrs. Bartrum one day that the doctor thought the child was looking very ill. The mother saw that Mrs. Polehampton thought the baby would die. But her own feeling was—"I *cannot* spare him, and I do not think God will take away my little lamb, when I have nothing else left."

That evening she laid him on her bed. He seemed to be sleeping comfortably. In the middle of the night he awoke, and grew restless. His mother spoke to him; he looked up and smiled. It was a sweet smile. His mother feared it was his *last*. She took him in her arms and walked about with him to hush him to sleep; but soon she felt him struggling, as if uneasy. She felt frightened, and called Mrs. Polehampton, who said, "Lay him down in your lap, and let him remain quite still." The mother did so, then turned away her head, that she might not see her child die, for his eyes were growing so bright that she knew he was dying. He gasped for breath a little while, and then fell asleep till the resurrection morn.

Mrs. Polehampton took the precious little body from the mother's knees and washed it and dressed it in a clean white night-gown, and laid it upon the bed.

The mother looked at him as he lay there. When she saw that his face was happy as an angel's, she felt that she *could spare him*, and that her little lamb was safe in her Saviour's bosom.

In the morning she went into the garden and gathered rosebuds and orange-blossoms to strew upon his pillow. A painter was sent for to draw his picture as he lay amongst the flowers,— his head leaning on one side, and a smile on his pale lips, a white rosebud in one hand, and a lock of his mother's hair in the other. He looked so sweet, that as his mother sat beside him, gazing on his happy countenance, she could not weep for him. For two short years she had watched over him with unceasing care : during seven months she had seen him suffer such troubles as babies seldom meet with,—troubles that had brought him to an early grave ; but now they were all past, and he would " hunger no more, neither thirst any more, neither would the sun light on him, nor any heat."

That afternoon the doctor fastened down the lid of the baby's coffin, and the mother was going to say, " Good night;" when she remembered there would be no night where baby was gone, but everlasting light and joys for evermore. She pressed the last kiss on his cold soft cheek, and looked at him for the last time.

The mourning coach was at the door. The mother and her friend, Mrs. Polehampton, and the kind Doctor Fayrer, went in the coach with the little coffin. Three other kind friends followed in another coach. When they reached the burying-ground, one of those friends, named Captain Boileau, assisted Doctor Fayrer to carry the precious babe to its tomb.

As the mother turned away from the open grave she said in her heart, "And now farewell, my own loved darling, till we meet in heaven! Thou hast soon passed through the waves of this troublesome world, and thou art safe

'In thy Father's sheltered home,
Where I know that sorrow cannot come.'"

When she returned home she found no joyous baby welcome, no little arms to clasp around her neck. She saw the frock last worn, the little hat and shoes lying about the room, and toys scattered on the floor; but "Where was baby?" She said unto God, "All Thy waves and Thy storms have gone over me. And now, Lord, what is my hope? Truly my hope is even in Thee."

She set sail for England the next day, Feb. 12th, 1858, leaving behind her what she most loved. But she was able to say, "The Lord gave and the Lord hath taken away, blessed be the name of the Lord." She believed her loved ones were happy in a secure resting-place, and she had these words written upon her baby's tombstone:—

"IS IT WELL WITH THY HUSBAND?
IS IT WELL WITH THE CHILD?
"AND SHE ANSWERED, IT IS WELL."
2 Kings, iv, 26.*

---

* This history is abridged from a most interesting book entitled, "A Widow's Reminiscences of the Siege of Lucknow," published by Nisbet. This work is remarkable for touching beauty and sweetness of spirit. How much better is it to place such works in the hands of youth than *fictions!*

THE CAPTIVES OF CAWNPORE.

DREADFUL were the sufferings of the captives of Lucknow. But in another city there were captives whose sufferings were still greater.

The name of Cawnpore will never be heard in Britain without a shudder and a thrill of horror.

There is another name that will never be heard without still greater abhorrence. It is the name of Nana Sahib.

This Nana was one of the most deceitful men who ever lived, a very son of him who is a murderer and a liar from the beginning, even Satan. But we cannot be surprised if Mahomedans are deceitful and cruel, for Mahomed himself was a deceiver and a murderer. Nana was a follower of that false prophet.

Nana wanted to be a great prince. He was not a prince, nor the son of a prince ; but he had been brought up in the house of a prince—called the Rajah of Bithoor, and he pretended that the Rajah had left him all his property and his power ; but this was quite false. He could not get the English Government to allow him to have all the possessions that he wanted, and on this account he hated bitterly all the English nation. Yet he pretended to love the English. He was very civil to them, invited them to his palace, and lent his elephants to English rulers whenever he was asked.

Though neither a prince nor the son of a prince Nana lived in a princely castle at Bithoor, a place six miles from Cawnpore. There he kept six great guns, and a great number of servants. Nana was very clever, and could speak and write English well. His manners, too, were like the manners of an English gentleman. All the English believed that Nana was their faithful friend, and that he would protect them if the Sepoys should rise up.

There were thousands of Sepoys at Cawnpore, and scarcely any English soldiers. When the English at Cawnpore heard of the slaughters at Meerut, at Delhi, and many other places, they began to feel frightened. The ladies and children were desired to leave the bungalows and come into a large strong building, once used as barracks for English soldiers. On the 21st of May the ladies were brought into this place; but the English officers continued to sleep in tents among the Sepoys.

The first night spent in the barracks was a very miserable one, for the place was hot, and crowded, and uncomfortable; the children were crying, and their mothers were alarmed and unable to sleep. One lady was so much terrified, that she went out of her mind.

It was a comfort to all when some English soldiers arrived at Cawnpore; but only a few came, not nearly enough to withstand the Sepoys, if they should rise up. Soon the English officers felt that it was not safe to go on sleeping in tents, and they joined the poor ladies in the barracks.

At last the dreadful night arrived when the Sepoys rose up. It was on June 4th, 1857, that the frightened ladies heard wild shouts and the shooting of pistols. Looking out of their windows they beheld fires blazing on every side. They soon heard that the bungalows were in flames, and the rebels were plundering, but *not slaughtering.*

Great was their joy when they were told that the rebels had rushed out of the city with their booty, shouting as they went, "To Delhi! To Delhi!"

And great was their horror the next day, when they were told that the rebels had *returned* to Cawnpore.

Who had brought them back? NANA, *the pretended friend of the English.* He had gone after the robbers, and had persuaded them to return to Cawnpore. He then wrote a letter to the General, Sir Hugh Wheeler, declaring that he intended to attack the garrison in the barracks. It was not till this letter came that the Nana's treachery was known. Up to that moment every one trusted in him as the friend of the English.

Nana had spoken the truth, when he had said he was going to attack the garrison. That very day (June 7) great guns began to pour their fire into the barracks; and day after day more guns and more enemies assaulted the place.

Terrible, indeed, were the sufferings of the poor captives. They soon found it hard to get out of the way of the bullets, which pierced the walls of the fortress in a thousand places. Some took shelter in holes they dug in the ground outside the walls, and covered over with boxes or boards; but though in these hiding-places they escaped the bullets, they found the heat almost unbearable.

The captives suffered much from thirst. It was dangerous to go out to fetch water from the well in the court. It was only during the evening that any one dare attempt it; but just for two hours after the sun had set—the firing was less frequent, and then captives with buckets crowded round the only well of water.

It was at the same hour that the dead bodies were carried to another well, and thrown down without coffins or mourners. Nor were dead bodies ever wanting, for day by day there were deaths from strokes of the sun, and from diseases of all kinds, and from shells and bullets.

The misery of the captives grew greater and greater. The stench of dead horses and the swarms of flies were insufferable. Fresh water failed entirely. A little corn was the only food. The walls seemed ready to fall from the immense number of holes the bullets had made.

The captives began to feel that it was of no use to resist any longer, and that the best way was to trust to the MERCY of the NANA!!

Alas! had they known the Nana better they would not have hoped for mercy from him. Even during the time the captives had been shut up, that Nana had been spilling the blood of ladies and children whom he had caught as they were fleeing from their enemies.

But the poor captives know nothing of these barbarous deeds, and therefore they hoped the Nana would spare their lives, if only they gave up the government money and their great guns.

Just as the English officers had almost determined to yield—they received a letter from the Nana, offering to send them away in safety, if they would only submit. They could hesitate no longer; and the very next day the Nana sent one of his chief officers to sign an agreement in writing.

The Nana promised to provide boats to convey the captives down the river Ganges to the great city of Allahabad, about two hundred miles off.

It was on June the 27th that the captives left their hateful abode. They were four hundred and fifty in number. How worn and pallid were the ladies; how puny and pining were the children! No one would have known them to be the same who entered that gloomy place five weeks ago. Many who had gone in *then* did not come out *now*, for they had died, and their bodies had been cast into the well.

This was the happiest morning the captives had seen for a long while. It seemed as if their sorrows had come to an end. There were doolies, and camels, and carts waiting at the gates to carry the ladies and children, and also the wounded soldiers. The other soldiers, with their officers, walked beside the rest, taking their muskets with them. An immense army of Sepoys accompanied them down to the river.

It was eight o'clock in the morning when they all reached the spot for embarking.

The Nana was there.

The captives stepped eagerly into the boats.

One boat had already pushed off.

Distant firing of guns was heard.

IT WAS THE NANA'S SIGN.

What was the horror felt by the captives when the Sepoys began to fire upon them from all sides, both with cannons and muskets! How dreadful were the shrieks of the women and

children! How great the confusion of the
soldiers! Some jumped into the water, but
Sepoys followed them close. Some reached the
opposite bank, but Sepoys were waiting for them
there. Every Englishman was murdered on the
spot, except those who escaped in the boat that
had already pushed off. The women and children
were not *killed*, but caught and sent back to the
city to be crammed into a little building without
beds, or baths, or any comfort of life.

What became of the poor creatures in the boat
that had pushed off? Sepoys pursued it on
both sides of the river,—and yet for two days
and two nights the boat went on its way. But
at last the wretched fugitives were OVERTAKEN.
They were lifted out of their boat into carts, and
driven back to Cawnpore, to be slaughtered there.

However, before the boat was overtaken, FOUR
had succeeded in getting away by swimming.
These FOUR were saved,—and these FOUR only,
of all the hundreds of men who left Cawnpore,
trusting to the promise of the treacherous Nana.

As for the poor captives who were brought
back in carts to Cawnpore, they were met by
the Nana at the entrance of the city.

He ordered them to be lifted out of the carts,
and to be seated upon the ground. There were
sixty men, twenty-five women, and four children.

Half dead with fatigue and terror, the poor

captives sat—expecting the worst. The Nana gave the word of command, "Separate the wives from their husbands!"

The captives had not expected so cruel a sentence as this. The fond wives, with their children clinging around them, rushed into the arms of their husbands, saying, "We will die together!" The Sepoys were obliged to use all their strength to tear them away. One wife, however, with her babe—they were not able, with all their endeavours, to tear away,—so closely did she cling.

The Nana was just going to say, "Fire!" when a voice was heard making an earnest request. Was he pleading for his life? No! a minister of God, named Moncrieff, was entreating to be allowed to offer up prayers with his dying friends.

The Nana, barbarous as he was, consented.

What prayers were then offered up! Did not many a sinner, soon to be slain, find mercy in that hour through the precious blood of the slaughtered Lamb?

The hands that had been lifted up in prayer now clasped the hands of their fellow-sufferers; each soldier gave a last farewell to his comrade.

The Nana spoke the word—the guns were fired—and in a moment the blood of sixty men and one woman flowed upon the ground; some died instantly, others were only wounded, and were killed afterwards by swords.

The poor women, after having seen a sight worse than death, were dragged along to a little house already overcrowded with prisoners. What a meeting took place between the ladies already shut up, and those just caught! What dismal tales of sorrow they had to tell one another!

But greater horrors were to come.

The captives had endured much misery in the barracks; but nothing compared with their misery now. They lay crowded together in rags and filth, without water to wash in, or beds to rest on, and with no food to eat but the coarsest bread.

One hundred and fifty women and children endured for a fortnight the most horrible torments from hunger, thirst, heat, sickness, and grief. Babies sickened in their mothers' arms and died. Mothers drooped and died. Those who died the *first* were counted the happiest.

There was only one hope remaining—British troops might come and deliver them.—And BRITISH TROOPS WERE ON THE WAY, HASTENING TO THEIR RELIEF. But, alas! they were stopped again and again by troops of Sepoys. The good General Havelock had to fight three great battles before he could reach Cawnpore.

He fought the third battle at a place twenty miles from Cawnpore.

The Nana's troops returned home that evening

in a savage mood. They asked leave to wreak their vengeance on the miserable captives.

Nana, with the joy of a demon, gave the order for a massacre.

That very evening these hounds of hell rushed into the loathsome abode. In their hands they held weapons of every kind, clubs and battle-axes, soldiers' bayonets and butchers' knives. What was the terror of the helpless captives at the sight of the murderers! Fierce were the struggles, and awful the screams, but not ONE was spared, neither fond mother nor tender babe, fair maiden nor little girl.

Could the brutal monsters sleep that night?

Whether they *slept* or not, I cannot tell; but they *repented* not.

Though they had *spared* NONE of the helpless captives, yet they had not *killed* ALL, for about a dozen women and a few children had crept under the dead bodies, and had escaped being murdered. When the murderers unlocked the doors of the slaughter-house in the morning, they found these poor wretches, all covered with blood, and they would have killed them, had not the terrified creatures rushed out of the house and thrown themselves into a well in the yard!

The very next day, July 17th, British troops under General Havelock entered the city.

The first question they asked was, " Where are the captives ?"

Great was their misery when they heard the horrible history. It was told them by an Englishman who had himself escaped two days before out of the bloody den.

The officers hastened to the hateful spot ; they passed through the front room and the court— into the back room, and as they stepped in—they found they were up to the ancles in blood. On the floor they saw scattered little shoes, crumpled bonnets, broken combs, torn books, and long tresses of fair hair.* The sight made them shudder. But how did they feel when they looked down the well, and beheld the heap of mingled bodies.

How did they FEEL ? They FELT that the murderers must be PUNISHED.

But *how* were they to be punished ? The chief murderer of all had gone to his palace in Bithoor, seven miles off. General Havelock, with his army, pursued him thither ; but when he arrived, lo !—the Nana and his army had fled, leaving behind them guns, horses, and cattle.

---

* Scraps of paper spotted with blood were found on the floor. On one of these a child had written its sad journal :— " Mamma died July 12 ; Alice died July 9 ; George died June 27 ; Uncle Willey died June 18 ; Aunt Lilly, June 17. Left barracks, June 27. Made prisoners as soon as we were at the river."

Havelock's army seized the spoil, and returned to Cawnpore, just to rest a little while before they set out for Lucknow, to relieve the captives pining in the Residency.   Through the mercy of God they *did* arrive in time to save *those* captives from destruction.

It was more necessary to save the Lucknow captives than to destroy the murderers of the Cawnpore captives.   Therefore Havelock left that work to another general.   His name was Neil.   When he arrived at Cawnpore he had a large trench dug round his camp, and having made himself as secure as he could, he gave orders that every rebel Sepoy should be seized and brought to him.

Every day some murderer was brought to him, and after he had been examined, and found guilty, he was condemned to be hanged; but FIRST—he was forced to go to the house of slaughter, and WIPE UP SOME OF THE BLOOD ON THE FLOOR.   This was a worse punishment than death; for the Hindoos imagine that, by touching the blood of Christians, they lose sharing in the pleasures of their gods, and that their souls will be made to pass, after death, into the bodies of cats and monkeys.

Ah! what a religion must theirs be, if they think it worse to *wipe up* blood than to *shed* blood! What a cruel, what a barbarous religion.

But while we blame these murderers, let us not excuse some murderers even more cruel than they.

Is not the SOUL more precious than the BODY? Must not he who murders the *soul* be worse than he who murders the *body*? What, then, shall we say of our own nation, who have long suffered the heathen to die in their sins, without telling them of that precious blood which can wash the sinner clean? How cruel were those English rulers who forbad English officers to teach the Sepoys the way of salvation!*

CIRCASSIA.

THIS is not a vast country, like China or Hindostan. It may be called a nook, it is so small compared with some great kingdoms : but it is famous on account of the beauty of the people. They are fair, like Europeans, with handsome features and fine figures. But their beauty has done them harm, and not good; for the cruel Turks purchase many of the Circassian women, because they are beautiful, and shut them up

---

* Extracted from " The Mutiny of the Bengal Army. By one who served under Sir Charles Napier," compared with that valuable work, " England and India," by the Honourable Baptist Noel.

in their houses. Perhaps you will be surprised to hear that the young Circassians think it a fine thing to go to Turkey—to live in fine palaces and gardens, instead of remaining in their own simple cottages. But I think that when they find themselves confined between high walls, they must sigh to think of their flocks and their farms at home, and more than all, of the dear relations they have left behind.

Circassia is a pleasant country, situated near the noble mountains of Caucasus. The snow on the mountains cools the air, and makes Circassia as pleasant to live in as our own England. Indeed, if you were suddenly to be transported into Circassia, you would be ready to exclaim, "Is not this England? Here are apple-trees, and pear-trees, and plum-trees, like those in my father's garden : those sounds are like the notes of the blackbird and thrush, which sing among the hawthorns in my native country."

But look again, you will see vines twining round the spreading oaks. You do not see such vines in England. But hark ! what do I hear ? It is a sound never heard in England. It is the yell of jackals.

MANNERS OF THE PEOPLE.—There is no country in the world where the people are as kind to strangers as in Circassia. Every family, however poor, has a guest-house. There is the family-

house, with its orchard, and stables, and at a
little distance, another house for strangers. This
is no more than a large room, with a stable at
one end. The walls are made of wicker-work,
plastered with clay. There is no ceiling but the
rafters, and no floor but the bare earth. Yet
there is a wide chimney, where a blazing fire is
kept up with a pile of logs. And there is a sofa
or divan, covered with striped silk, and many
neat mats to serve as beds for as many travellers
as may arrive. The wind may whistle through
the chinks, and the rain come through the roof,

Circassian Guest-house.

but the stranger is well warmed, and comfortably
lodged; and above all, he has the host to wait
upon him with more attention than a servant.
The supper is served as soon as the sun sets.

But where is the table? There is none worthy to be called a table. Is the supper placed on the floor? Not so. It is brought in on stools with three legs. They answer the purpose of tables, trays, and dishes, all in one. What is the fare served up? This is the sort of dinner provided. On the first table is placed a flat loaf; the gravy in the middle, and the meat all round. When this is taken away, another table is brought in with cheesecakes; a third with butter and honey; a fourth with a pie; a fifth with a cream; and last of all, a table, with a wooden bowl of curdled milk. The company have no plates; but each Circassian carries a spoon and a knife in his girdle, and with these he helps himself. The servants who stand by are not forgotten: a piece of meat or of pie-crust is often given to one of them; it is curious to see the man take it into a corner to eat it there. There are many hungry poor waiting at the door of the guest-house, ready to help the servants to devour the remains of the feast; and there is often a great deal of food left; for there are generally *ten* tables, and sometimes there are *forty* tables. The guests are expected to taste the food on each, however many there may be.

Instead of wine there is a drink called *shuat* handed to the guest: it is distilled from grain and honey. Vegetables are not much eaten in

Circassia : for greens are considered fit only for beasts : and there are no potatoes. Pies, and tarts, and tartlets of various kinds, are too well liked, and the finest ladies in the land are skilful in making them.

The family live in a thatched cottage, called "the family-house." It is not divided into rooms. If a man wants several rooms, he builds several houses.

As you approach the dwelling of a Circassian, you hear the barking of dogs, and upon coming nearer, you see women milking cows and feeding poultry, and boys tending goats and leading horses. If you go into the farm-yard you will see among the animals the buffalo—but no pig. There are, however, wild boars in the woods.

CIRCASSIAN WOMEN.—They are not shut up as Hindoo and Chinese, and Turkish ladies are. They do not indeed go into the guest-house to see strangers; but strangers are sometimes in-vited into the family-house to see them.

An Englishman, who visited a family-house, was introduced to the wife and daughter. They both rose up when he entered : nor would they sit down till he sat down ; and this respect ladies shew not only to gentlemen, but even to the poorest peasants. The only furniture in the house was the divan on which the ladies sat ; a pile of boxes containing the beds, which were to be spread on the floor at night ; and a loom for weaving cloth, and spindles for spinning.

The daughter, who was sixteen, was dressed in a skirt of striped silk, with a blue boddice, and silver clasps : and she wore a cap of scarlet cloth, adorned with silver lace—her light hair flowing over her shoulders : yet though so finely

Picture of Circassian Maiden.

arrayed, her feet were bare ; for she only put on her red slippers when she walked out. The mother was covered with a loose calico wrapper, and her face was concealed by a thick white veil. The visitor laid some needle cases at the ladies' feet, for it is not the custom for them to receive presents in their hands.

The needle-cases greatly delighted the young Hafiza and her mother. The present was well chosen, because the Circassian women are very industrious, supplying their husbands and brothers with all their clothes, from the woollen bonnet to the morocco shoe. The wool, the flax, and the hemp, are all prepared at home by the mothers and made into clothes by the girls, who first spin the thread, then weave the cloth, and finish by sewing the seams. Some girls are very clever in knitting silver lace for trimming garments. A girl named Dussepli was famous for her skill in this art ; indeed her name signifies " Shining as lace."

An Englishman went to the place where she lived, to buy some of her lace. He was shown into the guest-house, and he soon saw Dussepli approaching in a pair of high pattens. At first sight there was nothing pleasing in Dussepli, but when she spoke she seemed so kind and so true, that it was impossible not to like her. By her industry in knitting lace and dyeing cloth she helped to support her father, who was poor.

THE CIRCASSIAN MEN.—War is their chief occupation. Working in the fields is left to the women, and the little boys, and the slaves. There is, alas ! great occasion for the men to fight, as the land has long been infested with many dangerous enemies.

The Russians are endeavouring to conquer the Circassians: but the Circassians declare they will die sooner than yield. Long ago the enemies must have triumphed had it not been for the high mountains, which afford hiding places for the poor hunted inhabitants. Every man carries a gun, a pistol, a dagger, and a sword; and the nobles are distinguished by a bow and a quiver of arrows. The usual dress is of coarse, dark cloth, and consists of a tunic, trousers, and gaiters. The cap or bonnet is of sheepskin or goatskin.

The boys are taught from their infancy to be hardy and manly. They are brought up in a singular way. Instead of remaining at home, they are given, at three years old, into the care of a stranger: and the reason of this custom is, that they may not be petted by their parents.

The stranger is called "foster-father," and he teaches any boy under his care to ride well, and to shoot at a mark. The boy follows his foster-father over the mountains, urging his horse to climb tremendous heights, and to rush down dark ravines; and appeasing his hunger with a mouthful of honey from the bag fastened to his girdle. Such is the life he leads till he is a tall and a strong youth; and then he returns home to his parents. His foster-father presents him with a horse and weapons of war, and requires no payment in return for all his care.

Men brought up in this manner must be wild, bold, restless, and ignorant. Such are the Circassians. They care not for learning, as the Chinese do, but only for bravery. We cannot wonder at this, when we remember what enemies they have in their land. The Russians have built many strong towers, whence they shoot at all who come near. But not satisfied with this, they often come forth and rob the villages.

There was a Circassian (and he may be still alive), called Guz Beg; and he gained for himself the name of the "Lion of Circassia." He was always leading out little bands of men to attack the Russians. One day he found some Russian soldiers reaping in the fields, and when he came near they ran away in terror, leaving two hundred scythes in the field which he seized. But a great calamity befel this Lion. He had an only son. When he first led the boy to the wars he charged him never to shrink from the enemy, but to cut his way through the very midst. One day Guz Beg had ridden into the thick of the Russian soldiers, when suddenly a ball pierced his horse, and he was thrown headlong on the ground. There lay the Lion among the hunters. In another moment he would have been killed, when suddenly a youthful warrior flew to his rescue—it was his own son. But what could *one* do amongst *so many!* A troop of Circassian horse rushed to the spot, and bore away Guz Beg; but they were too late to save his son. They bore away the *body* only of the brave boy. Guz Beg was deeply grieved; but he continued still to fight for his country.

Circassian Lion—Guz Beg.

See those black heaps of ashes. In that spot there once lived a prince named Zefri Bey, with his four hundred servants; but his dwellings were burned to the ground by the Russians. That prince fled to Turkey to plead for help. What would have become of his wife and little girls if a kind friend had not taken them under his care? This friend was hump-backed, but very brave. Some English travellers went to visit him, and were received in the guest-house, and regaled with a supper of many tables. Next day the little girls came to the guest-house, and kissed their hands. The daughter of the hump-backed man accompanied them. The children were delighted with some toys the traveller gave them, and the kind young lady accepted needles and scissors. But where was the wife of Zefri Bey? A servant was sent to inquire after her, and found her in rags, lying on a mat, without even a counterpane, and weeping bitterly. Had no one given her clothes and coverings? Yes, but she gave everything away, for she had been used, as a princess, to make presents, and now she cared for nothing. Such are the miseries which the Russians bring upon Circassia.

THE GOVERNMENT.—There is no king of Circassia, but there are many princes.

The people pay great respect to these princes, standing in their presence, and giving them the first place at feasts, and in the battle field. But though the people honour them, they do not obey them.

There is a parliament in Circassia, but it does not meet in a house, but in a grove. Every man who pleases may *come,* but only old men may *speak*. If a young man were to give his opinions, no attention would be paid. The warriors sit on the grass, and hang up their weapons of war on the boughs above their heads, while they fasten their horses to the stems of the trees.

The speakers are gentle in their tone of voice and behaviour. The Circassians admire sweet winning speeches. They say there are three things which mark a great man ; a sharp sword, a sweet tongue, and forty tables. What do they mean by these? By a sharp sword they mean bravery ;—by a sweet tongue they mean soft speeches ;—and by forty tables they mean giving plentiful suppers to neighbours and to strangers. Are the Circassians right in this way of thinking? No—for though bravery is good, and speaking well is good, and giving away is good—these are not the greatest virtues ; and people may be brave and speak well and give away much, and yet be wicked ; for they may be without the love of God in their hearts. What are the greatest virtues ? These three—Faith, Hope, and Charity. These are graces which come from God.

SERVANTS.—There are slaves in Circasssia called serfs. But they are so well treated, that they are not like the slaves of other countries. They live in huts round their master's dwelling ; they work in the fields, and wait upon the guests, and share in the good fare on the little tables.

When a Circassian takes a Russian prisoner, he makes him a slave, and gives him the hardest work to do. Yet the Russians are much happier with their Circassian masters than in their own country.

Once a Circassian said to his Russian slave, "I am going to send you back to Russia." The man fell at his master's feet, saying, "Rather than do so, use me as your dog; beat me, tie me up, and give me your bones to pick." The master then told him that he had not spoken in earnest, and that he would not send him away, and then the poor fellow began to shout and to jump with joy.

BROTHERHOODS.—There is a very remarkable plan in Circassia, unlike the plans in other countries. A certain number of men agree to call themselves "brothers." These brothers help each other on every occasion, and visit at each other's houses frequently. They are not received in the guest-house, but in the family-house, and are treated by all the family as if they were really the brothers of the master.

A brotherhood sometimes consists of two thousand, but sometimes of only twenty persons.

RELIGION.—Circassia, though beautiful, is an unhappy country. The Russians keep the people in continual fear; this is a great evil. But There is another nation who have done the Circassians still greater harm. I mean the Turks. And what have they done to them? They have persuaded them to turn Mahomedans. The greatest harm that can be done to any one is, to give him a false religion. There are no grand mosques in Circassia, because there are no towns; but in every little village there is a clay cottage, where prayers are offered up in the name of Mahomed. There can be no minaret to such a miserable mosque: so the man who calls the hours of prayer climbs a tall tree, by the help of notches, and getting into a basket at the top, makes the rocks and hills resound with his cry. How different shall be the sound one day heard in every land, when all people shall believe in Jesus! Then shall the inhabitants of the rock sing—then shall they shout from the top of the mountains, and give glory unto the *Lord*, and not to Mahomed. (Isa. xlii, 11, 12.)

But though the Circassians call themselves Mahomedans, they keep many of their old customs, and these customs shew that they once heard about Christ. It is their custom to dedicate every boy to God; but not really to *God*, for in truth they dedicate him to the *cross*. Let me give you an account of one of the feasts of dedication.

The place of meeting was a green, shaded by spreading oak-trees. In the midst stood a cross.

Each family who came to the feast brought a little table, and placed it before the cross ; and on each table there were loaves, and a sort of bread called "pasta." There was a blazing fire on the green, round which the elder women sat, while the younger preferred the shade of a thicket. The priest took a loaf of bread in one hand, and in the other a large cup of *shuat* (a kind of wine), and holding them out towards the cross, blessed them. While he did this, men, women, and children knelt around, and bowed their heads to the ground. Afterwards, the *shuat* and the bread were handed about amongst the company. But this was only the beginning of the feast. Afterwards, a calf, a sheep, and two goats, were brought to the cross to be blessed. Then a little of their hair was singed by a taper, and then they were taken away to be slaughtered. Now the merriment began : some moved forward to cut up the animals, and to boil their flesh in large kettles on fires kindled on the green ; many young men amused themselves with racing, leaping, and hurling stones, while the elder people sat and talked. When the meat was boiled, it was distributed among the sixty tables, and then the priest blessed the food. And then the feasting began. Does it not seem as if the Circassians must once have learned about Jesus crucified, and about His supper of bread and wine, and about the Jewish feasts and sacrifices ? Once, perhaps, they knew the true religion, but they soon forgot it; 'and though they still remember the *cross*, they have forgotten *Christ* ; and though they still bless the bread and the cup, they know nothing of redeeming love. Do you not long to send missionaries to Circassia ? Well, some good Scotch missionaries went there some years ago, but, alas ! the Russians sent them away. Their thatched cottages may still be seen, and their fruitful orchards, but they themselves are gone. There are, however, a few German Christians in Circassia. They are not missionaries, but only farmers, therefore the Russians allow them to remain. They have a little church, where the Bible is read, and God is worshipped. You will be glad to hear a few Circassians may be seen amongst the congregation : they were converted by the Scotch missionaries, and they have remained faithful amongst their heathen neighbours.

Circassia is situated on a spot between two seas :—

The Black Sea, and

The Caspian Sea.

What a wonderful place is the Caspian Sea! It is like a lake, only so immensely large, that it is called a sea. The waters of lakes are fresh, like those of rivers ; but the waters of the Caspian are salt, yet not so salt as the salt sea. The shores of the Caspian are flat, and unwholesome. You might think, as you stood there, that you were by the great ocean, for there are waves breaking on the sands, and water as far as the eye can reach; but there is no freshness in the air as by the real sea.

The mountains of Caucasus run through Circassia. They are quite low, compared to the Himalaya; they are about the height of the Alps, and the tops are covered with snow. But the valleys between these mountains are not like the Swiss valleys, which are broad and pleasant; these valleys are narrow and dark, and not fit to live in, yet they are of great use as hiding-places for the Circassians. When pursued by a Russian, a Circassian will urge his horse to dash down the dark valley, and lest his horse should be alarmed at the sight of the dangerous depth below, he will cover the animal's eyes with a cloak. Thus many a bold rider escapes from a cruel soldier.

GEORGIA.

WHEN you hear of Circassia, you will generally hear of Georgia too, for the countries lie close together, and resemble one another in many respects. Yet though so near, their climate is different; for Circassia lies *beyond* the mountains of Caucasus, and is therefore exposed to the cold winds of the north. But Georgia lies *beneath* the mountains, and is sheltered from the chill blasts. Georgia is, therefore, far more fruitful than Circassia; but the people are less fair, and less industrious.

The sides of the hills are clothed with vines, and houses with deep verandahs are scattered amongst the vineyards, and women wrapped in long white sheets may be seen reposing in the porticoes, enjoying the soft air and lovely prospect. While Circassian ladies are busy weaving and milking, the Georgian ladies loll upon their couches, and do nothing. Which do you think are the happier? These Georgian ladies, though very handsome, are much disfigured by painted faces and stained eyebrows. Their countenances, too, are lifeless and silly, as might be expected, since they waste their time in idleness. Over their foreheads they wear a kind of low crown, called a tiara.

There is no country where so much wine is drunk as in Georgia; even a labourer is allowed five bottles a-day. The grapes are exceedingly fine, quite different from the little berries called grapes in Circassia. The casks are very curious— they are the skins of buffaloes; and as the tails

and legs are not cut off, a skin filled with wine
looks like a dead, or a sleeping buffalo.

And what is the religion of Georgia ?   It is
the Russian religion, because the Russians have
conqured the country.   They cannot conquer
the brave and active Circassians, but they have
conquered the soft and indolent Georgians.   The
Georgians are called Christians, but the Greek
Church, which is the Russian religion, is a Christ-
ianity laden with ceremonies, and darkened by
false doctrines.

TIFLIS.

There is but one town in Georgia.   It is beautifully situated on the steep banks of a river,
with terraces of houses, embosomed in vineyards.
So little do the people care for reading, that
there is not a bookseller's shop in the town, and
it is very seldom that a book-case is seen in a
house ; for the Georgians love show, and enter-
tainments, and idleness, but not study.

TARTARY.

THIS is one of the largest countries in the world,
yet it does not contain as many people as the
small land of France.   How is this ?   You will
not be surprised that many people do not live

there, when you hear what sort of a country it is.

Fancy a country quite flat, as far as eye can see, except where a few low sand-hills rise; a country quite bare, except where the coarse grass grows; a country quite dry, except where some narrow muddy streams run. Such is Tartary. What is a country without hills, without trees, without brooks? Can it be pleasant? This flat, bare, dry plain, is called the steppes of Tartary. In one part of Tartary there is a chain of mountains, and there are a few towns and trees, but *very few*. You may travel a long while without seeing one.

Nothing can be so dreary as the steppes appear in winter time. The high wind sweeping along the plain, drives the snow into high heaps, and often hurls the poor animals into a cold grave. Sledges cannot be used because they cannot slide on such uneven ground. But if the *white* ground looks dreary in winter, the *black* ground looks hideous in summer; for the hot sun turns the grass black, and fills the air with black dust, and there are no shady groves, no cool hills, no refreshing brooks. There must, indeed, be a *little* shade among the thistles, as they grow to twice the height of a man; but how different is such shade from the shade of spreading oaks like ours! Instead of nice fruit, there is bitter wormwood growing among the grass, and when the cows eat it their milk becomes bitter.

WILD ANIMALS.—The most common is a pretty little creature called the sooslik. It is very much like a squirrel.

But can it live where squirrels live,—in the hollows of trees? Where are the trees in the steppe? The sooslik makes a house for itself by digging a hole into the ground, just as rabbits do in England. Will it not surprise you to hear that wolves follow the same plan, and even the wild dogs? The houses the dogs make are very convenient, for the entrance is very narrow, and there is plenty of room below.

There are some very odious animals on the steppe:—snakes and toads. Yes, showers of toads sometimes fall. But neither snakes nor toads are as great a plague as locusts. These little animals, not bigger than a child's thumb, are more to be dreaded than a troop of wolves. And why? Because they come in such immense numbers. The eggs lie hid in the ground all the winter. Oh, if it were known *where* they were concealed, they would soon be destroyed! But no one knows where they are till they are hatched. In the first warm days of spring the young animals come forth, and immediately they begin crawling on the ground in one immense flock, eating up all the grass as they pass along; in a month they can fly, and then they darken the air like a thick cloud; whenever any green appears, they drop down and settle on the spot. The noise they make in eating can be heard to a great distance, and the noise they make in flying is like the rustling of leaves in a forest. They cannot be destroyed: but there are two things they hate,—smoke and noise,—and by these they are sometimes scared and induced to fly away.

PEOPLE AND CUSTOMS.—Besides the *wild* animals, there are *tame* animals, which inhabit the steppe with men and women who take care of them. They are all wanderers, both men and beasts. You can easily guess why they wander. It is to find sufficient grass for the cattle.

Every six weeks the Tartars move to a new place. Yet one place is so like another, that no place appears new :—there is always the same immense plain—without a cottage or an orchard, a green hill or a running brook, to make any spot remembered. It is great labour to the Tartar women to pack up the tents and to place them on the backs of the camels, and then to unpack and to pitch the tents. It is a great disgrace to the men to suffer the women to work as hard as they do; but the men are very idle, and like to sit by their tents smoking and drinking, while their wives are toiling and striving with all their might. The women have the care of all the cattle : and the men attend only to the horses. Perhaps they would not even do this, were it not that they are very fond of riding; and such riders as the Tartars are seldom seen.

To give you an idea how they ride, I will describe one scene that took place on the steppe.

Some travellers from Europe were on a visit to a Tartar prince (for there are *princes* in the desert,) and they were taken to see a herd of wild horses. The prince wished to have one of these wild horses caught. It is not easy to do this. But Tartars know the way. Six men mounted tame horses, and rushed into the midst of the wild horses. Each of the men had a great noose in his hand. They all looked at the prince to know which horse he would have caught. When they saw the prince give a sign, one of the men soon noosed a young horse. The creature seemed terrified when it found that it was caught: his eyes started out, his nostrils seemed to smoke. Presently a man came running up, sprang upon the back of the wild horse, and by cutting the straps round his neck, set him at liberty. In an instant the horse darted away with the swiftness of an arrow; yet the man firmly kept his seat. The animal seemed greatly alarmed at his strange burden, and tried every plan to get rid of it;—now suddenly stopping,—now crawling on the grass, like a worm,—now rolling,—now rearing,—now dashing forward at a fast gallop through the midst of the herd; yet all would not do; the rider clung to the horse as closely as ever.

But how was the rider ever to get off his fiery steed? That would be difficult indeed; but help was sent to him by the prince. Two men on horseback rode after him, and between them they snatched away the man from the trembling and foaming horse. The animal, surprised to find his load suddenly gone, stood stupified for a moment, and then darted off to join his companions. What *this* man did,—*many* Tartars can do; and even *little boys* will mount wild horses, and keep on by clinging to their manes: *women*, too, will gallop about on wild horses.

In Circassia the customs are very different; for though *men* ride so well, *women* there never ride at all; and surely it is far better not to ride than to be as bold as a Tartar woman.

Food.—What can be the food of the Tartars? Not bread (for there is no corn,) nor fruit, nor vegetables. The flocks and herds are the food. The favourite meat is horse-flesh; though mutton and beef are eaten also. Then there is plenty of milk—both cow's milk and sheep's milk.   As there is milk, there are butter and cheese.   But it is very unwholesome to live on meat and milk without bread and vegetables. The water, too, is very bad; for it is taken from the muddy rivers, and not from clear springs. It is a comfort for the Tartar that he can procure tea from China.   This tea is indeed very unlike the tea brought to England; for it comes to Tartary in hard lumps, shaped like bricks. It is boiled in a saucepan with water, and then mixed with milk, butter, and salt.   Thus you see the Tartar needs neither tea-kettle, tea-pot, nor sugar-basin.

It would be well if tea and milk were the only drinks in Tartary; but a sort of spirit is distilled by the Tartars from mare's milk; and brandy also is brought from Russia.

TENTS.—A Tartar tent is very unlike an Arab

Tartar Tent.

tent. It is in the shape of a hut for the sides are upright, and the roof only is slanting, and there is a small hole at the top to let the smoke escape. Neither is it made of skins, but of thick woollen stuff called felt, which keeps the cold out. At night the entrance is closed, and the family sleep on mats around the fire in the midst.

APPEARANCE.—The Tartars are not handsome like the Turks and Circassians. They are short and thick; their faces are broad and bony, their eyes very small, and only half open ; their noses flat, their lips thick, their chins pointed, their ears large and flapping, and their skin dark and yellow.

Their dress is warm and well suited for riding in the desert. Different tribes have different dresses. The dress of the Kalmuck Tartars is— a yellow cloth cap trimmed with black lamb's-skin, red boots with high heels, wide trousers, a tight jacket, and over all a loose tunic, fastened round the waist. The women dress like the men ; but they let their hair grow in two long tresses, while the men shave part of their heads and keep only *one* lock of hair hanging on their shoulders.

You see that the Tartars are much like the Chinese in their persons and dress; but they are a much stronger, bolder people, and much more ignorant. No wonder, therefore, that many years ago the Tartars got over the Chinese wall, and took possession of the Chinese throne. You must not forget that the Emperor of China is a Tartar.

GOVERNMENT.—To whom does Tartary belong? Has it a king of its own. No. Once it had many kings, called khans; but now the khans have lost their power, and are only *called* khans to do them honour.

There are many different tribes, and each tribe keeps to a certain part of the land, and never ventures to wander beyond its own bounds.

RELIGION.—The religion is the same as that which is so common in China, the religion of Buddha; but in some parts of Tartary there is the religion of Mahomet. It is sad to think that far more people in the world worship Buddha, the deceiver, than Jesus the Son of God. The Tartars think to please their false gods by making a loud noise. It would astonish a stranger to hear their jingling bells, shrill horns, squeaking shells, bellowing trumpets, and deafening drums. How unlike is their senseless noise to the sweet sound of a Christian hymn!

The Tartars think also to please their gods by glaring colours; so their priests dress in red and yellow, and bear flags, adorned with strips of gay silk. A band of priests looks something like a regiment of soldiers.

The chief priests are called Grand Lamas, and they are worshipped as gods; but their situation is not very pleasant, for they are not allowed to walk without help. Whenever they attempt to walk, they are held up by a man on each side, as if they were infants: and usually they are drawn in cars, or carried in palanquins. From want of exercise they become very weak and helpless. When they die their bodies are burned, and the ashes are gathered up and made into an idol. Thus they continue to be gods after they are dead. There are many Grand Lamas in Tartary.

As the Tartars are always moving about, a tent serves for a temple; and the idols are carried in great chests. They cannot walk, therefore they must be carried. What use are such gods?

The Tartars have found out a way of praying without any trouble; and it is a way that suits idols very well. They get some prayers written, and place them in a drum, and then turn the drum round and round with a string. This they call praying; and while they are thus praying, they can be chattering, smoking, and even quarrelling. The princes have a still easier way of offering up prayers. They write prayers upon a flag, and then place it before their tents for the wind to blow it about. This is *their* way of praying to their gods. And what, my dear child, is *your* way of praying to your God?

Have missionaries visited the Tartars?

Yes; I will tell you of two German missionaries, who tried to convert a tribe of Tartars, called the Kalmucks, living near the Caspian Sea and the river Volga. These good men were treated with great contempt by the Tartars. They translated the Gospel of St. Matthew into the Tartar language. One of the Tartars instead of thanking them, observed, "I wonder you should take so much trouble to prepare a book that we shall never read." When the precious book was given to the Tartars, some of them returned the books; and when it was read to them, they scornfully said, as they turned away, "It is only the history of Jesus."

At last one Tartar, named Sodnom, believed in Jesus. He said to the missionaries, "Now the Tartars, from my example, may turn to the Lord: for as when sheep are to be washed, each is afraid to enter the water till *one* has been in, so it may be with my countrymen.

Sodnom read every evening in the Testament to his family in the tent. At first his wife was displeased, and said that her husband wasted the firewood in making a light to read a book that was of no use. But afterwards she listened, and kept the children quiet. The neighbours also listened, and *twenty-two* turned to the Lord.

Then the prince and the priests grew angry,

and said the Christians must leave the camp.
Where could the Christians go? There was a
village called Sarepta, where some Germans

Tartars leaving the Camp.

lived. There they determined to go, though it
was two hundred miles off. One of the missionaries led the way on horseback; the Tartars
followed on foot: then came camels bearing the
tents and the women, while a bullock-cart contained the young children. The flocks and herds
were driven by the bigger children.

The good Germans in Sarepta received the
Tartars with great joy. One gray-headed man
of eighty-three came to meet them, leaning upon
his staff. He said he had been praying that he
might see a *Christian* Tartar before he died. He

heard these Tartars sing hymns to the praise of Jesus, and he felt his prayers were answered. Two days afterwards he died. Like old Simeon he might have said, "Lord, now lettest Thou Thy servant depart in peace, for mine eyes have seen Thy salvation."

The Christians went to live in a small island in the river Volga. When the river was frozen, the Germans went over the ice to visit them. Sodnom gave them tea mixed with fat in a large wooden bowl; and to please him the kind Germans drank some, though they did not like it. Many Tartars assembled in Sodnom's tent, and, seated on the ground smoking their pipes, talked together about heavenly things; and before they parted they put away their pipes and, folding their hands, sang hymns in their own language. The Germans, in taking leave, divided a large loaf among the company; for bread is considered quite a dainty by the Tartars.

The change that had taken place in these Tartars filled the Germans with joy; and more missionaries would have gone to teach the heathen Kalmucks, had not the Emperor of Russia forbidden them.

ASTRACAN.

This city is on the Caspian Sea. It is very unpleasant, on account of the heat and the gnats.

Not only Tartars dwell there, but many people of all nations, Russians, Hindoos, and Armenians. The chief trade of Astracan is in the fish of the sea and the salt of the shores. *

BOKHARA, IN TARTARY.

This is a kingdom in the midst of Tartary. It lies at the south of the Caspian Sea. It is not like the rest of Tartary, for it is a sweet green spot. Travellers have said that it is the most beautiful spot in the world, but that is not true. The reason that travellers have said so, is that, after passing through a great desert, they have been charmed at seeing again running streams and shady groves.

But though Bokhara is a beautiful place, it is a wicked place.

The king is one of the greatest tyrants in the world. He is called the Amir.

The city where he dwells is called Bokhara (which is also the name of the whole country.) His palace is on a high mound, in the midst of splendid mosques and mansions. Amongst these grand buildings is the prison, a place of horrible cruelty. There the prisoners lie in the dark and

* Taken from Xavier De Hell's " Travels
Smith's "History of Missionaries."

the damp. One use of the prison is to keep water cool for the king in the summer ; it feels therefore just like a cellar.

But the worst dungeon is filled with stinging insects, called "ticks," reared on purpose to torment prisoners. In order to keep the ticks alive when no prisoners are there, raw meat is thrown into the place. There is also a deep pit into which men are let down with ropes : as once the holy Jeremiah was in Jerusalem.

Once a fortnight the prisoners are judged by the Amir. Even when the ground is covered with snow they stand with bare feet, waiting for hours till the Amir appears.

Can so cruel a monarch be happy ? No. He lives in constant fear of his life.

He is afraid of drinking water, lest it should be poisoned. All that he drinks is brought from the river in skins, and sealed, and guarded by two officers ; it is then taken to the chief counsellor, called the Vizier, and tasted by him and his servants ; it is then sealed again, and sent to his majesty.

The Amir's dinner, when it is ready, is not placed on the royal table, but locked up in a box, and taken to the Vizier to be tasted, before it is served up in the palace.

But it is not the Amir only who is afraid of poison. No one will accept fruit from another, unless that other tastes it first. It must be very terrible to live in the midst of such murderers as the people of Bokhara seem to be.

The Amir is so much afraid of people making plans to destroy him, that he chooses to see all the letters that are written by his subjects; if a husband write to his wife, the letter must first be shewn to the Amir. There are boys, too, going about the city listening to all that is said, that they may let the Amir know if any one speaks against him.

But while the Amir is watching his people, *they* are watching *him;* for his chief officers hire men to listen to the Amir's conversation, that they may know if he intends to kill them. Yet every person *appears* to approve all the Amir does, saying on every occasion, "It is the act of a king; it must be good." They are such people as Jeremiah describes in the Bible, "their tongue is as an arrow shot out, it speaketh deceit; one *speaketh* peaceably to his neighbour, but in his *heart* he lieth in wait." (Jer. ix, 8.)

APPEARANCE.—The people in Bokhara are much handsomer than other Tartars; their complexions are fairer, and their hair is of a lighter colour. They wear large white turbans, and several dark pelisses, with high-heeled boots. These high heels prevent their walking well, and most people, both men and women, ride;

but the ladies always hide their faces with a veil of black hair-cloth.

The large court of the palace is filled from morning to night with a crowd of noisy people, most of them mounted on horses and donkeys.

In the midst of the court is the fruit-market. It is wonderful to behold the quantity and beauty of the fruits. The same fruits grow in Bokhara as in England, only they are much finer. *Such* grapes, plums, and apricots, mulberries, and melons, are never seen in Europe, and they are made more refreshing by being mixed with chopped ice. Large piles of ice stand all the summer long in the market-place, and even beggars drink iced water. But hot tea is preferred before any other drink. In every corner of the market there are large urns of hot tea, and small bowls of rich milk, surrounded all day by a thirsty crowd. How much better is this sight than the gin palaces of London!

But there is one great inconvenience in Bokhara, for which all its fruits can scarcely make amends. There is bad water. For Bokhara is not built on the banks of a river, or amongst running brooks; all the water is brought by canals, from a small stream near the town, and when the canals are dried up by the heat, there is no water, except in the tanks. This stagnant water produces a disease called the Guinea worm. In this complaint the skin is covered with painful swellings, and when they burst, a little flat worm is discovered in each, which must be drawn out before the poor sufferer can recover.

RELIGION.—It is the Mahomedan. The Amir is a strict observer of his religion. Every Friday he may be seen going to prayers in his great mosque. The Koran is carried before him, and four men with golden staves accompany him, crying out, "Pray to God that the Commander of the Faithful may act justly." As he passes by, his people stroke their beards to show their respect. Bokhara is reckoned by Mahomedans a very religious city; for in every street there is a mosque; every evening people may be seen crowding to prayers; and if boys are caught asleep during service, they are tied together, and driven round the market by an officer, who beats them all the way with a thick thong.

There is a school, too, in almost every street of Bokhara, and there the poor boys sit, from sunrise till an hour before sunset, bawling out their foolish lessons from the Koran; and during all that time they are never allowed to go home, except once for some bread. They have no time for play, except in the evening, and no holiday except on Friday. Seven years they spend in this manner, learning to read and write. When they leave school, if they wish to be counted very wise, they go to one of the colleges ; for there are many in Bokhara. Some spend all their lives in these colleges, living in small cells, and meeting in a large hall to hear lectures about the Mahomedan religion. It is a happy thing however, that in summer the students go out to work in the fields ; for how much better is it to work with the hands than to fill the head with the wicked inventions of Mahomed !

The Mahomedans, however, are very proud of their religion, because they *say*, they do not worship idols (yet they do worship at Mecca a black stone, and other like things in other places). They imagine that *all* Christians are idolaters, for they know that the Russians bow down to pictures.

Once the Vizier of Bokhara conversed a long while with two Englishmen about their religion.

He asked them, " Do you worship idols ?"

The Englishmen replied, " No."

The Vizier would not believe them, but said, " I am sure you have images and crosses hung round your necks."

Upon which they opened their vests to show there was nothing hidden.

Then the Vizier smiled, and said to his servants, " They are not bad people."

As the servants were preparing tea, the Vizier

took a cup, and said to the travellers, " You must drink with us, for you are people of the Book," meaning the Bible.

Yet you must not suppose, because the Vizier seemed to approve these Christians, that he, and the Amir, would allow missionaries to settle in the kingdom.

It is dangerous for Englishmen to visit Bokhara. When they do come, they must be very careful not to give offence, or they will lose their lives. Englishmen are more dreaded than any other people, because it is known in Bokhara that they have conquered Hindostan, and therefore the Amir fears lest they should conquer his kingdom also. As soon as an Englishman enters Bokhara, he is forbidden to write a letter, for fear he should contrive some plan to bring enemies there. Neither is he allowed to ride in the streets; none but Mahomedans are allowed to ride in *them*, though any one may ride *outside* the city.

Several Englishmen have been cruelly murdered in Bokhara.

Colonel Stoddart was let down with ropes into a dark deep pit, full of horrible insects, and he was kept there two months. Afterwards he was let out of the *pit*, but not let out of the *city*. No, he was kept there for several *years* as a prisoner. At last Captain Conolly came, and he also was shut up, and in the end, both Stoddart and Conolly were sentenced to die.

They were led with their hands tied behind them to a place near the palace, to be executed. Conolly, as he was dragged along, cried out, "Woe, woe, to me, for I have fallen into the hands of a tyrant!" At the place of execution the two Englishmen kissed each other.

Then Conolly said to his friend, "We shall see each other in Paradise, near Jesus."

These were their last words. Immediately afterwards their heads were cut off with a knife.

The bleeding heads were brought to the cruel Amir. A dervish standing near was bold enough to say to his monarch these words: "The blood of these murdered men will cry up to the Most High against you!"

The Amir was enraged, and ordered the dervish to be beaten and banished. But he has often had reason to think of those words, and he has been heard to say, "The wounds of my heart for having slain those English people will never heal;" for all kinds of troubles have happened to him since that murder.

A clergyman, named Joseph Wolff, travelled all the way from England, and all alone, on purpose to inquire after the lost Englishmen. The Amir was surprised at his coming, and said, "I have taken thousands of *Persians* and made them slaves, and no one came from Persia to inquire what was become of them; but as soon as I take two ENGLISHMEN prisoners, behold a man comes all this long way to inquire after *them !*"

The Amir did not know how precious are the lives of Englishmen in the eyes of their countrymen.

Joseph Wolff found it hard to get away from Bokhara. He was kept a long while in prison, and he feared he should be slain; for when he asked the Amir to give him the bones of Stoddart and Conolly to take to England, this was the Amir's answer: " I shall send YOUR bones !" *Their* bones indeed he could not have; as they had been cast into a well full of the bones of murdered men. After all, he was permitted to leave Bokhara; for the Lord graciously inclined the tyrant to let him go.

How can missionaries be sent to such a country ?

Bokhara is the only large town in the kingdom.

The sea of Aral lies to the north of the kingdom: it is an immense lake, but not nearly so large as the Caspian Sea.

The river Oxus flows into the Caspian. It is famous for its golden sands.

The great trade of Bokhara is in black woolly lambs'-skins, to make caps for the Persians : the younger the lamb the more delicate the wool. Thus many a pretty lambkin dies to adorn a Persian noble.

The best raisins in the world come from Bokhara.*

***

THE TOORKMAN TARTARS.

You have heard a great deal of the Tartars, and you have been told that they are a quiet and peaceable nation. But not *all ;* there is a tribe of Tartars called the Toorkmans, of a very different character. They wander about in the country between Bokhara and Persia, and their chief employment is to steal men from Persia, and to sell them in Bokhara as slaves. A whole troop, mounted on horses, rush sword in hand upon a Persian city, and return to the camp with hundreds of beasts and human creatures as their captives.

Some English travellers once met five men chained together, walking with sad steps in the deep sands of the desert. They were Persians just caught by the Toorkmans, and on their way to Bokhara. When the Englishmen saw these

* Taken from Sir Alexander Burnes, and from Kanikoff the Russian, and from the Rev. Joseph Wolff.

poor captives, they uttered a sorrowful cry, and the Persians began to weep. One of the travellers stopped his camel to listen to their sad tale; and he heard that a few weeks before, while working in the fields, they had been seized and carried off. They were hungry and thirsty; for the Toorkmans cruelly starve their slaves, in order that they may be too weak to run away. The traveller gave them all he had, which was a melon to quench their thirst.

But the worst part of the Toorkmans' conduct remains yet to be told. When they have taken many captives, they usually *kill* the old people, because they would not get much money for them in Bokhara; and they choose *one* of their captives to offer up as a thank-offering to their god!! Who is their god? The god of Mahomed. But though they are Mahomedans, they have no mosques, and are too ignorant to be able to read the Koran.

Robbery is their whole business. For this purpose they learn to ride and to fight. They understand well how to manage a horse, so as to make him strong and swift. They do not let him eat when he pleases, but they give him three meals a day of hay and barley, and then rein him up that he may not nibble the grass, and grow fat; and sometimes they give him no food at all, and yet make him gallop many miles. By this management the horses are very thin, but very *strong*, and able to bear their masters eighty miles in a day when required; and they are so swift that they can outrun their pursuers.

It is not surprising that the Toorkmans do not eat these thin horses, though other Tartars are so fond of horse-flesh. They prefer mutton. When they invite a stranger to dinner, they boil a whole sheep in a large boiling-pot; then tear up the flesh, mix it with crumbled bread, and serve it up in wooden bowls. Two persons eat from one bowl, dipping their hands into it, and licking up their food like dogs. The meal is finished by eating melons.

These coarse manners suit such fierce and wild creatures as the Toorkmans. It is their boast that they rest neither under the shadow of a TREE nor of a KING: meaning that they have neither trees nor kings to protect them in the desert.

The men wear high caps of black sheep-skin, while the women wear high white turbans. The tents are adorned with beautiful carpets; not only the floors, but the sides, and it is the chief employment of the women to weave them. As for the men, they spend most of their time in sauntering about among the tents; for the fierce dogs guard the flocks. But when their hands are idle, their thoughts are still busy in planning new robberies and murders.

It was by such men that the earth was inhabited when God sent the flood to destroy it. It is written, "The earth was filled with VIOLENCE."

Is there any man brave enough to go to these men to warn them of the judgment to come, and to tell them of pardon for the penitent, through the blood of Jesus?"

THIBET.

THIS land is full of mountains. What Switzerland is in Europe—*that* Thibet is in Asia—a land of mountains. But what are the mountains of Switzerland compared with the mountains of Thibet? They are but *hillocks* in comparison. It is an awful thing to go to Thibet. It is enough to frighten a stout heart to climb those slippery hills.

And is it worth while to make a journey to Thibet? Is the country so beautiful as to make one wish to see it?

It is grand rather than beautiful.

Are there curious sights to be seen there?

Yes, most curious.

There is a city in Thibet called Lassa, where lives the *greatest* person in the whole world, and the most *miserable*.

* Extracted from Sir Alexander Burnes' "Bokhara."

Greater than the Pope of Rome?

Yes; greater far. But understand what I mean.—Not *really* great, only *considered* great by a multitude of foolish people; by the people of China, and Japan, and Tartary, and many other countries. Millions and millions call him god, and worship him.

And who is this great man?

Is he a man?

Often he is only a child—almost a baby.

The people of Thibet choose some child, and say he is their god Buddha. He is called the Grand Lama. He is called god as long as he lives; and when he dies, another child is chosen to be god in his stead.

There are many Lamas, and there are many Grand Lamas; but there is one Grand Lama, grander and greater than all.

This Grand Lama is the king of Thibet. It has been said that Thibet belongs to China; but it does not. The Chinese have tried to conquer Thibet, but they have never been able to do so. Those high snowy mountains are like great walls round the country to keep enemies out. The Blue Mountains are on the north, and the Himalayan Mountains are on the south.

The Chinese want to have power in Thibet. They send an ambassador to Lassa, and this ambassador watches all that is done, and sends word to the Emperor of China; and the people of Thibet are afraid of offending the Emperor.

Once a year, too, the people of Thibet send presents to the Emperor. A great company, with camels and oxen, come with these presents across the mountains. This company is called the Thibetian Embassy. There is no difficulty in finding presents, for there are rich treasures in Thibet. There is gold in the rocky mountains; there is musk (that fine perfume) in the body of the wild musk-deer; and there are pastille-sticks for burning incense, made of gums flowing from trees, and mixed with musk and gold-dust. Pastille-sticks are burned in great quantities before the idols of China. These are presents for a mighty king, and the Emperor of China accepts them from the people of Thibet.

It is very seldom that travellers go from Europe to Thibet. One reason is, the snowy mountains are so hard to cross. Another is, that the Chinese try to keep them out. The people of Thibet are ready to receive strangers—all strangers except the English; and they are afraid of receiving *them*, because they have heard of their conquering the nations of India, and they are in terror lest the English should come from Calcutta, across the Himalayas, and conquer them.

How, then, can *we* hear about Thibet?

Two Frenchmen have lately visited that land, and written an account of their travels. They were Roman Catholic priests. They went to Thibet to teach the people about Jesus. But Roman Catholics teach many things that are displeasing to Jesus—such as worshipping the Virgin Mary, and bowing down to images. While we are glad that they tell the heathen about the crucified Saviour, we are sorry that they tell them also about the Pope, and penance and purgatory.

These two French priests were brave men, or they never would have ventured to go to Thibet.

How did they go there?

They did not go by themselves. That would have been impossible. They would have lost their way, and perished from cold or hunger, or they would have been slain by robbers. After waiting some time in Tartary, at last they heard that the great Thibetian Embassy would soon be going back to their own country. "Oh," thought the priests, "we will go with them." So they began to get everything ready for their journey. They knew that they must take food with them, as they would find none among the cold mountains. They bought tea, butter, flour, and barley-meal. Had you seen their tea you would not have known it to be tea. The tea-leaves were squeezed into a hard lump about the size of a brick. To make tea a little bit is broken off, crumbled into powder, and boiled in a kettle of water. When the water is almost black, a little salt and a little milk are added. How should you like salt instead of sugar? When people wish to make very good tea, instead of putting cream, they put butter into it. Buttered tea is considered a great treat. The priests bought five bricks of tea for their journey. The barley-meal that they bought was almost black. It was called *tsamba*. It was to be put into a cup, and made up into a paste with the finger, for tea-spoons are never used in Tartary or Thibet. The priests took eight sacks of this barley-meal, and two sacks of flour, with a quantity of butter.

To carry their food, as well as their books, tents, and clothes, they bought four camels. One servant could lead them all, for each was fastened to the tail of another, and a servant led the foremost. Another servant rode on a black mule. Both these servants were called cameleers. The priests were to ride upon white horses, and to go last of all.

When did the party set out?

They set out in the month of September, and travelled till they came to a great lake, called the Blue Sea, and there they pitched their tents, and waited patiently till the Embassy should

pass that way on their return to their own
country. The Blue Sea may well be called a
SEA, for it is about a hundred miles in length,
so that it appears like the great sea, for the land
on the other side cannot be seen. The grass
grows so fresh and high on its shores that numbers of Tartar shepherds feed their flocks all
around. This was a good place for the priests
to wait for the caravan. They took care to keep
near the shepherds' tents for fear of robbers, and
they moved whenever the shepherds moved.
For a whole month the priests waited, while
their horses and camels grew fat by feeding on
the rich pastures.

At last a sound was heard. A great troop
was seen in the distance. What a multitude!
Two thousand men, with five hundred oxen,
twelve hundred camels, and twelve hundred
horses. This troop was the Thibetian Embassy
returning from China. Such a troop of travellers is called a caravan. All the men of the
troop were not Thibetians, for there were three
hundred Chinese soldiers, and two hundred
Tartars to defend the caravan from robbers.

It was October when this great company left
the shores of the Blue Sea to go to Thibet. It
was pleasant weather when they set out, but
winter was coming on, and the journey became
less and less pleasant every day.

The noise of the caravan as it passed through the desert was wonderful to hear. The neighing of horses, the bellowing of oxen, the shrieking of camels, and the shouting of men, and above all the ringing of bells, were mingled together in strange confusion. At night the tents were pitched, but long before the morning came a cannon was fired to rouse the sleepers. Everybody rose, and lighted fires to boil their kettles. After a hasty breakfast the tents were folded up, and the caravan set out.

Mountain Pass in Thibet.

At last the travellers reached high mountains covered with snow. Those were the mountains of Thibet.

And now their sufferings began. For want of grass, some of the beasts died by the way. But what the horses felt the most was the COLD. It was thought well to dress them up in pieces of carpet, and to twist coarse camel's hair round their heads, like a turban. At any other time people would have laughed to see horses thus disguised; but no one could laugh on those cold mountains; they could hardly keep from crying. The oxen were of a kind that has coarse long hair. The right name for these oxen is yaks. The camels, too, have plenty of hair over their bodies and they like cold much better than heat.

What trouble the camels gave in crossing rivers! There were several rivers on the way, and they were all frozen. The horses and the yaks went readily across, but not so the camels. Their feet are like sponges, so that they cannot walk on slippery ground. These soft feet are just suited to walk upon sand, but not on wet ground, nor on hard ground. The men tried to prevent the camels from slipping by strewing sand on the ice: yet sometimes, in spite of all this care, a camel stumbled and fell down. When once a camel is on the ground it is very hard to get him to rise, for he is more obstinate than a donkey. The men tied ropes to the fallen camels and dragged them across the ice, and then put a carpet on the bank, and coaxed the creatures to tread upon it, if they *would*,—but often they would *not* : and then the camels were left to perish on the ice. Such was the consequence of obstinacy. ⁁ :

Men, as well as beasts, perished by the way. The priests once observed a man sitting on a great stone. They thought he was resting. "How foolish," said they to each other, "for a man to loiter in that manner, when the weather is so cold!" They called to him, but he answered not. They got off their horses and went up to him, and they saw he was a young Lama of their acquaintance. His eyes were shut, and icicles hung down from his mouth and nose. The priests thought he was dead, but as they looked he opened his eyes. "Let us try to save his life," said the kind priests. They wrapped him in a blanket, and placed him on their servant's black mule. He could just sit on the mule, and that was all. The priests led him to a tent, and placed him in a warm corner. Then they went to tell the young man's friends what they had done.

Did the friends seem pleased? No; for though they thanked the priests with many low bows, they added, "It is no use trying to save

his life. We left him on the way, because we
knew he must die. The cold will get to his
heart, and then he will die." These friends
accompanied the priests to the tent, and when
they entered they found that their words had
come to pass—the young Lama was dead.

Many a traveller was left to perish by the
way. A wooden cup of tea and a small bag of
barley-meal were always placed beside the frozen
men. But food was of no use to those who could
not eat.

Forty men, one by one, were thus left to die
among the mountains.

At last one of the priests fell ill. His feet
and hands were frozen; he could not sit upon
his horse. Did the other priest leave him to die?
No; he found a way of carrying him along.
He wrapped him in a blanket, and packed him
on the back of a camel, as if he had been a
bundle, and took great care of him, hoping he
might recover.

Who would have thought that this sick priest,
looking like a bundle, should be the means of
saving part of the company from robbers? Yet
so it was. How did this happen? Some of the
camels of the caravan lingered behind with their
masters, not being able to keep up with the rest.
Among these slow travellers was the sick priest.
One day some robbers came galloping up

towards this small party. They were terrible to look at; clothed in wolf's skin, with thick black hair hanging over their shoulders, and half hiding their faces, eyes glaring like the eyes of a lion, and two sabres stuck in each of their girdles. There were twenty-seven of these fierce men, and only eighteen travellers. The robbers saw the priest wrapped up in the coloured blankets, and inquired, "What is that"? One of the Thibetians replied, "It is a Lama from the western sky, and his prayers are very powerful." This Thibetian *really* thought that the priests were Lamas. The robbers felt afraid to hurt people who had such a great Lama to help them, and so they all galloped away. After a while the robbers returned, but it was in such a friendly way that they were invited to drink tea, and eat *tsamba*. Such robbers as these are never seen in England.

After the escape from the robbers, the priests took care not to linger behind the rest of the caravan, lest they should really be robbed.

And now the travellers have to mount higher hills than they had ever mounted before. Hill after hill they climb; it seems like a ladder of hills, one above the other, till at last they reach Tant-La—a high land or terrace, flat like a table, yet higher than any land in all Asia. Just as the Caspian Sea is the *lowest* land, so Tant-la is the *highest* land in all Asia.

The prospect is grand and fine,—the air is pure and cold. O how cold! Many had thought that this cold air would kill the sick priest, but to the surprise of all he began to get better as soon as he got upon the heights. There was, however, so little grass on this high land that many of the beasts died: and the servant's little black mule was among the number. The eagles were hovering in the air, ready to feast upon the dead.

It was pleasant when the sun shone as it often did and made the snow sparkle ; and it was easy to walk in this sparkling snow, which did not sink, but was as hard as lumps of white sugar.

During twelve days the caravan travelled along these snowy heights and then began to descend. Six days they had been going *up* the hills ; but they were only four coming *down*. They went from one high mountain to another a little lower, as if they had been going down a giant's staircase.

And now they reached the great valley of Thibet, and here they found shepherds dwelling in black tents, feeding their flocks on the rich grass. What a pleasant change from the bare and lonely mountains ! The travellers pitched their tents, and began to boil their tea, while their half-starved beasts were grazing around.

Suddenly a troop of horsemen were seen galloping towards the spot. The French priests remembered the robbers who had once overtaken them : and, filled with terror, they rushed out of their tent, crying, " Robbers ! robbers !" But the other travellers laughed at their fears, saying, " There are no robbers here ; these are shepherds." So the priests gladly returned to their tents to sip their buttered tea, after their long fatigues.

Presently the shepherds appeared at the doors of the tents. They might have been taken for butchers ! Joints of mutton dangled from their saddles. The priests purchased eight ; for the cold would prevent the meat spoiling; each joint was as hard as a stone. Instead of giving money for the meat, the priests gave in exchange a pair of boots, a sword, and a saddle. All those articles were made in Pekin, and everything Chinese is highly prized in Thibet.

The hungry priests set about boiling their mutton. They made a fire of *argols*, which are dry lumps of manure, the only fuel used in Thibet, where trees are few, and coals are not found. Upon this fire they placed two legs of mutton in a boiling pot. At last their servant declared that the mutton was quite ready. Just then a cry was heard of " Fire, fire !" The priests rushed out of the tent, as much frightened as at the shepherds in the morning but

this time no one laughed at their fears. The
dry grass had caught fire, and the flames were
spreading on every side. To save the tents
from catching fire—people snatched up carpets,
and endeavoured to stifle the flames. But these
furious flames were hastening with all speed
towards the spot where the camels were feeding.
The horses and the oxen fled in dismay; but
the stupid camels never stirred, even when the
fire had taken hold of them. The priests, with
carpets in their hands, ran to save their own
four camels, and managed to put out the fire
which was consuming their long thick hair.
Three were only singed, but the fourth was
almost broiled. It would not be able to bear
any burden for a long while, if ever again. It
was a pitiable object to behold.

How great is the stupidity of camels! How
hard it is to save them from perishing either by
fire or by water! Do not these camels resemble
sinners who refuse to flee from the wrath to
come?

Mercifully the flames were put out, though not
till they had burned up a square mile of grass.

For several days the travellers proceeded
through the valley among herds of yaks and
flocks of sheep, tended by herdsmen and shepherds. At last they arrived at a large village.
Here black tents were mingled with mud huts;

but there were no fields, no gardens: the inhabitants were all shepherds and herdsmen.

It was thought advisable to sell the camels to these villagers; for the rest of the way would be over the rocky ground not suited to the soft spongy feet of camels. The priests sold their four camels. In exchange they hired six long-horned oxen. They did not buy them, but only hired them. A driver who came with the oxen, was to take them back. The priests dismissed at the same time one of their camel-drivers. They had one servant only left, and no animals of their own but their two white horses. The travellers hoped to arrive at their journey's end in a fortnight.

At last they came to a village where they beheld, for the *first time* since they had entered Thibet, farm-houses, with fields and gardens. They were charmed at the sight, as it was a sign that they were not far from the great city to which they were bound. These farm-houses were tall, and white, and overshadowed by high trees. In front of each was a handsome terrace, and on the roof a small tower, adorned with flags.

What did those flags signify?

They were the signals of idolatry. The writing on those flags were prayers to Buddha. Instead of repeating prayers, the people let their prayers float on high, while they dance, and sing, and eat, and drink below. These are the evening amusements of the villagers in the front of the farm-houses.

In this village the long-haired oxen were exchanged for strong and active donkeys—able o climb the tremendous mountain that yet remained to be crossed. It was the last, and it was the steepest and the roughest, and altogether the worst. Yet, as it was the *last*, who would not climb it with good courage? The Thibetians believe that when they have gained the top—all their past sins have been pardoned; therefore they climb it with all their hearts.

The priests had to get off their white horses and go on their hands and knees. In the middle of the night they began to ascend, and they reached the top at ten in the morning. But when they got to the top they could not see the city of Lha-sa, for many crooked rocky paths were yet to be trodden. Just before the sun set that day the travellers found themselves on a spot whence they saw below the GREAT CITY.

After a journey of four months they first beheld the great Lha-sa commonly called Lassa. This was in January 1846. Lassa is a beautiful city. High trees surround it like a green wall. The tall houses are of dazzling whiteness, and their flat roofs are crowned with small towers.

The temples have high domes, covered with gold. But rich as thou art, O Lassa, thou art poor indeed, for thou hast no heavenly treasure; and fair as thou art, thou art dark indeed, for thou hast no heavenly light!

What makes Lassa so famous?

Not its *size*; for it is a small city, only two miles across, and six miles round.

Nor its *strength*; for its walls were destroyed in a war with the Indians.

Nor is it the *beauty* of Lassa (though it is beautiful) that makes it famous—but its *god*. The greatest of all the living Buddhas lives at Lassa. This god is called the Talé-Lama—which means the Lama that has a *talé*—or *ocean* of greatness. There are many grand Lamas, but none like him.

Lha-sa is called the mountain of Spirits; for Lha means mountain, and Sah means spirits. The Buddhists consider it the most sacred city in the world. It is the holy city of Thibet, even as Benares is the holy city of Hindostan.

The evening when the priests arrived at Lassa they went to the house of some Tartar friends to sleep; but the next morning they set out to search for lodgings.

They were pleased with the clean and broad streets. They admired the whiteness of the houses, which are whitewashed every year, and

also, the borders of red and yellow that adorned
the doors and windows.　Red and yellow are
sacred colours, and those which are worn by
Lamas.　But what disappointment the strangers
felt when they entered these gaudy dwellings!
Inside was all filth and disorder.　These houses
were like the Pharisees of old, who were in appearance so holy, but in reality so unholy.

It was hard to fix on lodgings where the
houses were so loathsome.　At last the priests
chose two rooms at the top of a high house.　In
this house there were fifty lodgers.　There were
a great many stories, and it was fatiguing to
climb so many stairs—it was even dangerous;
as they were steep and narrow, and there were
no banisters.　Yet it was best to be at the top
of a house, because it is only in the roof that
there is a chimney; for in Thibet there are no
chimneys in the walls.

I must now describe the rooms the priests
hired.　One was large and square.　In it there
was a small window with wooden bars instead
of glass, and another window in the roof, and
that window was the chimney.　It is true that
snow came in at this opening: but it was better
to have snow in the room than smoke.　Under
this hole an earthen plan was placed.　This was
the fire-place.　*Argols* were burned in it, instead
of wood or coals.　Two goat-skins spread on the

floor near the fire served for seats in the day and beds at night.

The priests tried to arrange their things neatly in their lodging, and not to throw them about anywhere, like the Thibetians. They placed their saddles, their boots, and their folded tents in one corner, and they hung up their old ragged robes against the wall. It was necessary to have a heap of *argols* to supply the fire with fuel. As for tables, chairs, beds, or chests of drawers, there were none in the room.

Adjoining the large room there was a small room. It contained a brick stove, and was to be the kitchen. The servant was to sleep there. His name was very long indeed. The first syllables of it were Sam-dod. By this name we may call him.

He was a young man, with a dark Tartar complexion, and a flat Tartar face. Though brought up to be a Lama, he had escaped when a boy from his master, and had wandered about the country—till he became a servant to the priests. He had been baptized by the priests, and he called himself a Christian. But he was not a faithful servant nor a good man, whatever he might call himself. He had been cameleer to the priests, but he was now their cook. He was groom also to the white horses, that were kept in a stable in the court till grown fat enough to be sold.

When the priests were settled in their lodgings they had time to rest after their long journey. They occupied themselves in learning the language of Thibet; for till they knew it better, they could not teach their religion to the people.

When they went into the town they observed the strange customs, and made inquiries respecting all they saw.

The most remarkable building near Lassa is the palace of the Talé-Lama. It is built on a hill one mile from the town. This hill is of a curious shape—the shape of a sugar-loaf; so steep, and so pointed,—and it looks the more strange, because it rises up suddenly in the midst of flat ground. This mountain is the Buddha-La, or Buddha-Mountain. On the top is a high and magnificent temple, with a splendid golden dome and golden pillars. That is the palace of the Grand Lama. All around are smaller palaces, with gilt roofs for lesser Lamas. The way to this mountain is planted with three rows of trees.

This sacred road is generally crowded with pilgrims from many countries, going to worship the Talé-Lama. The pilgrims chatter not, they stare not, they laugh not, as they walk; but they repeat their prayers in a low voice upon their beads.

The priests wished much to visit the Talé-Lama in his palace; but they were not allowed, on account of the small-pox having broken out in the city, and its being reported that the disease had been brought by the caravan from China. This was not true; but the report deprived the priests of the sight of the sacred child. They heard he was nine years old, and that he had been shut up for six years.

The Talé-Lamas often die when they are young; and it is suspected that the man who has the care of them causes them to be secretly murdered.

When one Talé-Lama dies another is chosen. And how?

The difficulty is to find out in what little child, or babe, the spirit of Buddha is gone to live. Now this *cannot* be found, because there is no such spirit, and no such babe. But it comes into the head of some father to *say* that the spirit is in his child. That father goes to the grown-up Lamas, on Buddha-La, and tells them what he thinks.

When three such babies have been heard of, their parents bring them on a certain day to the city of Lassa. The chief Lamas meet together in the Buddha-La, and fast and pray for a week. Then they take three golden fishes—write on them the names of the three babies, and cast the fishes into a golden urn. The eldest of the Lamas puts his hand into the urn, and draws out a fish. He reads out the name written on it.

The parents of the babe are told of the great
honour that has come to their child. The un-
fortunate infant is carried through the city in
great pomp, and placed in the golden temple, to
be for ever shut up there, while other children
are playing in the fields.

Unhappy little boy throned upon his cushions!

Does he really believe that he is a god?

The little beggars under the hedges are happier far than such a god as this!

The town of Lassa is very unlike Buddha-
La. Instead of praying pilgrims—there are
noisy traders—in every street,—some selling
and some buying, and all pushing and brawling
as they go.

There is also the noise of snarling and barking from the multitudes of dogs that run about
the streets—tall, lean, frightful animals.

On what do you think they feed?

On all the offal and refuse of the town, on the
dead bodies of beasts and birds. But not on
these only. They also feed on the FLESH OF MEN.
These dogs are kept for the purpose of eating the
dead. These dogs are, in fact, the graves of men.
It is considered more *honourable* to be eaten
after death than to be buried. Some dead
bodies are burned, some are drowned, some are
laid on mountain-tops; *none are buried.* MOST
bodies are eaten by dogs; the poor by common

dogs, the rich by valuable dogs kept in the Lamas' houses. The flesh is cut up in small pieces before it is devoured. The men of Thibet do not believe in the resurrection, or they would not thus use dead bodies. They believe the spirit goes from one body into another, and that the body perishes for ever.

There are three things for which Thibet is famous.

These are *poulou*, pastilles, and pottery.

Poulou is a woollen cloth; and, strange to say, it is spun and woven by men only, and not by women; for it is the women who keep the shops and stalls, and the men who spin and weave. Red *poulou* is the dress of all the Lamas, even of those in China; so you may suppose what a quantity is wanted. Coarse *poulou* is cheap, but fine *poulou* is very dear indeed.

Pastille is sweet-smelling stuff rolled into the shape of sticks. It is made by burning sweet-smelling wood, then gathering up the ashes, and mixing them with musk, and with gold-dust. The use of these sticks is to be burned as incense in honour of idols. When once lighted they continue to burn like candles, spreading sweet odours all around. Their colour is pink, and they are about as long as a walking-stick.

The pottery is not of earth, but of roots of

trees. The cups in Thibet are all made of this wood. They are carried about by every one in a little bag, fastened to his girdle, or else worn in the bosom of his vest. Nothing else is wanted for a meal but a cup; and whether it is tea, or broth, or pudding, the cup will do.

These CUPS, these STICKS, and this CLOTH are the manufactures of Thibet, and are much celebrated. Lamas wear the finest cloth, burn the sweetest sticks, and drink out of the prettiest cups that are made; for they are luxurious persons, who always expect to be served, and never to serve.

Though there are quantities of gold and silver in Thibet, it is not the *natives* who work these metals, but Indians from the other side of the Himalayan mountains, and who live in Lassa for the purpose of adorning the temples with golden roofs.

These are the *things* for which Thibet is famous. But who are the *people*, and what are they like.

They are Tartars; not Mantchow Tartars, who once conquered China, but Mongol Tartars. They have the true Tartar face, and may be known by their small black eyes, high cheekbones, flat nose and wide mouth. Their skin is tawny, their figure light and active, their disposition frank, open, and lively. As they walk

along they may generally be heard humming a
tune. They let their long black hair flow over
their shoulders, and they wear a blue cap on
common days, and a high red hat on great days.
Their robes are full, and sometimes of one
colour, and sometimes of another; but the sash
is red, and the little bag for the cup is green.

The women dress very nearly as the men do,
except that they wear a short tunic of various
colours over the robe, and instead of a blue cap
a yellow. But the women have one custom quite
peculiar to themselves. No women in any other
country do the same. In some countries women
hide their faces, and in others paint them; but
who ever heard of women daubing their faces
over with a dark sticky stuff, like currant jelly,
on purpose to make themselves look ugly? But
this is the custom and *the law.* The *thicker* the
black paste is laid on—the *better* is the woman.
Daubed with this black paste—women are allowed to go about where they please, and are not
shut up, as in China and India. These black-faced
women make themselves very useful: in the
country they plough,—in the town they sell.

Soon after arriving at Lassa, the priests went
to a cup-shop to buy cups. A woman well
blacked over with varnish kept the shop. She
took out of a drawer two small boxes: each
contained a cup wrapped up in paper.

The price? Twenty pounds each! The priests were astonished, for they saw no particular beauty in those cups.

Have you no others at a lower price? O yes, said the woman. Here are two very cheap.

The price was half an ounce of silver each, (which is equal to *four shillings*.) The priests thought these cups quite as pretty as the others, and they bought them. When they showed them to their acquaintance, they heard that these cups were not worth more than *two* shillings each; but in Thibet all the shopkepers impose upon strangers.

There are *wooden* cups to be had worth forty pounds.

But even people who buy *such* cups live upon very poor fare—nothing more than tea and black barley. Meat is considered quite a delicacy, and too good to be eaten often. When meat is served up, some is boiled, and some is *raw.*

Rich as Thibet is in gold, it is really poor. The chief cause of this—is the bad government.

It is a great disadvantage to be governed by a Talé-Lama, who is of no more use than an image. The man who takes care of him, the Nome Khan, is, in fact, the king of Thibet, though he is not nearly as great, or as much honoured, as the Talé-Lama.

I told you before that the Chinese long to get

Thibet into their power. They keep a close watch over it, hoping to get it some day. They always have an ambassador at Lassa. It is his place to keep strangers out of the country, lest they should come and conquer it.

The Chinese ambassador heard of the two French priests, and he determined to turn them out as soon as he could. You shall hear how cunningly he set about the work.

A Visit from Spies.

One day, as the French priests were sitting on their goat-skins by their little furnace, a Chinese entered the room. It was not the ambassador. It was not so great a man as he.

"I am a merchant," said the man. "I am come to buy some of your goods."

"We have nothing to sell," said the priests.

"Nothing!" said the Chinaman. He looked surprised.

"Yes," said the priests, "here are two old saddles. We are going to sell our horses, therefore we do not want the saddles."

While they were talking about the price—another Chinaman entered, and then—another, and then—two Lamas of Thibet. All said they came to buy; and they began to search every corner for something to buy: but could find nothing. After asking many questions, the five visitors went away without buying anything.

When they were gone, the priests said to each other, "Did those men come to *buy?* We think they came to *spy,* and not to *buy.*"

Thus saying, they sat down to dinner. They ate boiled beef out of wooden cups.

They had rinsed the cups, and filled them with buttered tea, when the two Lamas returned.

"Follow us," said they; "the Regent wants to speak to you in his palace."

Who was this Regent? Perhaps you think he was the Nome Khan, who took care of the little Lama. No he was not. The Nome Khan was too young to reign, being only eighteen. So the chief man *next* to him was Regent. He was *not* a Lama.

The priests put on their fox-skin caps, and

with their servant, followed the messengers to the Regent's palace.

After crossing a large court, they entered by a gilt door the room where the Regent was sitting. He was dressed in a yellow robe trimmed

The Regent.

with fur; his black hair was turned up, and fastened with three small gold combs, and one of his ears was adorned with a diamond ring. His red cap, with its coral ball, was lying on a green cushion by his side. He himself was seated on a tiger's skin. Behind him stood four quiet Lamas, two sly Chinamen, and one grave Mahomedan, with a long beard and a turban.

The priests were commanded to sit down on a
red carpet.   The Regent spoke to them kindly.

" Whence do you come ?"

" From the Western sky."

" Do you come from Calcutta ?"

" No ; from France."

" Are you a Peling ?"

(Peling means stranger, and it is the name by
which Englishmen are called in Thibet.)

" No ; we are Frenchmen."

" Can you write ?"

" Better than we can speak."

" Here is paper.   Write something in your
own language."   The priests wrote in French,
"What shall it profit a man, if he gain the whole
world, and lose his own soul ?"   They wrote
the same words in Thibetian underneath.

The Regent read the words, and said, " They
are as good as the words in my prayer-books."

As good!   Are they not a great deal BETTER?
Are they not the words of Jesus ?

The men who stood behind the Regent heard
the words, and began to praise the priests for
their wonderful wisdom.

At this moment a sound was heard in the
court-yard.   The Regent said, " I perceive that
the Chinese ambassador has just arrived."   So
saying, he left the room with all his train, and
the priests were left alone in the room.

Presently a young Chinaman entered, and bade them follow him to see the ambassador.

The priests obeyed.

They found the ambassador sitting on a throne covered with red cloth (for the Chinese do not sit on the floor as Turks and Tartars do.)

A black writing-table was before the throne. Crowds of Chinamen and Thibetians stood around.

The ambassador did not speak as kindly as the Regent had spoken. He asked the priests where they had been, and looked displeased at their answers. But he looked still more displeased when he looked at the servant, for he had heard that he had become a Christian.

" Don't you know that the Emperor forbids his subjects to follow the religion of the Lord of heaven ?"

The servant answered boldly, " It is the only true religion."

After asking many more questions, the ambassador said at last, "It is night. It is suppertime. You may go. To-morrow, if I want you, I will send for you."

The priests willingly left the room. But they were not allowed to go home. A Lama led them up a steep and high staircase, along a balcony near the top of the house, and then into a splendid and well-lighted room. The walls, the floor, and the ceiling, were painted and gilt. A good supper was set out on the table.

The Regent was there. He spoke as kindly as before, and tried to calm the fears of the priests; but he could not make himself well understood till a kind man entered who knew Chinese, and who could interpret the Regent's Thibetian into Chinese; for the priests knew the Chinese language well, but the Thibetian very little.

While they were at supper, the Regent, pointing to some pictures on the walls, asked the priests whether they could paint such pictures.

" We cannot paint. We are priests, and we teach the religion of Jehovah."

" But can you draw MAPS ?"

" No, we cannot."

" You surprise me," replied the Regent. " I thought that all from the Western sky could draw and paint. If you can, confess it."

The priests persisted in declaring that they could not.

" I am glad to hear it; for I must tell you that the Chinese cannot bear strangers to come here and draw maps; and they are afraid that you are come here in order to draw maps of Thibet, and that when by these maps your Emperor has learned the way, he will send an army here and conquer Thibet, as the Pelings conquered

India. And when you have conquered Thibet, the Chinese fear you will attack China next."

The priests then replied,—

"Though we cannot draw maps, we have maps in our lodgings: but they are printed maps that we brought from France."

After much conversation, the Regent arose, saying it was time to go to rest.

The priests proposed to return to their lodgings, but the Regent insisted on their sleeping in the palace. The truth was—they were PRISONERS.

A servant led them through many rooms into a small one, containing two couches. But how could the poor priests lie down to rest, when people began crowding into the room? They came from all parts of the palace to see the strangers; doors might be heard opening and shutting in the long passages, for many who had gone to bed got up in order to gratify their curiosity. The priests bore the staring and the whispering for some time, but at last they politely requested their visitors to depart. Every one bowed but no one stirred. The priests then, kneeling, repeated aloud their evening prayer. All were silent; but still no one stirred. At last the priests put out the lights. The crowd, surprised, burst out a-laughing and groped out of the room. When the intruders were gone—the priests in the dark lay down on their couches.

But the priests did not laugh as they lay there, for they were filled with anxiety respecting what was going to be done to them. At last they slept, but not soundly.

As soon as it was light, the door was gently opened, and the priests saw the same gentleman who had interpreted for them last night in the Chinese language. He was not a Chinese, but a native of Cashmere, a Mahomedan with a long beard and a turban. He sat down between the two couches, and kindly inquired after the health of the priests. The Regent had sent him to tell the priests, in Chinese, that the property at their lodgings was going to be examined; but that, if they had no MAPS, they had nothing to fear.

As soon as this kind visitor had left the room, the priests arose and ate the breakfast he had brought them—cakes and dried fruit; which they preferred to the food the Regent had sent them—buttered tea, rolls stuffed with mincemeat, and sugar.

Three Lamas now entered, and summoned the priests to go to their lodgings. A crowd of people accompanied them along the streets. The Regent, mounted on a magnificent white horse, followed by a troop of horsemen, arrived at the lodgings at the same time as the priests. He climbed the steep and narrow stairs. Unlocking the padlock on the door, the priests invited him to enter their humble abode.

A gilt chair had been brought from the palace, and on this the Regent sat in the middle of the room. The trunks, the ragged robes, the old boots, and even the saucepans, were brought out and a list was taken by a writer sitting at the Regent's feet. Then the Regent, with the gold seal of the Talé-Lama, and a stick of red-sealing-wax, marked all the articles, that they might all be examined before the Chinese judgment-seat.

Men were called out of the street to carry the things (for *every one* in Thibet is *obliged* to serve the governors;) the Lamas walked by the side of these porters to guard them; the Regent and his troop of horse followed; and the poor priests came last.

The judge was waiting in the judgment-hall. Who was he? The Chinese ambassador, Ki-chang. The priests were desired to open their own trunks. Every one was curious to see their contents. There were many books. There were also images, and crosses, and pictures, holy beads for repeating prayers, and holy vases for holy water, and many such vain and sinful ornaments. The crowd were filled with admiration. The Thibetians expressed theirs in a frightful way, by putting out their tongues, and scratching one ear. The Chinese made many bows. Even the Regent and the ambassador, forgetting how great they were, opened their mouths like wondering children. What delighted them most—were the pictures, which were coloured prints.

The pictures reminded them of MAPS.

"Where are your maps?"

Three maps were shown. One of the old World, one of the New, and one of China, with Thibet.

"But we did not draw these maps ourselves," said the priests; "they were printed in France."

"O yes, I see that," said Ki-chang, who was proud of knowing the difference between a print and a drawing.

Yet he knew very little about maps; for he could not find the places in them, neither could the Regent.

"Where is Lassa?" said they. "Where is Calcutta."

The priests pointed to the places.

The Regent appeared frightened to see that these places were so near each other, for he dreaded the Pelings coming over from Calcutta to conquer Thibet.

"But then," said he, "there are those high mountains between."

The Thibetians imagine that there is a Lama near those mountains who, by his prayers, keeps the snow always falling, and so keeps the Pelings from coming over.

When Ki-chang had examined all the things he allowed the priests to return to their lodgings.

The porters who had brought the things carried them back.

Great was the joy of the priests.

Just as they were thinking of preparing their dinner the kind Mahomedan entered, with two servants carrying provisions. He brought a message from the Regent. It was to say that he would buy the two horses. The money was paid down immediately. The horses had been taken the night before to the Regent's stables. The price paid for each horse was a lump of silver, worth four sovereigns of our money.

The priests presented their own servant, Samdod, with one of these lumps of silver as his wages—the *first* he had received. He showed his delight by tossing it in the air, while he cried out, "This is a famous day!" Such was his way of thanking.

It had been a famous day both to master and servant, and the next was more famous; for when the priests went to the palace to thank the Regent for all his kindness, they were invited to leave their lodgings, and to come and live in a house belonging to him, without paying any rent. Into this comfortable house they removed that very evening.

The largest room in it they prepared as a

chapel. They papered it neatly, and then, alas! they adorned it with images. They set up a crucifix, and bowed down and worshipped it. Many people heard of the chapel, and came to see it, and listened to the priests when they explained the various images and ornaments. But they did not see much difference between the priest's religion and their own. The priests told them that Buddha was a false god, and that Christ was the true God. Surely Christ ought not to be worshipped in the *same way* as Buddha is worshipped; for Christ is God, and "God is a Spirit, and they that worship Him must worship Him in spirit and in truth." But Buddha is nothing in the world, and any sort of worship does for him.

But though these priests taught a false *way* of *worship*, yet they told the people the truth about Christ dying for men. One Chinese doctor, when he heard it, was much struck. He listened attentively while the priests spoke of Jesus coming from heaven, lying in a manger, dying on a cross, ascending up to heaven, and sitting at the right hand of God; and he said, "I believe." The priests gave him a gilt crucifix to wear round his neck; but this did not satisfy him; he wanted a *prayer*. They promised to send him some books of Christian prayers in Chinese; but the young man said, "I want a short and easy prayer, which I can learn immediately, and repeat often." So the priests taught him this prayer: "Jesus, Saviour of the world, have mercy on me." For fear of forgetting even these few words he wrote them on a piece of paper and put it in a purse hanging to his girdle.

Whenever this Chinaman met the priests in the streets, as he drew near he repeated this prayer. He let all men see he was a Christian, by letting the crucifix be seen.

Often he came to the chapel to be instructed. What a pity that his teachers did not know better what to teach him! What a pity that he was taught to worship images instead of to pray for the Holy Spirit! What a pity that he was taught to look to saints, and to angels, and to Mary for help, instead of to Christ ALONE! What a pity he was taught to make the sign of the cross, to sprinkle himself with holy water, and to count prayers upon beads! Yet, if he truly loved the Saviour, we are sure that the Saviour loved him: for He has said, "I love them who love me." This Chinaman was a very amiable man; and even before he heard of Christ used to visit the sick poor, and give them medicines without money.

The Regent continued to show the priests great respect, and invited them to sup with him every evening, when he asked them many ques-

tions about their religion.　Having heard their
account of it, he observed, "It is very much
like the Buddhist's religion."

––––––––––––

Suddenly the priests experienced a great
change in their condition.

One day Ki-chang, the Chinese ambassador,
sent for them, and after talking to them for
some time in a coaxing manner, he ended by
saying,––

"Thibet is too cold for you.　You had better
return to your own kingdom of France."

They assured him that they were quite satisfied with Thibet.

Then Ki-chang let them know that he *commanded* them to leave the country.

They entreated to know the reason.

He replied,––

"Your religion has been forbidden by the
Grand Emperor."

That was reason enough ; for the Emperor of
China need render no reason but his own will.

Full of grief, the priests went to complain to
the Regent.　He told them not to be afraid.

"Whatever the Chinese ambassador may say,
the governors of Thibet do not object to strangers
coming into the country, especially such men as

you are—men of prayer, just like the Lamas. Never fear. I will protect you."

The priests were much comforted by these words.

But princes cannot always do what they wish for their favourites.

The kind Regent entreated the ambassador to let the priests remain.

"No," said Ki-chang; "my Emperor has sent me here to protect the Talé-Lama. But what will become of *him* if these men teach the people to worship the Lord of heaven?"

The Regent tried from day to day to persuade the ambassador, declaring that he *never* would consent to sending away the priests. There was danger of a quarrel arising between these two great men.

The priests, hearing how violent the dispute had grown, determined to end it by LEAVING THIBET of their own accord.

They went to the Regent and told him they were going away.

He seemed sorry; but he said,—

" I fear I cannot keep you; for the Talé-Lama is but a child, and the ambassador takes advantage of this to do as he will; and we cannot resist, for China is stronger than Thibet."

So the priests went to Ki-chang, and told him they were going away.

PT. I   T

Was he sorry? No indeed.

"You cannot do better," said he. "It will be better for you, better for me, better for everybody. You must go in eight days, and you must go by way of China."

"No, indeed," said the priests. "We must go the nearest way. We must go through *India*. If we go that way we shall reach Calcutta in one month; if we go the other way we shall not reach Canton for *eight* months.

But Ki-chang persisted in saying—

"You cannot go through India." .

What was his reason against their going through India?

His reason was—he knew that he must send some of his soldiers to protect the priests; and he did not like that they should go to Calcutta lest the Pelings should come back with them, and learn the way to Thibet. For the Pelings are looked upon as a very encroaching nation, who want to conquer all countries, even as they have conquered India.

The priests were obliged to go the way that Ki-chang said; for how could they go without soldiers to guard them?

They had only *one week* more to spend in Thibet.

It was the month of March, and that is the *first* month of the year in that country.

NEW-YEAR'S DAY came. A sad new-year's day
it was for them; for they had set their hearts
upon Thibet, and lo! they were forced to go.

In a strange way this day was kept by the
noisy inhabitants of Lassa.

The priests were asleep in their beds when
they were awakened by a terrible uproar in the
streets. The sound of bells and shells, cymbals
and tambourines, resounded from every quarter.
The priests would have borne these noises; but
soon they heard loud knocks at the door of their
bed-room. When they did not answer, the
knocks became louder and louder. At last they
were obliged to rise and open the door. A troop
of men entered : one had in his hand a basin of
boiling water, wherein floated small balls of
honey and butter. Another man gave the priests
a silver hook, and desired them to fish and eat.

"We do not eat at night," replied the sleepy
pair.

No excuse was accepted.

"Fish and eat," was the command.

So the priests fished up *one* ball and ate it.

No sooner were these intruders departed than
others came with more balls, and these also
must be swallowed. When day came it was
no better, for then buttered tea and barley-meal
were brought.

The priests looked out of window and they

saw children dancing and singing in the streets, dressed in green robes adorned with bells, while men with black masks and white beards were twirling and tumbling.

But the strangest sight of all was the dance of spirits on Buddha-La, the hill where the Talé-Lama dwelt. Long cords were let down from the top to the bottom of that steep hill. Up these cords—men with the nimbleness of monkeys climbed, and then let themselves slip down with the swiftness of arrows, as though they would mimic the angels, always ascending and descending from heaven to earth.

When *new-year's day* was over—the *uproar* was not over; for during the *first week* of the year the Lamas from all parts of the country come into the town. What a number of Lamas there are in Thibet, Tartary, and China! Tens of thousands arrived every day; some on oxen, and some on horses, and some on asses. They *said* they came to worship in a temple in the midst of Lassa, and to purchase Buddhist books at the printing-house, and to implore the blessing of the Talé-Lama in his palace. But they seemed more like madmen than worshippers; for they were roaring and shouting in the streets, pushing and pulling one another, and often fighting with clenched hands.

Meanwhile the priests with heavy hearts were

preparing to depart. They took down the images in their chapel, sighing to think that so few of the heathen had been persuaded to worship them. They thought, because these were the images of the blessed Mary, of the holy apostles, and of the true Saviour, that it was good to worship them. They understood not the Lord's second commandment. They forgot that even the serpent which Moses had made, and which had healed so many dying men, was not to be worshipped. No. Hezekiah destroyed it, because people worshipped it. He said, "It is a piece of brass!" (2 Kings xviii, 4.)

As the priests were taking down their images they offered up a prayer that God would send better missionaries than they were to teach the heathen of Thibet.

Say "Amen" to this prayer. May the Lord send Protestant missionaries, with Bibles, and not images!

But there are idolaters who call themselves Protestants.

Who are they?

Men who love gold and silver more than righteousness. These priests were not *such* idolaters; for when the Regent offered them a great heap of silver they refused to accept it, lest they should seem covetous. They would only accept a dictionary of the languages of Asia. They presented the Regent with a microscope, as a token of gratitude for all his kindness.

They were not allowed to take their servant with them; for he was a subject of the Chinese Emperor, and it was not lawful for him to be a Christian.

The day for leaving Lassa arrived. Early in the morning two Chinese soldiers came to summon the priests and to lead them to the house of their master. Was it to the house of Ki-chang? No; but to the house of a Mandarin who was returning to China, and who was appointed to take charge of the priests. This man's name was Ly. He was not a judge, as many mandarins are, but a captain.

To this man's house the priest were conducted. A sumptuous breakfast was spread on the table; not buttered tea or barley-meal, but Chinese food with Chinese chop-sticks. The priest had been so long use to eat with their fingers that they had almost forgotten the use of sticks.

Ly himself looked old; for his hair was gray, his teeth were gone, his eyes were weak, and his skin withered. Yet he was not really old; he was diseased. This was plain from the enormous size of his legs.

What had brought him to this state?

It was BRANDY. Ly was now resolved to drink no more of that fiery poison; but it was

TOO LATE. Many things that are lost may be found again. But health seldom is.

After breakfast, Ly took the priests to the house of Ki-chang to take leave. Fifteen soldiers accompanied them.

Ki-chang giving charge to the Soldiers.

Ki-chang made a long speech to the priests, and tried to show how well he was treating them· He said,—

"You will have horses to ride upon. You will not need tents, for a lodging will be provided for you every night—as well as food by the way. Servants will wait upon you. Soldiers will guard you. May the star of happiness guide you!

Ki-change then gave a charge to Ly. Among other things he said,—

"Treat the strangers well; never drink brandy."

Last of all Ki-chang spoke to the soldiers.. This he did in a sharp voice,—

"And you, soldiers" (at these words the fifteen, as if moved by one string, fell upon their knees, with their face bent towards the ground, and so they remained during the whole speech,) "be respectful and obedient ! Do you clearly understand ?"

"Yes, we do."

"Do not injure the flocks, nor the fields. Do you clearly understand ?"

"Yes, we do."

"Do not quarrel with one another. Do you clearly understand ? "

"Yes, we do."

"Whosoever conducts himself ill will be punished. Do you clearly understand?"

"Yes, we do."

Then the fifteen struck the ground thrice with their foreheads, and rose to depart. All returned to the house of Ly. Eighteen horses were waiting ready saddled in the court. The best was for Ly, the two next for the priests, and the rest for the soldiers.

At the door Ly parted from his wife, a Thibetian woman. It is the wicked custom of the Chinese to marry wives while in Thibet, and to leave them there when they go away.

Ly did not seem grieved at leaving his wife behind. He said calmly,—

"We are going to part. You stay in this place, and sit quietly in your room when I am gone."

Parting of Ly with his wife.

"Go in peace," replied the wife, "and take care of the swellings in your legs!"

She then put her hands to her eyes, as if she was crying.

Ly turned towards the priests and said,—

"What strange women these Thibetians are! See, I have left her a well-built house, and good furniture, and yet she is going to cry!"

What an unfeeling man was this Ly! He cared for nothing but silver and brandy.

The travellers rode through the streets of Lassa, avoiding as much as they could the riotous troops of Lamas.

Outside the town a group of people were assembled. They were waiting to bid farewell to the priests. Among them was the young Chinese doctor, who carried in his purse that little prayer to Jesus. The priests dismounted to speak a few sorrowful words to their affectionate friends, and then rode on, without the hope of ever seeing them again.

On the way they found a troop of horsemen waiting to accompany them. The Regent had appointed a grand Lama with seven men to guard the travellers through Thibet. Thus the company consisted in all—of twenty-six horsemen, besides the drivers of a herd of oxen laden with baggage.

It was on the 15th of March, 1846, that the priests left Lassa, having spent only *two months* in that idolatrous city.

They passed first through a valley abounding in fields and farm houses, and they met Lamas singing and dancing on their way to Lassa.

In the evening they stopped at a house in the village, and they found the people prepared to receive them, having had orders from the Regent. It was pleasant when tired with their journey, to sit on green woollen cushions, around a basin with a blazing fire of *argols*, and to drink hot buttered tea, and eat *tsamba*.

But they had many hardships to endure during their three months' journey through Thibet. Often they had to sleep in wretched sheds. They had to cross mountains so thickly covered with snow that the oxen, after leaping from a high place, often sunk so deep as not to be seen at all for a few moments. When going *up* the Mountain of Spirits, the priests had to get off their horses and cling to their tails; and when going *down* they had to let their horses loose that they themselves might roll down like balls; and when they got to the bottom they had to catch their horses.

But this mountain was not the *most* dangerous; there were mountains so slippery that it was best *not* to dismount, but to trust to the horses' feet, at the edge of high precipices, while the dark waters rolled and rumbled far below. Three well-laden oxen, in passing along one of the mountain ledges, lost their footing, tumbled over, and were never seen again. Was not this terrible sight enough to fill with horror the horsemen who followed the herd?

In the valleys there are Thibetian chieftains who live like country gentlemen.

One of these chieftains, named Proul Tamba, came to see Ly as he was stopping at a village

on the way. This proud chieftain rode on horseback, and was followed by four horsemen. He
wore a robe of green silk, trimmed with wolf-
skin, and a fox-skin cap, purple leather boots,
and a red girdle, with a long sabre. His black
hair hung low over his shoulders.

The chieftain invited the travellers to call at
his house as they passed, and then he galloped
away to prepare for their arrival.

The house was as tall as a castle. A canal
with a row of high trees surrounded it. A draw-
bridge was let down for the travellers to cross
the canal. By the great gate, on the other side,
Proul was waiting for his guests. Servants
having tied the horses to posts in the court-
yard,—the guests entered a large saloon. At
one end were three statues of Buddha, with large
lamps burning above them; for this room was a
chapel as well as a parlour. The great beams of
the ceiling were covered with gold, and the walls
were adorned with coloured flags, written over
with sentences about Buddha.

In one corner there was a low table, with four
large red cushions on the floor. Proul invited
Ly and the priests to sit down. The door
opened, and a lady appeared. She was full-
dressed : her long black hair was adorned with
gold spangles, coral beads, and mother-o'-pearl
buttons, and her face was well daubed with black

paste. In her arms she bore an immense tea-
pot. Cups were not necessary, as each person
carried his own in his girdle, and held it out to be
filled with well-flavoured, well-buttered tea. The
lady quitted the room and returned with two
gilt plates of grapes and nuts. The travellers
could scarcely eat these fruits, for the grapes
were sour and the nuts hard. They had grown
in Thibet, and no good fruit can grow in that
country. The poor guests would have left the
house very hungry if no other food had been
brought; but two servants soon entered, bearing
in their hands a low table, with a kid roasted
whole, and a haunch of venison. After this
excellent supper, the guests presented their host
with a scarf and departed. It is the custom to
carry scarves made of thin gauze, and to give
them as a sign of friendship to those you wish to
please. They are called scarves of blessing.

Though Proul had been so polite to Ly, yet
he could not bear the Chinese—nor can any of
the Thibetian chieftains.

One day the priests observed some of their
fellow travellers stop, get off their horses, and
bow three times down to the ground. They inquired the reason, and they heard that a hermit
Lama lived in a mountain-cavern close by, and
that he was counted one of the holiest of men.
He had lived alone in that cavern for twenty-two

years, and had never once all that time quitted
his gloomy abode.   Nor did he allow any one to
visit him—except *once in three years*—when he

Hermit of the Mountain.

received visits during *one week* from those who
wanted to ask him questions about the future.
It was believed that he could tell all that would
happen.

How did he get food from day to day?

Charitable persons who lived near—brought
tea and barley-meal to the foot of the mountain,
and the hermit let down a cord from his cavern,
(which was near the top,) and drew up the food

through a small opening in his cave. No other presents would he receive. When other presents were brought him by those who visited him once in three years, he gave them away to the poor.

He declared that he wanted nothing but his tea and *tsamba,* and his yellow robe lined with sheep-skin—not even a cap for his shorn head. It was *believed* that he only ate once in six days; but had he done so, he would have soon died. It was also *believed* that he was *always* praying, night as well as day. He had nothing else to do but to count prayers on his beads, and to read his books, full of false stories about Buddha.

Many Lamas had dug cells near him in the mountain, and they called themselves his disciples, though they saw him only once in three years. *Proul Tamba's father was one of these hermits!!* He had given up his house and lands to his son and had turned hermit, thinking to save his soul.

One day the travellers overtook a family travelling to China. There was a Thibetian woman riding on a fine donkey, with a babe fastened to her back by leathern straps. As she rode she led a horse by a cord. She watched the steps of this horse with tender care, for on either side a pannier was fixed, with a smiling child in each, peeping from underneath the cover. The father came last, on horseback, with a boy

of twelve years old behind him.   This man was
a Chinese soldier; he was bringing his Thibetian
wife into China.   He was not an unfeeling man,
like Ly; he loved his wife and children, and he
would not leave them in Thibet.

Family travelling in Thibet.

Ly's Chinese soldiers began to laugh at him
"The man must be mad," said they.   "To bring
things into China would be wise; but to bring
that large-footed *woman*, and those little bar-
barians—how foolish! Does he mean to show
them as sights when he gets home?"

The priests approved the man for his affectionate conduct, and for not following the wicked
customs of his country.

From this time the family travelled with the

caravan. In crossing high mountains, it was sad to see how much the little creatures in panniers were frightened; they cried with terror when they found their horse sinking in the snow, and themselves almost buried under it.

Ly had been getting worse and worse during the whole journey. Once, when he attempted to walk with his swollen legs, he fell down, and was picked up by his soldiers. Riding on horse-back was too fatiguing for him, yet he would not hire a palanquin, because he did not like to part with any of his silver. At last he was so ill that he *could* ride no more, and he hired a palanquin.

One morning the travellers were setting out as usual, after their night's rest. They had mounted their horses—when the Chinese soldiers observed that their master was not there. So one of them went to look for him. He pushed open the door, and beheld the mandarin stretched on his bed, with his mouth open and teeth clenched. He rushed out of the room, pale with terror, and whispered to his fellow-travellers, "Ly is dead!"

The priests ran into the room, and putting their hands to his heart, they found that Ly was *not* quite dead; they heard the rattle in his throat, and saw him die immediately. The water in his legs had risen up to his chest, and had suffocated him. The soldiers brought

a cloth to wrap their master in. It was the
present of some Grand Lama, and was covered
with words and pictures of Buddha; and it was
supposed that it would cause the dead man's
soul to pass into the body of a happy animal.
In this wrapper the body was carried on men's
shoulders to the town in China where Ly was
born. No wife nor child—nor soldier—nor
servant—lamented his death. As he lived, so
he died—unbeloved—a drunkard and a miser.

It was the month of June when the travellers
climbed the LAST mountain of Thibet, yet the
snow was falling thick and fast.

But now they reached the sunny plains of
China, with its fields of rice and plantations of
tea—how different from the pastures for herds
and flocks in Thibet! But the religion is the
SAME. In China also there are temples of
Buddha, and dwellings of Lamas.*

AFFGHANISTAN.

THIS land is not a desert. Yet there are but few
trees, and because there is so little shade, the
rivulets are soon dried up. Yet it might be a
fruitful land, if the inhabitants would plant and
sow. But they prefer wandering about in tents,

---

* Abridged from Huc's " Travels in Thibet."

and living upon plunder, to settling in one place and living by their labour. The Tartar has good reason for roaming over his plains, because the land is bad; but the Affghan has no reason, but the *love* of roaming.

The plains of Affghanistan are sultry, but the mountains are cool; for their tops are covered with snow. The shepherds feed their flocks on the plains during the winter; but in the spring they lead them to the mountains to pass the summer there. Then the air is filled with the sweet scent of clover and violets. The sheep often stop to browse upon the fresh pasture; but they are not suffered to linger long. The children have the charge of the lambs; an old goat or sheep goes before to encourage the lambs to proceed, and the children follow with switches of green grass. Many a little child who can only just run alone enjoys the sport of driving the young lambs. The tents are borne on the backs of camels. The men are terrible-looking creatures, tall, large, dark, and grim, with shaggy hair and long black beards. They wear great turbans of blue check, and handsome jackets, and cloaks of sheep-skin; they carry in their girdles knives as large as a butcher's, and on their shoulders a shield and a gun.

Besides these wild wanderers, there are some Affghans who live in houses.

Cabool, the capital, is a fine city, and the king dwells in a fine citadel. The bazaar is the finest

Amir of Cabool.

in all Asia. It is like a street with many arches across it : and there people sell all kinds of goods.

But what is a fine *bazaar* compared to a beautiful *garden ?* Cabool is surrounded by gardens : the most beautiful garden is the king's. In the midst is an octagon summer-house, where eight walks meet, and all the walks are shaded by fruit-trees. Here grow, as in Bokhara, the best fruits to be found in an English garden, only much larger and sweeter. The same kind of birds, too, which sing in England, sing among the branches, even the melodious nightingale. It is the chief delight of the people of Cabool to wander in the gardens: they come there every evening, after having spent the day in sauntering about the bazaar: for they are an idle people, talking much and working little.

The noise in the city is so great that it is difficult to make a friend hear what you say: it is not the noise of rumbling wheels, as in London, for there are no wheeled carriages, but the noise of chattering tongues.

The Affghans are a temperate people; they live chiefly upon fruit, with a little bread; and as they are Mahomedans, they avoid wine, and drink instead iced sherbets, made of the juice of fruit. In winter, excellent *dried* fruits supply the place of fresh.

But the Affghan, though living on fruits, is far from being a harmless and amiable character; on the contrary, he is cruel, covetous, and treacherous. Much British blood has been shed in the valleys of Affghanistan.

We cannot blame the Affghans for defending their own country. It was natural for them to ask, "What right has Britain to interfere with us?"

A British army was once sent to Affghanistan to force the people to have a king they did not like, instead of one they did like.

I will tell you of a youth who accompanied his father to the wars.

This boy looked forward with delight to going as a soldier to a foreign land, and his heart beat high when the trumpet sounded to summon the troops to embark. Joyfully he quitted Bombay, crossed the Indian Ocean, and landed near the mouth of the Indus. When the army began its march towards Affghanistan, he rode on a pony by his father's side.

At first it seemed pleasant to pitch the tent in a new spot every day, to rest during the heat, and to travel in the dead of the night, till the sun was high in the sky. But soon this way of life was found fatiguing, for the heat was great, and the water scarce. The air, too, was clouded by the dust the troops raised in marching; and green grass was seldom seen, or a shady tree under which to rest. The food, too, was dry and stale, and no fresh food could be procured, for the Affghans, before they fled, had destroyed the corn and fruit growing in the fields, that their enemies might not eat them. The camels, too, which bore the baggage of the British army, grew ill from heat and thirst; for it is not true that camels can live *long* without water; in three or four days they die. Besides this, the hard rocks in the hilly country hurt their feet, and hastened their death. Many a camel died as it was seeking to quench its thirst at a narrow stream in the valley, and its dead body falling into the water, polluted it. Yet this water the soldiers drank, for they had no other, and from drinking it they fell ill. The father of the youthful soldier was one of these, and he was compelled to stop on the way for several weeks; and because the heat of a tent was too great, he took shelter in a ruined building. Here his son nursed him with a heavy heart. Where was the delight the youth had expected to find in a soldier's life?

At last the British army reached a strong fort built on the top of a hill; Guznee was its name. Its walls and gates were so strong that it seemed impossible to get into the city; yet the British knew that if they did *not*, they must die either by the Affghan sword, or by hunger and thirst among the rocks. For some time they were much perplexed and distressed. At last a thought came into the mind of a British captain, " Let us blow up the gates with gunpowder." The plan was good; but how to perform it, there was the difficulty. Soon all was arranged. In the night some sacks of gunpowder were laid very softly against the gates; but as no one could set fire to the sacks when *close* to them, a long pipe of cloth was filled with gunpowder, and stretched like a serpent upon the ground; one end of the pipe touched the sack, and the other end was to be set on fire. But before the match was applied, a British officer peeped through a chink in the gates to see what the Affghans were doing within. Behold! they were quietly smoking and eating their supper, not suspecting any danger! The match was applied—the gunpowder exploded, and the strong gates were shattered into a thousand pieces; the army rushed in sword in hand, and the Affghans fled in wild confusion.

Where was our young soldier? He was running into the fort between two friendly soldiers, who kindly helped him on; each of them was holding one of his arms, and assisting him to keep up with the troops, rushing through the gates. As he ran, he heard horrible cries, but the darkness hindered him from seeing the dying Affghans rolling in the dust, only he felt their soft bodies as he hastily passed over them. He heard his fellow-soldiers shouting and firing on every side. Some fell close beside him, and others were wounded, and carried off on the shoulders of their comrades, screaming with agony.

Half an hour after the gates were fired, the city was taken. The news of the victory spread among the Affghans on the mountains and the plains, and the whole country submitted to the British.

The army soon marched to Cabool, that proud city. No one opposed their entrance, and the bazaar, and the king's garden, and the royal citadel, were visited by our soldiers.

After spending two months in beautiful Cabool, resting their weary limbs and feasting on fine fruits, the army was ordered to return home. They began to march again towards the coast, a distance of fifteen hundred miles, over cragged rocks and scorching plains.

In the course of this terrible journey, the father of the young soldier again fell ill, and was forced to stop by the way. His affectionate son nursed him night and day; closed his eyes in death, and saw him laid in a lowly grave in the desert. With a bleeding heart the youth embarked to return to Bombay.

During the voyage a furious storm arose, and all on board despaired of life. *Then* it was the youth remembered the prayers he had offered up by his dying father's bed; *then* it was he felt he had not turned to God with all his heart; and *then* it was he vowed, that if the Lord would spare him this *once*, he would seek his face in truth. God heard and spared.

And did the youth remember his prayers and vows? He did,—though not at *first*,—yet after a little while he *did*. He read the *word* of God, he prayed for the *Spirit* of God, and at length

he enjoyed the *peace* of God; and now he
neither fears storm nor sword, because Christ is
his shelter and his shield.

BELOOCHISTAN.

Beloochees.

JUST underneath Affghanistan lies Beloochistan,
by the sea coast. It is separated from India by
the river Indus. You may know a Beloochee
from an Affghan by his stiff red cotton cap, in
the shape of a hat without a brim: whereas, an
Affghan wears a turban. Yet the religion of
the Beloochee is the same as that of the Affghan,
namely the Mahomedan; and the character is
alike, only the Beloochee is the fiercer of the two:
the country also is alike, being wild and rocky.

Beloochistan has *not* been conquered by the British; it has a king of its own.

BURMAH.

Of all the kings in Asia, the king of Burmah is the greatest, next to the emperor of China. He has not indeed nearly as large a kingdom, or as many subjects, as that emperor; but, like him he is worshipped by his people. He is called " Lord of life and death," and the " Owner of the sword," for instead of holding a *sceptre* in his hand, he holds a golden sheathed *sword*. A sword indeed suits him well, for he is very cruel to his subjects. Nowhere are such severe punishments inflicted. For drinking brandy the punishment is, pouring molten lead down the throat; and for running away from the army, the punishment is, cutting off both legs, and leaving the poor creature to bleed to death. A man, for choosing to be a Christian, was beaten all over the body with a wooden mallet, till he was one mass of bruises; but before he died he was let go.

Every one is much afraid of offending this cruel king. The people tremble at the sound of his name; and when they see him they fall down with their heads in the dust. The king makes any one a lord he pleases, yet he treats even his

lords very rudely. When displeased with them
he will hunt them out of the room with his drawn
sword. Once he made forty of his lords lie
upon their faces for several hours, beneath the
broiling sun, with a great beam over them to keep
them still. It was well for them that the king did
not send for the men with spotted faces. Who
are those men? The executioners. Their faces
are always covered with round marks tattooed in
the skin. The sight of these spotted faces fills
all the people with terror. Every one runs away
at the sight of a spotted face, and no one will
allow a man with a spotted face to sit down in
his house. In what terror the poor Burmese
must live, not knowing when the order for death
will arrive! Yet the king is so much revered,
that when he dies, instead of saying, "He is
dead," the people say, "He is gone to amuse himself in the heavenly regions."

The king has a great many governors under
him, and they are as cruel as himself. A missionary once saw a poor creature hanging on a cross.
He inquired what the man had done, and finding
that he was not a murderer, he went to the governor to entreat him to pardon the man. For
a long time the governor refused to hear him: but
at last he gave him a note, desiring the crucified
man to be taken down from the cross. Would
you believe it? the Burmese officers were so cruel

that they would not take out the nails, till the missionary had promised them a *piece of cloth* as a reward! When the man was released, he was nearly dead, having been seven hours bleeding on the cross : but he was tenderly nursed by the missionary and at last he recovered. Yet all the agonies of a cross had not changed the man's heart, and he returned to his old ways of life as a thief. Had he believed in that Saviour who was nailed to a cross for his sins, he would, like the dying thief, have repented.

Though the Burmese are so unfeeling to each other, they think it wrong to kill animals, and never eat any meat, except the flesh of animals that have died of themselves. Even the fishermen think they shall be punished hereafter for catching fish ; but they say, " We must do it, or we shall be starved." You may be sure that such a people must have some false and foolish religion ; and so they have, as you will see.

RELIGION.—It is the religion of Buddha. This Buddha was a man who was born at Benares, in India, more than two thousand years ago ; and people say, that for his great goodness he was made a *boodh,* or a god. Yet the Burmese do not think he is alive now ; they say he is resting as a reward for his goodness. Why, then, do they pray to him, if he cannot hear them ? They pray because they think it is

very good to pray, and that they shall be rewarded for it some day.   What reward do they
expect ?   It is this—to *rest* as Buddha does—
to sleep for ever and ever.   This is the reward·
they look for.   Every one in Burmah thinks he
had been born a great many times into the
world,—once as an insect,—then as a bird,—
then as a beast; and he thinks that because he
was very good,—as a reward he was made a *man.*
Now he thinks that if he is very good as a *poor*
man, he shall be born next time the son of a *rich*
man ; and that at last he will be allowed to rest
like Buddha himself. What is it to be good ? The
Burmese say that the greatest goodness is making an idol, and next to that, making a pagoda.
You know what an idol is, but do you know
what a pagoda is ?   It is a house, with an idol

Burmese Pagoda.

hidden inside; but it has no door, nor window, therefore no one can get into a pagoda. Some pagodas are very large, and others very small. As it is thought so very good to make idols and pagodas, the whole land is filled with them; the roads in some places are lined with them; the mountains are crowned with them.

Next to making idols and building pagodas, it is considered good to make offerings. You may see a father climbing a steep hill to reach a pagoda, his little one by his side, and plucking green twigs as he goes. He reaches the pagoda and strikes the great bell, then enters the idol-house near the pagoda, and teaches his young child how to fold its little hands, and to raise them to its forehead, while it repeats a senseless prayer; then leaving the green twigs at the idol's feet, the father descends with his child in his arms. How many little ones, such as Jesus once took in His arms, are taught every day to serve Satan!

The people who are thought the best in Burmah are the priests. Any one who pleases may be a priest. The priests pretend to be poor, and go out begging every morning with their empty dishes in their hands; but they get them well filled, and then return to their handsome house, all shining with gold, in which they live together in plenty and in pride. They are expected to dress in rags, to show that they are poor; but, not liking rags, they cut up cloth in little pieces, and sew the pieces together to make their yellow robes; and this they call wearing rags. They pretend to be so modest, that they do not like to show their faces, and so hide them with a fan

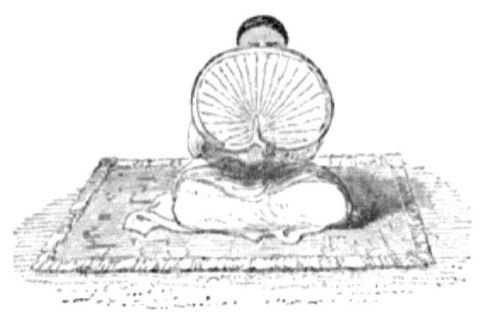

Burmese Priest preaching.

even when they preach; for they *do preach* in their way, that is, they tell foolish stories about Buddha. The name they give him is Guadama, while the Chinese call him Fo. They have five hundred and fifty stories written in their books about him; for they say he was once a bird, a fly, an elephant, and all manner of creatures, and was so good, whatever he was, that at last he was born the son of a king.

CHARACTER.—The Burmese are a blunt and rough people. They are not like the Chinese and the Hindoos, ready to pay compliments to strangers. When a Burmese has finished a visit, he says, "I am going," and his friend replies,

"Go." This is very blunt behaviour. But all blunt people are not sincere. The Burmese are very deceitful, and tell lies on every occasion indeed, they are not ashamed of their falsehoods. They are also very proud, because they fancy they were so good before they were born into this world. When they do kind actions, it is in the hope of getting more merit, and this bad motive spoils all.

They are kind to travellers. In every village there is a pretty house called a Zayat, where travellers may rest. As soon as a guest arrives, the villagers hasten to wait upon him;—one brings a clean mat, another a jug of water, and a third a basket of fruit. But why is all this attention shown? In the hope of getting merit.

The Burmese resemble the Chinese in their respect to their parents. They are better than the Chinese in their treatment of their children, for they are kind to the *girls* as well as to the boys; neither do they destroy any of their infants. They are temperate also, not drinking wine,— having only two meals in the day, and then not eating too much. In these points they are to be approved. They are, however, very violent in their tempers; it is true they are not very easily provoked, but when they are angry they use very abusive language. Thus, you see, they are by no means an amiable people.

APPEARANCE.—In their persons they are far less pleasing than the Hindoos; for instead of *slender* faces and figures, they have broad faces and thick figures. But they have not such dark complexions as the Hindoos.

They disfigure themselves in various ways. To make their skins yellow, they sprinkle over them a yellow powder. They also make their teeth black, because they say they do not wish to have white teeth, like dogs and monkeys. They bore their ears, and put bars of gold, or silver, or marble through the hole.

The women wear a petticoat and a jacket. The men wear a turban, a loose robe, and a jacket; they tie up their hair in a knot behind, and tattoo their legs, by pricking their skin, and then putting in black oil. They have the disagreeable custom of smoking, and of chewing a stuff called " coon," which they carry in a box.

Every one (except the priests) carries an umbrella, to guard him from the sun; the king alone has a white one; his nobles have gilded umbrellas; the next class have red umbrellas; and the lowest have green.

FOOD.—Burmah is a pleasanter country than Hindostan, for it is not so hot, and yet it is as fruitful. The people live chiefly upon rice; but when they cannot get enough, they find abundance of leaves and roots to satisfy their hunger.

ANIMALS.—There are many tigers, but no lions. The Burmese are fond of adorning their houses with statues of lions; but never having seen any, they make very strange and laughable figures. The pride of Burmah is her elephants, but they all belong to the king, and none may ride upon one but himself and his chief favourite. Carriages are drawn by bullocks, or buffaloes;

Burmese Gentleman in a Bullock-Carriage.

and there are horses for riding; so the Burmese can do very well without the elephants. The king thinks a great deal too much of these noble animals. There was a white elephant that he delighted in so much, that he adorned it with gold and jewels, and counted it next to himself in rank, even above the queen.

HOUSES.—The Burmese build their houses on posts, so that there is an empty place under the floors. Dogs and crows may often be seen walking under the houses, eating whatever has fallen through the cracks of the floor.

The king allows none but the nobles to build houses of brick and stone; the rest build them of bamboos. This law is unpleasant; but there is another law which is a great comfort to the poor. It is *this;*—any one may have land who wishes for it. A man has only to cultivate a piece of spare land, and it is counted his, *so long* as he continues to cultivate it; therefore all industrious people have gardens of their own.

THE KARENS.

Among the mountains of Burmah, there are a wild people called the Karens, very poor and very ignorant; yet some have attended to the voice of the missionaries. They are not so proud as the Burmese; for they have no gods at all, and no books at all : they have not filled their heads with five hundred and fifty stories about Gaudama; therefore they are more ready to listen to the history of Jesus.

The Karens live in houses raised from the ground, and so large is the place underneath, that they keep poultry and pigs there. Every year they move to a new place, and build new houses, clear a new piece of ground, by burning the weeds,—then dig it up, and sow rice. Thus they wander about, and they number their years by the number of houses they have lived in.

Of all the Eastern nations, they sing and play the most sweetly, and when they become Christians, they sing hymns very sweetly indeed.

There is one Christian village among the mountains, called Mata, which means "Love;" and every morning the people meet together in the Zayat, or travellers' house, to sing and pray. Before they were Christians, the Karens were in constant fear of the Nats (not *insects*, but evil spirits); and sometimes, in order to please their Nats, they were so cruel as to beat a pig to death. The Christian Karens have left off such barbarous practices, and have become kind and compassionate. When the missionaries told them that they ought to love one another, some of them went secretly the next day to wait upon a poor leper, and upon a woman covered with sores. Another day, without being asked, they collected some money and brought it to the missionaries, saying they wished to set free a poor Burman who had been imprisoned for Christ's sake. It is cheering to the missionaries to see them turning from their sins.*

AVA.

This city was once the capital of Burmah, and then it was called the "golden city." But

---

* Taken from "Travels in Eastern Asia." By the Rev. Howard Malcolm.

now the king lives in another city, and the
glory of Ava has passed away.

MAULMAIN.

This city, though in Burmah, may be called a
British city, because the British built it; for they
have conquered great part of Burmah. There are
missionaries there. One there was named Judson, who turned more than a hundred Burmese
to the Lord. But he passed through great
troubles. His wife and his little girl shared in
these troubles.

I will now relate the history of the short life
of little Maria Judson.

THE MISSIONARY'S BABE.

The missionary's babe, little Maria, was born
in a cottage by the side of a river, and very
near the walls of the great city of Ava, where
the king dwelt.

It was a wooden cottage, thatched with straw,
and screened by a verandah from the burning
sun. It was not like an English cottage, for it
was built on high posts, that the cool air might
play beneath. It contained three small rooms,
all on one floor. The country around was
lovely; for the green banks of the river were
adorned with various coloured flowers, and with
trees laden with fine fruits.

In this pretty cottage the infant Maria was lulled in her mother's arms to sleep, and often the tears, rolling down the mother's cheeks, fell upon the babe's fair face. Why did the mother weep? It was for her husband she wept. He was not dead, but he was in prison. He was a missionary, and the king of Ava had imprisoned him in the midst of the great city. Was his wife left all alone with her babe in her cottage? No, there were two little Burmese girls there. They were the children of heathen parents, and they had been received by the kind lady into her cottage, and now they were learning to worship God. Their new names were Mary and Abby. There were also two men servants, of dark complexion, dressed in white cotton, and wearing turbans. It was a sorrowful little household, because the master of the family was absent, because he was in distress, and his life was in danger. Every day his fond wife visited him in his prison.

She leaves her babe under the care of Mary, and sets out with a little basket in her hand. After walking two miles through the streets of Ava she comes to some high walls—she knocks at the gate—a stern-looking man opens it. The lady, passing through the gates, enters a court. In one corner of the court there is a little shed, made of bamboos, and near it, upon a mat, sits a pale and sorrowful man. His countenance brightens when he perceives the lady enter. She refreshes him with the nice food she has brought in her basket, and comforts him with sweet and heavenly words ;—then hastens to return to her babe.   As soon as she enters her cottage, she sinks back, half fainting, in her rocking chair, while she folds again her little darling in her arms.   Happy babe! thy parents are suffering for Jesus—and they are blessed of the Lord, and their baby with them.

Greater sorrows still soon befell the little family.   One day a messenger came to the cottage, with the sad tidings that the bamboo hut had been torn down, the mat and pillow taken away, and the prisoner, laden with chains, thrust into the inner prison.   The loving wife hastened to the governor of the city to ask for mercy ; but she could obtain none, only she was permitted to see her husband.   And *what* a sight!   He was shut up in a room with a hundred men, and without a *window!*   Though the weather was hot, no breath of air reached the poor prisoners, but through the cracks in the boards.   No wonder that the missionary soon fell ill of a fever.   His wife fearing he would die, determined to act like the widow in the parable, and to weary the unjust judge by her entreaties.   She left her quiet cottage, and built a hut of bamboos at the governor's gate, and there she lived with her babe, and the little Burmese girls. The prison was just opposite the governor's gate, so that the anxious wife had now the comfort of being near her suffering husband. The governor was wearied by her importunity, and at last permitted her to build again a bamboo hovel for the prisoner in the court of the prison. The sick man was brought out of the noisome dungeon, and was laid upon his mat in the fresh air. He was supplied with food and medicine by his faithful wife, and he began to recover.

But in three days a change occurred. Suddenly the poor wife heard that her beloved had been dragged from his prison, and taken—she knew not where. She inquired of everybody she saw, "Where is he gone?" but no answer could she obtain. At last the governor told her that his prisoner was taken to a great city, named A-ma-ra-poora. This city was seven miles from Ava. The wife decided in a moment what to do. She determined to follow her husband. Taking her babe in her arms, and accompanied by the Burmese children and one servant, she set out. She went to the city up the river in a covered boat, and thus she was sheltered from the scorching sun of an Indian May. But when she arrived at Amarapoora, she heard that her husband had been taken to a village six miles off. To this village she travelled in a clumsy cart, drawn by oxen. Overcome with fatigue she arrived at the prison and saw her poor husband sitting in the court, chained to another prisoner, and looking very ill. He had neither hat, nor coat, nor shoes, and his feet were covered with wounds he had received, as he had been driven over the burning gravel on the way to the prison; but his wounds had been bound up by a kind heathen servant, who had torn up his own turban to make bandages.

When the missionary saw his wife approaching with her infant, he felt grieved on her account, and exclaimed, "Why have you come? You cannot live here?" But she cared not where she lived, so that she could be near her suffering husband. She wished to build a bamboo hut at the prison gate; but the jailor would not allow her. However, he let her live in a room in his own house. It was a wretched room, with no furniture but a mat. Here the mother and the children slept that night, while the servant, wrapped in his cloth, lay at the door. They had no supper that night. Next day, they bought food in the village, with some silver that the lady kept carefully concealed in her clothes.

A new trouble soon came upon them. Mary was seized with a small-pox of a dreadful sort. Who now was to help the weak mother to nurse the little Maria? Abby was too young to help.

The babe was four months old, and a heavy burden for feeble arms; yet all day long the mother carried it, as she went to and fro from the sick child to the poor prisoner. Sometimes, when it was asleep, she laid it down by the side of her husband. He was able to watch a babe asleep, though not to nurse a baby *awake*, owing to his great weakness and to his mangled feet.

Soon the babe herself was attacked by the small pox, and continued very ill for three months. This last trial was too much for' the poor mother. Her strength failed her, and for many weeks she lay upon her mat unable to rise. She must have perished, if it had not been for the faithful servant. He was a native of Bengal, and a heathen. Yet he was so much concerned for his sick mistress and imprisoned master, that he would sometimes go without food all day, while he was attending to their wants; and he did all—without expecting any wages.

The poor little infant was in a sad case, now its mother was lying on the mat. It cried so much for milk, that once its father got leave to carry it round the village, to ask the mothers who had babes to give some milk to his. By this plan, the little creature was quieted in the day, but at night its cries were most distressing.

The time at length arrived when these trials were to end. The king sent for the missionary, *not* to put him to death, as he had once intended, but to ask for his help. What help could he render to the king? The reason why the missionary had been imprisoned so long was, that a British army had attacked Burmah. The king had feared lest the missionary should take part with the enemy, and *therefore* he had shut him up. Now there were hopes of peace, and an interpreter was wanted to help the Burmese to speak with the British. The missionary knew both the English language and the Burmese, and he could explain to the king what the English general would say.

For this purpose he was brought to Ava. He was not now driven along the road like a beast, but relieved from his chains, and treated tolerably well. Yet he was still a prisoner.

The mother was now well enough to make a journey, though very weak. She returned to her cottage by the river side, and soon she had the delight of seeing her husband ENTER IT. It was seventeen months since he had been torn from it by the king's officers, and during all that time he had been groaning in irons. But he was not now allowed to remain in his cottage, but only to obtain a little food and clothing to take with him to the Burmese camp.

No sooner was he gone than his wife was seized with that deadly disease called spotted fever. What now would become of little Maria. Through the tender mercy of God, on the very day the mother fell ill, a Burmese woman offered to nurse the babe. Every day the mother grew worse, till at last the neighbours came in to see her die. As they stood around, they exclaimed in their Burmese tongue, "She is dead, and if the king of angels should come in, he could not recover her." *Their* king of angels could *not*, but *her* KING OF ANGELS could, for He can raise the dead. But this dear lady was *not* dead, though nearly dead.

The Lord of life showed her mercy. A friend entered the sick chamber. It was Dr. Price, a missionary and a prisoner, who had obtained leave from the king to visit the sick lady. He understood her case, and he ordered her head to be shaved, and blisters to be applied to her feet. From that time she began to recover, and in a month she had strength to stand up. The governor, who had once been so slow to hear her complaints, now sent for her to his house. He received her in his kindest manner. What was her joy when she found her husband there, not as a prisoner, but as a guest ! Many prayers had she offered up during her long illness, and they were now answered. The promise she had trusted in was fulfilled. This was *that* promise : "Call upon me in the day of trouble, and I WILL DELIVER THEE, and thou shalt glorify me."

But still brighter days were at hand. The king of Burmah had made peace with the British, and had agreed to deliver the missionaries into their hands. Glad, indeed, were they to escape from the power of the cruel monarch. Little Maria and her parents, as well as Mary and Abby, were conveyed in a boat down the river to the place where the English army had encamped. The English general received them with fatherly kindness, and gave them a tent to dwell in near his own. What a fortnight they spent in that tent ! It was a morning of joy, after a night of weeping. Little Maria was now, for the first time, dwelling with *both* her parents.

Soon afterwards she was taken to a new home in a town in Burmah, built by the English, called Amherst.* Here the missionary might teach the Burmese to know their Saviour, without being under the power of the cruel Burmese king.

It seemed as if the little family, so long afflicted, were now to dwell in safety, and to labour in comfort. But there is a rest for the

---

* Amherst is only thirty miles from Maulmain.

people of God, and to this rest one of this family was soon removed.

The missionary determined to go to Ava, to plead with the king for permission to teach his subjects. He parted from his beloved wife, little thinking he should never see her again.

During her husband's absence, she watched with deep anxiety over her little Maria. The child was pale, and puny, yet very affectionate and intelligent. Whenever her mamma said, "Where is dear papa gone?" the little creature started up, and pointed to the sea. She could not speak plainly, being only twenty months old.

Not long did she enjoy her mother's tender care. The poor mother, worn with her past watching and weeping, was attacked by fever. As she lay upon the bed, she was heard to say, "The teacher is long in coming, I must die alone, and leave my little one ; but as it is the will of God, I am content."

She grew so ill, that she took no notice of anything that passed around her ; but even then she called for her child, and charged the nurse to be kind to it, and to indulge it in everything till its father returned. This charge she gave, because she knew the babe was sick, and needed the tenderest care. At last the mother lay without moving, her eyes closed, and her head resting on her arm. Thus she continued for two days, and then uttered one cry, and ceased to breathe. Her illness had lasted eighteen days. Then she rested from her labours, and slept in Jesus.

What now became of little Maria? A missionary and his wife came to Maria's home, and took charge of the child. Maria fancied that kind Mrs. Wade was her own mother.

What a day it was when the poor father returned home! No wife to meet him, with love and joy; only a sickly babe, who had forgotten him, and who turned from him with alarm. Where could he go to but the grave, to weep there?

Little Maria was nursed with a mother's care, though not in a mother's arms; but her delicate frame had been shaken by her infant troubles, and care and comforts came TOO LATE. After drooping day by day, she died at the age of two years and three months, exactly six months after her mother. Her father was near, to close her faded eyes, and fold her little hands on her cold breast, and then to lay her in a little grave, close beside her mother's, under the Hope Tree.

The words of the poet would suit well the case of this much-tried infant :—

> " Short pain, short grief, dear babe, were thine;
>   Now, joys eternal and divine."

Many a missionary's babe lies in an early

tomb—babes dear to the Saviour, for their parents' sakes. Their deaths are precious in His sight, and their spirits are safe in His hands.

SIAM.

CROSS a river, and you pass from Burmah to Siam. These two countries, like most countries close together, have quarrelled a great deal, and now Britain has got in between them, and has parted them: as a nurse might come and part two quarrelsome children. Britain has conquered that part of Burmah which lies close to Siam, and has called it British Burmah; so Siam is now at peace.

But though these two countries have been such enemies, they are as like each other as two sisters. Siam is the little sister. Siam is a long narrow slip of a country, having the sea on one side, and mountains on the other.

The religion of Siam is the same as that of Burmah—the worship of Buddha. But in Siam he is not called Buddha: the name given him there is "Codom." You see how many names this Buddha has: in China he is Fo; in Burmah he is Guadama; in Siam he is Codom. Neither is he honoured in Siam in exactly the same way as in Burmah. Instead of building magnificent pagodas, the Siamese build magnificent image-houses, or temples.

The Siamese resemble the Burmese in appearance, but they are much worse-looking. Their faces are very broad and flat; and so large are the jaws under the ears, that they appear as if they were swollen. Their manner of dressing their hair does not improve their looks; for they cut their hair quite close, except just on the top of their heads, where they make it stand up like bristles; nor do they wear any covering on their heads, except when it is very hot, and then they put on a hat made of leaves, in the shape of a milk-pan. They do not disfigure themselves, as the Burmese do, with nose-rings and ear-bars; but they love ornaments quite as much, and load

Siamese Woman and Children.

themselves with necklaces and bracelets. Their dress consists of a printed cotton garment, wound round the body. This is the dress of the women as well as of the men; only sometimes the women wear a handkerchief over their necks.

In disposition the Siamese are deceitful and cowardly. It has been said of them, that as *friends* they are not to be *trusted*, and as *enemies* not to be *feared :* they cannot be trusted, because they are deceitful : they need not be feared, because they are cowardly. This is indeed a dreadful character ; for many wicked people are faithful to their friends, and brave in resisting their enemies.

No doubt the manner in which they are governed makes them cowardly ; for they are taught to behave as if they were worms. Whoever enters the presence of the king must creep about on hands and knees. The great lords require their servants to show them the same respect. Servants always crawl into a room, pushing in their trays before them ; and when waiting, they walk about on their knees. How shocking to see men crawl like worms, to gratify the pride of their fellow-men! The rule is, never to let your head be higher than the head of a person more honourable than yourself; if he stand, you must sit; if he sit, you must crouch.

The Siamese are like the Burmese in cruelty.

When an enemy falls into their hands, no mercy is shown.

A king of a small country, called Laos, was taken captive by the Siamese. This king, with his family, was shut up in a large iron cage, and exhibited as a sight. There he was, surrounded by his sons and grandsons, and all of them heavily laden with chains on their necks and legs. Two of them were little boys, and they played and laughed in their cage!—so thoughtless are children! But the elder sons looked very miserable; they hung down their heads, and fixed their eyes on the ground; and well they might; for within their sight were various horrible instruments of torture;—spears with which to pierce them;—an iron boiler in which to heat oil to scald them;—a gallows on which to hang their bodies, and—a pestle and mortar in which to pound the children to powder. You see how Satan fills the heart of the heathen with his own cruel devices. The people who came to see this miserable family rejoiced at the sight of their misery: but they lost the delight they expected in tormenting the old king, for he died of a broken heart; and all they could do *then* was to insult his body: they beheaded it, and then hung it upon a gibbet, where every one might see it, and the beasts and birds devour it.

What became of this unhappy family is not known.

But, though so barbarous to their *enemies*, the Siamese in some respects are better than most other heathen nations, for they treat their *relations* more kindly. They do not kill their infants, nor shut up their wives, nor cast out their parents. Yet they show their cruelty in this :— they often sell one another for slaves. They also purchase slaves in great numbers ; and there are wild men in the mountains who watch Burmans and Karens to sell them to the great chiefs of Siam. It is the pride of their chiefs to have thousands of slaves crawling around them.

BANKOK.

This is the capital of Siam. It is built on an island in a broad river, and part of it on the banks of the river. It ought therefore to be a pleasant city, but it is *not*, owing to its extreme untidiness. The streets are full of mud, and overgrown with bushes, amongst which all the refuse is thrown ; there are also many ditches with planks thrown across. There is only one pleasant part of the town, and that is where the Wats are built. The Wats are the idol-houses. Near them are shady walks and fragrant flowers, and elegant dwellings for the priests. The people think they get great merit by making Wats, and therefore they take so much trouble : for the Siamese are very idle. So idle are they, that there would be very little trade in Bankok if it were not for the Chinese, who come over here in crowds, and make sugar, and buy and sell, and get money to take back to China. You may tell in a moment a Chinaman's garden from a Siamese garden ; one is so neat and full of flowers ;—the other is overgrown with weeds and strewn with litter.

The most curious sight in Bankok is the row of floating houses. These houses are placed upon posts in the river, and do not move about as boats do ; yet if you *wish* to move your house, you can do so ; you have only to take up the posts, and float to another place.

Besides the floating houses, there are numerous boats in the river, and some so small that a child can row them. There are so many that they often come against each other and are overset. A traveller once passed by a boat where a little girl of seven was rowing, and by accident his boat overset hers. The child fell out of her boat, and her paddle out of her hand ; yet she was not the least frightened, only surprised : and after looking about for a moment, she burst out a-laughing, and was soon seen swimming behind her boat (still upside down) with her paddle in her hand. These little laughing rowers are too giddy to like learning, and they are not at all willing to come to the missionaries' schools; but some poor children, redeemed from slavery, are glad to be there, and have been taught about Christ in these schools.*

MALACCA.

THIS is a peninsula, or almost an island, for there is water almost all round it. In shape it is something like a *dog's* leg, even as Italy is something like a *man's* leg.

The weather in Malacca is much pleasanter than in most parts of India, because the seabreezes make the air fresh. There is no rainy season, as in most hot countries, but a shower cools the air almost every day. The country, too, is beautiful, for there are mountains, and forests, and streams.

Yet it is a dangerous country to live in, for the people are very treacherous. There are many pirates among them. What are pirates? Robbers by sea. If they see a small vessel, in a moment the pirates in their ships try to overtake it, seize it, take the crew prisoners, and sell them for slaves. The governors of the land do not punish the pirates; far from punishing them

* Extracted from the Rev. Howard Malcolm's "Travels."

they share in the gains. That is a wicked land indeed, where the governors encourage the people in their sins.

Malacca has no king of her own; the land belongs to Siam, except a very small part. The inhabitants are called Malays. They are not like the Siamese in character: for instead of being cowardly, they are fierce. Neither have they the same religion, for instead of being Buddhists, they are Mahomedans. Yet they know very little about the Koran, or its laws. One command, however, they have learned, which is—to hate infidels. They count all who do not believe in Mahomed to be infidels, and they say that it is right to hunt them; they are proud of taking Christian vessels, and of selling Christians as slaves.

There are some valuable plants in Malacca. There is one which has a seed called "pepper." There is a tree which has in the stem a pith called "sago." Who collects the pepper and the sago? There are mines of tin. Who digs up the tin? The idle Malays will not take so much trouble, so the industrious Chinese labour instead. The Chinese come over by thousands to get rich in Malacca. As there is not room for them in their own country, they are glad to settle in other countries. But though the Chinese set an example of *industry*, they do not set an example of *goodness :* for they gamble, and so lose their *money :* they smoke opium, and so lose their *health ;* and they commit many kinds of wickedness, by which they lose their *souls.*

As for the Malays, they are so very idle, that when trees fall over the river and block up the way, they will not be at the trouble of cutting a way through for their boats,—but will sooner creep *under* or climb *over* the fallen trees.

The capital of Malacca is Malacca, and this city belongs to the English ; but it is of little use to them, because the harbour is not good.

SINGAPORE.

This city also belongs to the English, and it is of great use to them, because the harbour is one of the best in the world. Many ships come there to buy and to sell, and, amongst the rest, the Chinese junks. The city is built on a small island, very near the coast. There are many beautiful country-houses perched on the hills, where English families live, and there are long flights of stone steps leading from their houses to the sea.

But many of the Malays have no home but a boat hardly large enough to lie down in. There they gain a living by catching fish, and collecting shells and coral, to exchange for sago, which is their food. These men are called "Ouranglout," which means "Man of the water." Does not this name remind you of the apes called "Ourang-outang," which means, "Man of the woods?" There are ourang-outangs in the forests of Malacca, and they are more like men, and more easily tamed than any other ape. Yet still how different is the *tamest* ape from the *wildest* man! for the one has an immortal soul, and the other has none.

The Malay language is said to be the easiest in the world, even as the Chinese is the most difficult. The Malay language has no cases nor genders, nor conjugations, which puzzle little boys so much in their Latin grammars. It is easy for missionaries to learn the Malay language. When they know it they can talk to the Chinese in Malacca in this language.

I will tell you of a school that an English lady has opened at Singapore for poor Chinese girls.

THE CHRISTIAN SCHOOL-GIRLS.

The two elder girls were sisters, and were called Chun and Han. Both of them, when they heard about Jesus, believed in Him, and loved Him. Yet their characters were very different, Chun being of a joyful disposition, and Han of a mournful and timid temper. They had no father, and their mother was employed in the school to take care of the little children, and to teach them needlework; but she was a heathen.

When Chun and Han had been three years in the school, their mother wanted them to leave, and to come with her to her home. The girls were grieved at the thought of leaving their Christian teacher, and of living in a heathen home; yet they felt it was their duty to do as their mother wished. But they were anxious to be baptized before they went, if they could obtain their mother's consent. Their kind teacher, Miss Grant, thought it would be of no use to ask leave *long* before the time, lest the mother should carry her girls away, and lock them up. So she waited till the very evening fixed for the baptism. Miss Grant had been praying all day for help from God, and the two sisters had been praying together: and now the bell began to ring for evening service. Now the time was come when the mother must be asked.

"Do you know," said Miss Grant to the mother, "that the children are going to church with me?"

"Yes," replied the mother, "wherever Missie

pleases to take them." Then the lady told her of the baptism, and entreated her consent. At last the heathen mother replied, "If you wish it, I will not oppose you." Miss Grant, afraid lest the mother should change her mind, hastened into her palanquin, and the sisters hastened into theirs. Looking back the lady perceived the mother was standing watching the palanquins. Seeing this, she stopped, saying, "Nomis, why should not you come, and see what is done ?" To the lady's surprise, the mother immediately consented to come ; and so this heathen mother was present at the baptism of her daughters. Their teacher (who was their *mother in Christ*), rejoiced with exceeding joy to see her dear girls give themselves to the Lord, and to hear them answer in their broken English, "All *dis* I do steadfastly believe."

Soon after their baptism, the girls went to live in their mother's house. To comfort them, Miss Grant promised to fetch them every Sunday, to spend the day with her. She came for them at five o'clock in the morning, before it was light, and took them back at nine, when it was quite dark. If she had not fetched them herself they would not have been allowed to go.

After awhile, they were *not* allowed to go. The reason was, that the heathen mother wanted Chun to marry a heathen Chinaman. Chun

refused to commit such a sin. Then her mother
was angry, mocked her, and prevented her going
to see Miss Grant. Still Chun refused. She saw
her mother embroidering her wedding-dresses,
but she still persisted that she would not marry
a heathen, especially as she would have to bow
down before an idol at her marriage. Chun grew
very unhappy, and looked very pale ; she wrote
many letters to her kind friends, and offered up
many prayers to her merciful God. And did
the Lord hear her, and did He deliver her ? He
did. A Christian Chinaman, who had been
brought up by a missionary, heard of Chun, and
asked permission to marry her. He had never
seen her, for it is not the custom in China for
girls to be seen.

Miss Grant was delighted at the thought of
her darling Chun marrying a Christian, and she
helped to prepare for the wedding. There was
no bowing down before an idol at that wedding,
but an English clergyman read the service.
Chun's face, according to the custom, was
covered with a thick veil, and even her hands
and feet were hidden. A few days after the
wedding, Miss Grant, according to the custom,
called on the newly married. She found the
room beautifully ornamented, like all Chinese
rooms at such times, but there were two ornaments seldom seen in China—two Bibles lying
open on the table.

Chun long rejoiced that she had so firmly refused to marry a heathen. One day Miss Grant said to her, playfully, "Has your husband beaten you yet?" (for she knew that Chinamen think nothing of beating their wives). Chun replied with a sweet look, "Oh, no! he often tells me, that *first* he thanks God, and then *you*, Miss, for having given me to him as his wife."

There was another girl at Miss Grant's school named Been. Sometimes she was called Beneo, which means Miss Been, just as Chuneo means Miss Chun. Miss Grant hoped that Been loved the Saviour, and hated idols, but she soon lost her, for her parents took her to their heathen home.

After Been had been home a short time her mother died. The neighbours were astonished to find that Been refused to worship her mother's spirit, and to burn gold-paper to supply her with money in the other world. While her relations were busily occupied in their heathen ceremonies, Been sat silent and alone. Soon afterwards, her father, who cared not for her, sold her to a Chinaman to be his wife, for forty dollars.

Miss Grant heard of her sad fate, and often longed to see her, but did not know where to find her. One evening, as she was paying visits in her palanquin, she saw a pair of bright black eyes looking through a hedge, and she felt sure that they were her own Been's. She stopped, and calling the girl, saluted her affectionately. She was glad she had found out where Been lived, as she would now be able to pay her a visit.

Soon she called upon her in her own dwelling;—a poor little hut in the midst of a sugar plantation. She brought, as a present, a New Testament in English, and in large print. Been appeared delighted.

"Do you remember how to read it?" inquired Miss Grant.

"Yes, how could I forget?" Been sweetly replied.

"Well then, read," said Miss Grant.

Been read, "I am the good shepherd, and know my sheep."

"Do you understand?" inquired the lady.

"Yes," said Been, and she translated the words into Malay.

As Miss Grant was rising to depart, she observed a hen gathering her brood under her wings.

"Of what does that remind you, Been?"

"I know," said the poor girl; "I remember what I learnt at school;" and then, in her broken English, she repeated the words: "As a hen *gaderet* her chickens under her wings, so would I have *gadered de*, but *dou* wouldest not."

At this moment Been's husband came in. The girl was glad, for she wanted Miss Grant to ask him, as a great favour, to allow her to spend next Sunday at the school. The husband consented. There was a joyful meeting indeed, on that Sunday, between Been, and Chun, and Han ; nor was their affectionate teacher the least joyful of the company.*

SIBERIA.

THIS is a name which makes people *shiver*, because it reminds them of the cold. It is a name which makes the Russians *tremble*, because it reminds them of banishment, for the emperor often sends those who offend him to live in Siberia.

Yet Siberia is not an ugly country, such as Tartary. It is not one dead flat, but it contains mountains, and forests, and rivers. Neither is Siberia a country in which nothing will grow ; in some parts there is wheat, and where *wheat* will not grow *barley* will, and where *barley* will not grow *turnips* will. Yet there are not many cornfields in Siberia, for very few people live there. In the woods you will find blackberries, and wild roses, like those in England ; and *red* berries, as well as *black* berries, and *lilies* as well as *roses*.

* Extracted from the Rev. Howard Malcolm's "Travels," and from the " History of the Society for Promoting Female Education in the East," and from " Tomline's Missionary Journal."

Still it must be owned that Siberia is a very cold country; for the snow is not melted till June, and it begins to fall again in September; so there are only two whole months without snow; they are July and August.

INHABITANTS. The Russians are the masters of Siberia, and they have built several large towns there. But these towns are very far apart, and there are many wild tribes wandering about the country.

One of these tribes is the Ostyaks. Their houses are in the shape of boxes, for they are square, with flat roofs. There is a door, but you must stoop low to get in at it, unless you are a very little child; and there is a window, with fish-skin instead of light. There is a chimney, too, and a blazing fire of logs in a hole in the ground. There is a trough, instead of a dining table, and out of it the whole family eat, and even the dogs sometimes. The house is not divided into rooms, but into stalls, like those of a stable; and deer-skins are spread in the stalls, and they are the beds; each person sits and sleeps in his own stall, on his own deer-skin, except when the family gather round the fire, and, sitting on low stools, warm themselves, and talk together.

In one of these snug corners an old woman was seen quite blind, yet sewing all day, and threading her needle by the help of her tongue.

She wore a veil of thick cloth over her head, as all the Ostyak women do, and as she did not need light, she hid her head completely under it.

But though the Ostyaks are poor, they possess a great treasure in their dogs, for these creatures are useful as horses, and much more sensible. They need no whip to make them go, and no bridle to turn them the right way; it is enough to *tell* them when to set out, and to stop, or to turn, to move faster, or more slowly. These dogs are white, spotted with black; the hair on their bodies is short, but long on their handsome curling tails. They draw their masters in sledges, and are yoked in pairs. There are some large sledges in which a man can lie down in comfort: to draw such a sledge twelve dogs are necessary ; but there are small sledges in which a poor Ostyak can just manage to crouch, and two dogs can draw it. When the dogs are to be harnessed, they are not caught, as horses are, but only called. Yet they do not like work better than horses like it, and when they first set out they howl, but grow quiet after a little while.

The driver is sometimes cruel to these poor dogs, and corrects them for the smallest fault, by throwing a stone at them, or the great club he holds in his hand, or at least a snowball : if a hungry dog but stoop down to pick up a morsel of food on the road, he is punished in this

manner. Yet it must be owned that the dogs
have their faults; they are greedy, and inclined
to thieving. To keep food out of their way, the
Ostyaks build store-houses on the tops of very
high poles. The dogs are always on the watch
to slip into their masters' houses. If the door
be left open ever so little, a dog will squeeze in,
if he can ; but he does not stay *long* within, for
he is soon thrust out with blows and kicks : the
women scream at the sight of a dog in the hut,
for they fear lest he should find the fish-trough.
Yet, after long journeys, the dogs are brought
into the hut and permitted to lie down by the
fire, and to eat out of the family-trough. At
other times they sleep in the snow, and eat whatever is thrown to them. When they travel, bags
of dried fish are brought in their sledges, to feed
them by the way. The puppies are tenderly
treated, and petted by the fire; yet many are
killed for the sake of their fleecy hair, which is
considered a fine ornament for pelisses.

The Ostyaks have another and a greater
treasure than dogs; they have rein-deer. Those
who live by fishing have dogs only, but those
who dwell among the hills have deer as well as
dogs. Rein-deer are like dogs in one respect —
they can be driven without either a whip or a
bit, which are so necessary for horses. But
though they do not need the lashing of a whip,

they require to be gently poked with a long pole; and though they do not need a bit, they require to be guided by a rein, fastened to their heads; because they are not like dogs, so sensible as to be managed by speaking.

But deer are very gentle, and are much more easily driven than horses. To drive horses four-in-hand is very difficult, but to drive four rein-deer is not. The four deer are harnessed to the sledge all in a row, and a rein is fastened to the head of one; when *he* turns all the rest turn with him. Usually they trot, but they *can* gallop very fast, even downhill. When they are out of breath, the driver lets them stop, and then the pretty creatures lie down, and cool their mouths with the snow lying on the ground.

Men ride upon rein-deer; not upon their *backs*, but upon their *necks;* for their backs are weak, while their necks are strong. Riders do not mount rein-deer as they do horses,—by resting on their backs, and then making a spring, for that would hurt the poor animals; they lean on a long staff, and by its help spring on the deer's neck. But it is not easy, when seated, to keep on; *you* would certainly fall off, for all strangers do, when they try to ride for the *first* time. The Ostyak knows how to keep his balance, by waving his long staff in the air, while the deer trots briskly along. But these

rein-deer have some curious fancies; they will
not eat any food but such as they pluck themselves from the ground. It would be of no use,
at the end of a long journey, to put them in
a stable;—they would not eat; they must be let
loose to find their own nourishment, which is
a kind of moss that grows wild among the
hills.

The rein-deer after he is dead, is of as much use
to the Ostyak as when he was alive; for his
skin is his master's clothing. Both men and
women dress alike, in a suit that covers them
from head to foot; the seams are well joined
with thread made of rein-deer sinews, and the
cold is kept quite out. The Ostyak lets no part
of his body be uncovered but just his face, and
that would freeze, if he were not to rub it often
with his hands, covered over with hairy rein-
deer gloves. The women cover their faces with
thick veils. The Ostyak wears a great coat
made of the skin of a white deer; this gives
him the appearance of a great white bear. He
carries in his hand a bow taller than himself.
His arrows are very long, and made of wood,
pointed with iron. With those he shoots the
wild animals. He is very glad when he can
shoot a sable; because the Russian Emperor
requires every Ostyak to give him yearly, as a
tax, the skins of two sables. The fur of the

sable is very valuable, and is made into muffs
and tippets, and pelisses for the Russian nobles.

But without his snow-shoes the Osytak
would not be able to pursue the wild animals,
for he would sink in the snow. These shoes are
made of long boards, turned up at the end like
a boat, and fastened to the feet. What a wild
creature an Ostyak must look, when he is hunting his prey, wrapped in his shaggy white coat,
his long dark hair floating in the wind—his
enormous bow in his hand, and his enormous
shoes on his feet!

What is the character of this wild man? Ask
what is his religion, and that will show you how
foolish and fierce a creature he must be. The
Ostyak says, that he believes in ONE God who
cannot be seen, but he does not worship him
alone; he worships other gods. And such gods!
Dead men! When a man dies, his relations
make a wooden image of him, and worship it for
three years, and then **bury it**. But when a *priest*
dies, his wooden image is worshipped *more* than
three years; sometimes it is *never* buried; for
the priests who are alive encourage the people
to go on worshipping dead priests' images, that
they may get the offerings which are made to
them.

But what do you think of men worshipping
DEAD BEASTS? Yet this is what the Ostyaks do

When they have killed a wolf or a bear, they stuff its skin with hay, and gather round to mock it, to kick it, to spit upon it, and then—they stick it up on its hind legs in a corner of the hut, and worship it! Alas! how has Satan blinded their mind!

And in what manner do they worship the beasts? With screaming,—with dancing,—with swinging their swords,—by making offerings of fur, of silver and gold, and of rein-deer. These rein-deer they kill very cruelly, by stabbing them in various parts of their bodies, to please the cruel gods, or rather cruel devils, whom they worship.

Has no one tried to convert the Ostyaks to God? The Emperor of Russia will not allow Protestant missionaries to teach in Siberia. He wishes the Ostyaks to belong to the Greek Church, and he has tried to bribe them with presents of cloth to be baptized; and a good many have been baptized. But what good can such baptisms do to the soul?

The Russians do much harm to their subjects, by tempting them to buy brandy. There is nothing which the Ostyaks are so eager to obtain as this dangerous drink. On one occasion a traveller was surrounded by a troop of Ostyaks, all begging for brandy; and when they could get none, they brought a large heap of

frozen fish, and laid it at the traveller's feet, saying, "Noble sir, we present you with this."
They did get some brandy in return. Then,
hoping for more, they brought a great salmon,
and a sturgeon as long as a man. They seemed
ready to part with all they had for the sake of
brandy.

Thus you see how much harm the Ostyaks
have learned from their acquaintance with the
Russians. The chief good they have got has
been,—learning to build houses ; for once they
lived only in tents.

THE SAMOYEDES.

This tribe lives so far to the north, that they
see very little of the Russians, though they belong to the Emperor of Russia. They live close
by the Northern Sea. Imagine how very cold
it must be. The Samoyedes inhabit tents made
of rein-deer skins, such as the Ostyaks used to
live in. They are a much wilder people than the
Ostyaks. The women dress in a strange, fan-
tastic manner : not contented with a rein-deer
dress, as the Ostyaks are, they join furs and skins
of various sorts together ; and instead of veiling
their faces, they wear a gay fur hat, with lappets ;
and at the back of their necks a glutton's tail
hangs down, as well as long tails of their own hair,
with brass rings jingling together at the end.

But if their taste in *dress* is laughable, their taste in *food* is horrible, as you will see. A traveller went with a Samoyede family for a little while. They were drawn by rein-deer, in sledges, and other rein-deer followed of their own accord. When they stopped for the night, they pitched the tent, covering the long poles with their rein-deer skins, sewed together. The snow covered the ground inside the tent, but no one thought of sweeping it away. It was easy to get water to fill the kettle, as a few lumps of snow soon melted. Some of the men slept by the blazing fire, while others went out, armed with long poles, to defend the deer from the wolves. There was in the party a child of two years old, with its mother. The child was allowed to help himself to porridge out of the great kettle. The traveller offered him white sugar; but at first he called it snow, and threw it away; soon, however, he learned to like it, and asked for some whenever he saw the stranger at tea. At night, the child was laid in a long basket, and was closely covered with furs; in the same basket he also travelled in the sledge.

One day the traveller saw a Samoyede feast. A rein-deer was brought and killed before the tent door; and its bleeding body was taken into the tent, and devoured, all raw as it was, with the heartiest appetite. It was dreadful to see the Samoyedes gnawing the flesh off the bones; their faces all stained with blood, and even the child had his share of the raw meat. Truly they looked more like wolves then men.

I might go on to tell you of many other tribes; but I must be content to mention just a few.

There is a tribe living in the eastern part of Siberia, called the Yakuts, and instead of deer and dogs, they keep horses and oxen; and strange to say, they *ride* upon the oxen, and *eat* the horses. A horse's head is counted by them to be a most dainty dish. The cows live in one room, and the family live in the next with the calves, which are tied to posts by the fire, and enjoy the full blaze. You may suppose that the calves need the warmth of the fire, when I tell you that the windows of the house are made of ice, but that the cold is so great that the ice does not melt.

There is a large tribe called the Buraets. They dwell in tents. They are Buddhists. At one time the Russians allowed missionaries to go to them. There was an old man named Andang, who used to attend the services very regularly. His wife accompanied him. One Sunday the preacher spoke much of heaven and its glories. The old woman on returning to her tent, said to her husband, "Old man, I am going home to-night." Her husband did not understand her meaning: then she said, " I love Jesus Christ, and I think I shall be with him to night." She lay down in her tent that night, but rose no more. In the morning the old man found her stiff and cold. He saddled his horses, and set off to tell the missionary. "Oh, sir," said he, with tears, "my wife is gone home!" When the missionary heard the account of her death, he felt cheered by the hope that the old woman, though born a heathen, had died a Christian, and had left her tent to dwell in a glorious mansion above; for how was it that she felt no fear of death, and how was it that she felt heaven was her home? Was it not because Jesus loved her, and because she loved Jesus.*

THE BANISHED RUSSIANS.

Siberia is the land to which the Emperor sends many of his people, when they displease him. In passing through Siberia, you would often see wagons full of women, children, and old men, followed by a troop of young men, and guarded by a band of soldiers on horseback. You might know them to be the banished Russians. What is to become of them? Some are to work in the mines, and some are to work in the factories. Some are to have a less heavy punishment; they

* "Juvenile Missionary Magazine, February 1850.

are to be set free, in the midst of Siberia, to support themselves in any way they can. Gentlemen and ladies have a small sum of money allowed them by the Emperor, and they live in the towns.

These people are called in Siberia, "the unfortunates." Some of them have not deserved to be banished; but some have been guilty of crimes.

Cities.

There are a few cities in Siberia, but only a few, and they have been built by the Russians.

The three chief cities are,—

Tobolsk, on the west, on the river Oby.
Irkutsk, in the midst, on the lake Baikal.
Yarkutsk, on the east, on the river Lena.

Of these Cities,

Tobolsk is the handsomest.
Irkatsk is the pleasantest.
Yarkutsk is the coldest.

It is not surprising that Tobolsk should be the handsomest, for there the governor of Siberia resides.

A great many Chinese come to Irkutsk to trade and bring quantities of tea.

Yarkutsk is the coldest town in the world; there may be others nearer the north, but none lie exposed to such cold winds. The inhabitants scarcely dare admit the light, for fear of increasing the cold; and they make only one or two very small windows in their houses. Yet in summer vegetables grow freely in the gardens.

The Ostyaks live near the Oby.
The Bureats live near lake Baikal.
The Yakuts live near the Lena.

THE URAL MOUNTAINS.

They are full of treasures; gold, silver, iron, copper, and precious stones. They are dug up by the banished Russians, and sent in great wagons to Russia, to increase the riches of the Emperor.*

* Taken from Erman's "Travels in Siberia."

KAMKATKA.

It is impossible to look at Siberia without being struck with the shape of Kamkatka, which juts out like a short arm. It is a peninsula. A beautiful country it is; full of mountains, and rivers, and woods, and waterfalls, and not as cold as might be expected. But there are not many people dwelling in it; for though it is larger than Great Britain, all the inhabitants might be contained in one of our small towns. And why are there so few in so fine a country? Because the people love brandy better than labour. They have been corrupted by the Russian soldiers, and traders, and convicts, and they are sickening and dying away.

A traveller once said to a Kamkatdale, "How should you like to see a ship arrive here from China, laden with tea and sugar?" "I should like it well," replied the man, "but there is one thing I should like better—to see a ship arrive full of *men*; it is men we want, for our men are sick: of the twelve here, six are too weak to hunt or fish.

But the ship that would do the most good to Kamkatka is a missionary ship. The Greek

Church is the religion; but *no* religion is much thought of in Kamkatka; hunting and fishing only are cared for. Yet I fear, if missionaries were to go to Kamkatka, the Emperor of Russia would send them away.

Where there are few men, there are generally many beasts and birds; this is the case in Kamkatka.

One of the most curious animals in Siberia is the Argalis, or mountain sheep. It is remarkable for its enormous horns, curled in a very curious manner. Think not it is like one of our quiet foolish sheep; there is no animal at once so strong and so active. It is such a climber, that no wolf or bear can follow it to the high places, hanging over awful precipices, where it walks as firmly as you do upon the pavement. Sometimes a hunter finds it among the mountains, and just as he is going to shoot it, the creature disappears :—it has thrown itself down a precipice! Is it dashed to pieces? No, it fell unhurt and has escaped without a bruise; for its bones are very strong, and its skin very thick.

The bears of Kamkatka live chiefly upon fish and berries, and seldom attack men. Yet men hunt them for their skins, and for their fat. The skins make cloaks, and the fat is used for lamps; but the flesh is thrown to the dogs. Many of the bears are very thin. It is only *fat* bears that can sleep all the winter in their dens without food; *thin* bears cannot sleep long, and even in winter they prowl about for food. Dogs are very much afraid of them. A large party of travellers, who were riding in sledges drawn by dogs, observed the dogs suddenly begin to snuff the air, and lo! immediately afterwards, a bear at full speed crossed the road, and ran towards a forest. Great confusion took place among the dogs; they set off with all their might; some broke their harness, others got entangled among the trees, and overturned their sledges. But the bear did not eacape; for the travellers shot him through the leg, and afterwards through the body; and the dogs feasted on *his* flesh, instead of the bear feasting on *theirs*.

Hunting seals is one of the occupations of the Kamkatdales. Three men in sledges, each sledge drawn by five dogs, once got upon a large piece of ice near the shore. They had killed two seals upon the ice, when they suddenly perceived that the ice was moving, and carrying them out to sea. They were already too far from land to be able to get back. They knew not what would become of them, and much they feared they should perish from cold and hunger. The ice was so slippery that they were in great danger of sliding into the sea. To prevent this, they stuck their long poles deep into the ice, and tied themselves to the poles. They were driven about for many days; but one morning—to their great joy—they found they were close to the shore. They did not forget to praise God for so mercifully saving their lives; though they were so weak from want of food, as scarcely to be able to creep ashore.

CHARACTER.—The Kamkatdales are generous and grateful. A poor family will sometimes receive another family into the house for six weeks: and when the food is nearly gone, the generous host, not liking to tell his visitors of it, serves up a dish of different sorts of meat and vegetables, mixed together; the visitors know this is a sign that the food is almost exhausted, and they take their leave.

Did I say the Kamkatdales are grateful? I will give you an instance of their gratitude. A traveller met a poor boy. He remembered his face, and said, "I think I have seen you before." "You have," said the boy; "I rowed you down the river last summer, and you were so kind as to give me a skin, and some flints; and now I have brought the skin of a sable as a present for you." The traveller, perceiving the boy had no shirt, and that his skin dress was tattered, refused the present; but seeing the boy was going away in tears, he called him back and accepted it. A

Chinese servant, who was standing by, pitied so much the ragged condition of the boy, that he gave him his own thin nankin shirts.[*]

CEYLON.

THIS is one of the most beautiful islands in the world. Part of it indeed is flat—that part near Hindostan; but in the midst—there are mountains; and streams running down their sides, and swelling into lovely rivers, winding along the fruitful valleys. Such scenes might remind you of Switzerland, the most beautiful country in Europe.

The chief beauty of Ceylon is her TREES.

I will mention a few of the beautiful, curious, and useful trees of this delightful island. The tree for which Ceylon is celebrated is the CINNAMON tree, and there are groves of it extending for sixty miles along the shore, and the sweet scent may be perceived far off upon the seas. If you were to see a cinnamon tree, you might mistake it for a laurel;—a tree so often found in English gardens. Cinnamon trees are never allowed to grow tall, because it is only the upper branches which are much prized for their bark. The little children of Ceylon may often

[*] Taken from " Travels of Peter Dobell."

be seen sitting in the shade, peeling off the bark with their knives; and this bark is afterwards sent to England to flavour puddings, and to mix with medicine.

There are also groves of cocoa-nut trees on the shores of Ceylon. A few of those trees are a little fortune to a poor man; for he can eat the *fruit*, build his house with the *wood*, roof it with the *leaves*, make cups of the *shell*, and use the oil of the *kernel* instead of candles.

The JACK TREE bears a larger fruit than any other in the world;—as large as a horse's head, —and so heavy that a woman can only carry one upon her head to market. This large fruit does not hang on the tree by a stalk, but grows out of the trunk, or the great branches. This is well arranged, for so large a fruit would be too heavy for a stalk, and might fall off, and hurt the heads of those sitting beneath its shade. The outside of this fruit is like a horse-chesnut, green and prickly; the inside is yellow, and is full of kernels, like beans. The wood is like mahogany,—hard and handsome.

But there is a tree in Ceylon, still more curious than the jack tree. It is the TALPOT TREE. This is a very tall tree, and its top is covered by a cluster of round leaves, each leaf so large that it would do for a carpet for a common-sized room; and one single LEAF, cut

in three cornered pieces, will make a TENT!
When cut up, the leaves are used for fans and
books. But this tree bears no fruit till just
before it dies,—that is till it is *fifty* years old :
THEN—an enormous bud is seen, rearing its
huge head in the midst of a crown of leaves ;
the bud bursts, with a loud noise, and a yellow flower appears,—a flower so large, that it
would fill a room ! The flower turns into fruit.
THAT SAME YEAR THE TREE DIES.

PEOPLE.—And who are the people who live
in this beautiful land ?

In the flat part of the island, towards the
north, the people resemble the Hindoos, and
speak and think like them ; and they are called
Tamuls.

But among the mountains of the south a different kind of people live, called the Cingalese.
They do not speak the Tamul language, nor do
they follow the Hindoo Religion. They follow
the Buddhist religion. You know this is the
religion of the greater part of the nations. Ceylon is full of the temples of Buddha. In each
temple there is an inner dark room, very large,
where Buddha's image is kept,—a great image
that almost fills the room.

The priests in their yellow cloaks, with their
shaven heads and bare feet, may be seen every
morning begging from door to door : but *proud*

beggars they are,—not condescending to *speak,*
—but only standing with their baskets ready to
receive rice and fruit; and the only thanks they
give—are their blessings.

There is another worship in Ceylon, and it is
more followed than the worship of Buddha, yet
it is the most horrible that you can imagine. It
is the worship of the DEVIL! Buddha taught,
when he was alive, that there was no God, but
that there were many devils: yet he forbad
people to worship these devils; but no one minds
what he said on the point.

There are many *devil-priests.* When any one
is sick, it is supposed that the devil has caused
the sickness, and a devil-priest is sent for. And
what can the priest do? He dances,—he sings,
—with his face painted,—small bells upon his
legs, and a flaming torch in each hand; while
another man beats a loud drum. He dances—
he sings—all night long,—sometimes changing
his white jacket for a black, or his black for a
white,—sometimes falling down, and sometimes
jumping up,—sometimes reeling, and sometimes
running,—and all this he does to please the
devil, and to coax him to come out of the sick
person. This is what he *pretends,*—but in *reality*
he seeks to get money by his tricks. The people
are very fond of these devil-dancers; it *tires*
them to listen to the Buddhist priests, mum-

bling out of their books, the five hundred and fifty histories of Buddha; but it *delights* them to watch all night the antics of a devil-priest.

What is the character of these deceived people? They are polite and obliging, but as deceitful as their own priests. They are not even *sincere* in their wrong religion, but are ready to *pretend* to be of any religion which is most convenient. The Portuguese once were masters of Ceylon, and they tried to make the people Roman Catholics. Then the Dutch came, who tried to force them to be Protestants. Many infants were baptized, who grew up to be heathen priests. Now the English are masters of Ceylon; they do not *oblige* the people to be Christians, yet many pretend to be Christians who are not.

A man was once asked, "Are you a Buddhist?"

"No," he replied.

"Are you a Mahomedan?"

"No."

"Are you a Roman Catholic?"

"No."

"What is your religion?"

"Government religion."

Such was his answer. This man had no religion at all,—he only wished to obtain the favour of the governor. But will he obtain the favour of the Governor of the world, the King of kings ?

We have said nothing yet about the appearance of the Cingalese. Both men and women wear a piece of cloth wound round their waists, called a *comboy ;* but they do not, like the Hindoos, twist it over their shoulders ; they wear a jacket instead. Neither do the men wear turbans, as in India, but they fasten their hair with a comb, while the women fasten theirs with long pins. The Cingalese ladies and gentlemen imitate the English dress, especially when they come to a party at the English governor's house. Then they wear shoes and stockings instead of sandals ; the gentlemen contrive to place a hat over their long hair, by first taking out the combs ; yet they still wind a *comboy* over their English clothes. The Hindoos do not thus imitate the English, for they are too proud of their own customs. Hindoo ladies never go into company ; but Cingalese ladies may be seen at parties, arrayed in coloured satin jackets, and adorned with golden hair-pins, and diamond necklaces.

You have heard of the foolish ideas the Hindoos entertain about castes. It is the Brahmin priests who teach *them* these opinions. The Buddhist priests say nothing about castes ; yet the Cingalese have castes of their *own* ; but not the *same* castes as the Hindoos. There are

twenty-one castes in all; the highest caste consists of the husbandmen, and the lowest of the
mat-weavers.

Below the lowest castes are the OUTCASTS!
The poor outcasts live in villages by themselves,
hated by all. When they meet anyone who
are not outcasts, they go as near to the hedge
as they can, with their hands on the top of their
heads, to show their respect. These poor creatures are accustomed to be treated as if they
were dogs. What pride there is in man's heart!
How is it one poor worm can lift himself up so
high above his fellow-warm, though both are
made of the same dust, and shall lie down in the
same dust together.

KANDY.

This town is built among the high mountains.
It was built there for the same reason that the
eagle builds her nest on the top of a tall rock,—
to get out of the reach of enemies. But the
proud king, who once dwelt there, has been conquered, and now England's Queen rules over
Ceylon. No wonder that the proud king had
enemies, for he was a monster of cruelty. His
palace is still to be seen. See that high tower,
and that open gallery at the top! There the
last king used to stand to enjoy the sight of his
subjects' agonies. Those who had offended him

were killed in the court below,—killed, not in a common manner, but in all kinds of barbarous ways,—such as by being cut in pieces, or by

A Chief of Kandy.

swallowing melted lead. At length the Cingalese invited the English to come and deliver them from their tyrant; the English came and shut him up in prison till he died, and now an English governor rules over Ceylon.

The greatest curiosity to be seen at Kandy is a TOOTH! a tooth that the people say was taken out of the mouth of their Buddha. It is kept in a splendid temple, on a golden table in a golden box of great size. There are seven boxes, one inside the other, and in the innermost box, wrapped up in gold there is a piece of ivory, the size of a man's thumb,—that is the tooth of Buddha ! Every day it is worshipped, and offerings of fruit and flowers are presented.

COLOMBO.

This is the chief *English* town of Ceylon, as Kandy is the chief *Cingalese* town. The English governor lives here, but he has a house at Kandy too, where he may enjoy the cool mountain air. There is a fine road from Colombo to Kandy, broader and harder than English roads ; yet it is cut through steep mountains, and winds by dangerous precipices. But there are labourers in Ceylon stronger than any in England. I mean the ELEPHANTS. It is curious to see this huge animal meekly walking along with a plank across its tusks, or dragging wagons full of large stones. Among the mountains there are herds of *wild* elephants : sometimes a hundred may be seen in one herd. There are no elephants in the world as courageous as those of Ceylon, yet they are very obedient when tamed. If you wished to visit the mountains, you might safely ride upon the back of the sure-footed elephant, and all your brothers and sisters, however many, might ride with you.

MISSIONARIES.—There are some in Ceylon,

and some of the heathen have obeyed their voice.

There was once a devil-priest. Having been detected in some crime, he was imprisoned at Kandy, and while in prison he read a Christian tract, and was converted. Thus, (like Onesimus, of whom we read in the Bible,) he escaped from *Satan's* prison, while shut up in *man's* prison. When he was set free, he was baptized by the missionary at Kandy, and he chose to be called Abraham. What name did he choose for his son, a boy of fourteen? Isaac. He buried his conjuring books, though he might have sold them for eight pounds. His cottage was in a village fifteen miles from Kandy. He had left it a *wicked* man; he returned to it a *good* man.

After some time, a Missionary went to visit Abraham in his cottage. A good Cingalese was his guide. The walk there was beautiful, along narrow paths, amidst fields of rice, through dark thickets, and long grass. No one in Abraham's village had ever seen the fair face of an Englishman; and the sight of the missionary alarmed the inhabitants. Abraham's family was the only Christian family in that place. How glad Abraham felt at the sight of the missionary,—almost as glad as the *first* Abraham felt at the sight of the three angels. When the missionary entered, Abraham was teaching his wife, for she was soon to be baptized. By what name? By the name of Sarah. There were seven children in the family. How hard it must be for Abraham to bring them up as Christians, in the midst of his heathen neighbours! Even his brothers hate him, wound his cattle, and break down his fences. Once they pointed a gun at him, but it did not go off. Abraham's comfort is to walk over to Kandy every Saturday, to worship God there on Sunday with the Christians; and he does not find fifteen miles too far for his willing feet. May the Lord preserve Abraham faithful in the midst of the wicked!

BORNEO.

This is the largest island in the world, except one. Borneo is of a different shape from our Britain; but if you could join Britain and Ireland in one, both together would not be so large as Borneo. Yet how unlike is Borneo to Britain; Britain is a Christian island. Borneo is a heathen island. Yet Borneo is not an island of *idols*, as Ceylon is. *All* heathens do not worship idols. I will tell you who live in Borneo, and you will see why there are so few idols there.

Many people have come from Malacca, and

settled in Borneo; so the island is full of Malays. These people have a cunning and cruel look, and no wonder;—for many of them are PIRATES ! It is a common custom in Borneo to go out in a large boat,—to watch for smaller boats,—to seize them,—to bind the men in chains,—and to bring them home as slaves. There are no seas in the world so dangerous to sail in as the seas near Borneo, not only on account of the rocks, but on acccount of the great number of pirates. What is the religion of Borneo? It is Mahomedanism. But the Malays do not follow the laws of Mahomed as the Turks do. They do not mind the hours of prayer, nor do they attend regularly at the mosque. This is not surprising, for they do not understand the Koran. Mahomed wrote in Arabic, and the Malays do not understand Arabic. Why do they not get the Koran translated ? Mahomet did not wish the book to be translated. Why, then, do not the Malays learn Arabic ? I wonder they do not; but I suppose they are too idle, and too careless. The boys go to school, and learn to read and write their own easy language—the Malay ; and they learn also to repeat whole chapters of the Koran, but without understanding a word. Still they think it a great advantage to know these chapters, because they imagine that, by repeating them, they can drive away evil spirits.

The Malays observe Mahomed's law against eating pork; but many of them drink wine, though Mahomed forbids it. However, they follow Mahomed in not having dancing at their feasts; indeed, their behaviour at feasts is sober and orderly, for they amuse themselves chiefly by singing, and repeating poems. They have only two meals a-day, and they live chiefly upon rice, which they eat sitting crossed-legged on the floor. They get tea from China, and drink many cups during the day, in the same way as the Chinese.

The ladies are treated like the ladies of Turkey, and shut up in their houses, to spend their time in folly and idleness.

The men scarcely work at all, but employ the slaves they have stolen at sea to labour in their fields. Their houses are not better than barns, and not nearly as strong; for the sides and roof are generally made only of large leaves. They are built upon posts, as in Siam. It is well to be out of the reach of the leeches, crawling on the ground.

The Malays dress in loose clothes, trousers, and jacket, and broad sash; the women are wrapped in a loose garment, and wear their glossy black hair flowing over their shoulders. The rich men dress magnificently, and quite cover their jackets with gold, while the ladies delight to sparkle with jewels.

BRUNI.

This is the capital. It is often called Borneo, and it is written down in the maps by this name. It is one of the most curious cities in the world; for most of the houses are built in the river, and most of the streets are only water. Every morning a great market is held on the water. The people come in boats from all the country round, bringing fruit and vegetables to sell, and they paddle up and down the city till they have sold their goods.

The Sultan's palace is built upon the bank, close to the water; and the front of his palace is open; so that it is easy to come in a boat, and to gaze upon him, as he sits cross-legged on his throne arrayed in purple satin, glittering with gold.

There is a mosque in Bruni; but it is built only of brick, and has nothing in it but a wooden pulpit; and hardly anybody goes there; though a man stands outside making a loud noise on a great drum, to invite people to come in.

THE DYAKS.

These are a savage people who inhabit Borneo. They lived there before the Malays came, and they have been obliged to submit to them. They are savages indeed. They are darker than the Malays; yet they are not black; their skin is only the colour of copper. Their hair is cut short in front, but streams down their backs; their large mouths show a quantity of black teeth, made black by chewing the betel-nut. They wear very little clothing, but they adorn their ears, and arms, and legs, with numbers of brass rings. Their looks are wild and fierce, but not cunning like the looks of the Malays. They are not Mahomedans; they have hardly any religion at all. They believe there are some gods, but they know hardly anything about them, and they do not want to know. They neither make images to the gods, nor say prayers to them. They live like the beasts, thinking only of this life; yet they are more unhappy than beasts, for they imagine there are evil spirits among the woods and hills, watching to do them harm. It is often hard to persuade them to go to the top of a mountain, where they say evil spirits dwell. Such a people would be more ready to listen to a missionary than those who have idols, and temples, and priests, and sacred books.

Their wickedness is very great. It is their chief delight to get the heads of their enemies There are a great many different tribes of Dyaks, and each tribe tries to cut off the heads

of other tribes. The Dyaks who live by the sea
are the most cruel; they go out in the boats to
rob, and to bring home, not *slaves*, but HEADS!
And how do they treat a head when they get
it? They take out the brains, and then they
dry it in the smoke, with the flesh and hair still
on; then they put a string through it, and fasten
it to their waists. The evening that they have
got some new heads, the warriors dance with
delight,—their heads dangling by their sides;
—and they turn round in the dance, and gaze
upon their heads,—and shout,—and yell with
triumph! At night they still keep the heads

Dyak with Heads.

near them; and in the day, they play with
them, as children with their dolls, talking to

PT. I   B B

them, putting food into their mouths, and the
betel-nut between their ghastly lips. After
wearing the heads many days, they hang them
up to the ceilings of their rooms.

No English lord thinks so much of his
pictures as the Dyaks do of their heads. They
think these heads are the finest ornaments of
their houses. The man who has *most* heads is
considered the *greatest* man. A man who has
NO HEADS is despised! If he wishes to be respected, he must get a head as soon as he can.
Sometimes a man, in order to get a head, will
go out to look for a poor fisherman, who has done
him no harm, and will come back with his head.

When the Dyaks fight against their enemies,
they try to get not only the heads of *men*, but
also the heads of *women* and CHILDREN. How
dreadful it must be to see a poor BABY'S HEAD
hanging from the ceiling! There was a Dyak
who lost all his property by fire, but he cared
not for losing anything, so much as for losing
his PRECIOUS HEADS; nothing could console him
for THIS loss; some of them he had cut off
himself, and others had been cut off by his
father, and left to him!

People who are so bent on killing, as these
Dyaks are, must have many enemies. The Dyaks
are always in fear of being attacked by their
enemies. They are afraid of living in lonely

cottages; they think it a better plan for a great many to live together, that they may be able to defend themselves, if surprised in the night. Four hundred Dyaks will live together in one house. The house is very large. To make it more safe, it is built upon *very high posts*, and there are ladders to get up by. The posts are sometimes forty feet high; so that when you are in the house, you find yourself as high as

House of Sea Dyaks.

the tall trees. There is one very large room, where all the men and women sit, and talk, and do their work in the day. The women pound the rice, and weave the mats, while the men make weapons of war, and the little children play about. There is always much noise and confusion in this room. There are a great many doors along one side of the long room; and each of these doors leads into a small room where a family lives; the parents, the babies, and the girls sleep there, while the boys of the family sleep in the large room, that has just been described.

You know already what are the ornaments on which each family prides itself,—the HEADS hanging up in their rooms! It is the SEA Dyaks who live in these very large houses.

The HILL Dyaks do not live in houses quite so large. Yet several families inhabit the same house. In the midst of their villages, there is always one house where the boys sleep. In this

Skull-House.

house all the HEADS of the village are kept. The house is round and built on posts, and the entrance is underneath, through the floor. As this is the best house in the village, travellers are always brought to this house to sleep. Think how dreadful it must be, when you wake in the night, to see thirty or forty horrible heads dangling from the ceiling! The wind, too, which comes in through little holes in the roof, blows the heads about; so that they knock

Head of a Dyak.

against each other, and seem almost as if they were still alive. This is the HEAD-HOUSE.

These Hill Dyaks do not often get a new head; but when they do, they come to the Head-house at night, and sing to the new head while they beat upon their loud gongs. What do they say to the new head?

"Your head, and your spirit, are now ours. Persuade your countrymen to be slain by us. Let them wander in the fields, that we may bring the heads of your brethren, and hang them up with your head."

How much Satan must delight in these prayers! They are prayers just suited to that great MURDERER and DESTROYER!

The Malays are enemies to all the Dyaks; and they have burnt many of their houses, cut down their fruit-trees, and taken their children captives. The Dyaks complain bitterly of their sufferings. Some of them say, "We do not live like men, but like monkeys; we are hunted from place to place; we have no houses; and when we light a fire, we fear lest the smoke should make our enemies know where we are."

They say they live like monkeys. But why do they behave like tigers?

An English gentleman, named Sir James Brooke, has settled in Borneo, and has become a chief of a large tract of land. His house is near the river Sarawak. He has persuaded the Sultan of Borneo to give the English a VERY LITTLE island called the Isle of Labuan. It is a desert island. Of what use can this small island be to England? English soldiers may live there and try to prevent pirates infesting the seas. If it were not for the pirates, Borneo would be able to send many treasures to foreign countries. It is but a little way from Borneo to Singapore, and there are many English merchants at Singapore, ready to buy the precious things of Borneo. Gold is found in Borneo, mixed with the earth. But I do not know who would dig it up, if it were not for the industrious Chinese, who come over in great numbers to get money in this island. Diamonds are found there, and a valuable metal called antimony.

The sago-tree, the pepper plant, and the sugar-cane, and the cocoa-nut tree are abundant.

The greatest curiosity that Borneo possesses are the eatable nests. These white and transparent nests are found in the caves by the sea shore, and they are the work of a little swallow. The Chinese give a high price for these nests, that they may make soup for their feasts.

ANIMALS.—Borneo has very few large animals. There are, indeed, enormous alligators in the rivers, but there are no lions or tigers; and even the bears are small, and content to climb the trees for fruit and honey. The majestic animal which is the pride of Ceylon is not found in Borneo; I mean the elephant.

Yet the woods are filled with living creatures. Squirrels and monkeys sport among the trees.

The leaps of the monkeys are amazing; hundreds will jump one after the other, from a tree as high as a house, and not one will miss his footing; yet now and then a monkey has a fall. The most curious kind of monkey is found in Borneo—the Ourang-Outang; but it is one of the least active; it climbs carefully from branch to branch, always holding by its hands before it makes a spring. These ourang-outangs are not as large as a man, yet they are much stronger. All the monkeys sleep in the trees; in a minute a monkey makes its bed by twisting a few branches together.

Beneath the trees—two sorts of animals, very unlike each other, roam about,—the clumsy hog, and the graceful deer. As the *largest* sort of *monkeys* is found in Borneo, so is the *smallest* sort of *deer*. There is a deer that has legs only eight inches long. There is no more elegant creature in the world than this bright-eyed, swift-footed little deer.*

JAPAN.

THIS country is like China in many respects. The people are like,—the religion is like,—and many of the laws are like.

* Taken from Keppel, Mundy, Belcher, and Marryat.

In Japan there *was* a law to prevent strangers landing on the shore; but in Japan, as well as in China, that law has lately been altered. An agreement has just been made with Britain, promising to allow our nation to land on *certain spots*, and to go as far as *thirty* miles up the country, and to build houses and churches, and to exchange our goods for theirs. This is a wonderful alteration. Curious people are anxious to know all about Japan;—and Christian people are very anxious to let Japan know all about Jesus.

There is an Emperor of Japan. He rules with great strictness, and insists on obedience to his laws. He used to make his subjects observe strictly that law about having nothing to do with strangers. There was not always such a law. Once the Spanish and Portuguese priests were allowed to live in Japan, and while they lived there, they persuaded numbers to become Roman Catholics. But at last an Emperor of Japan arose who began to be afraid lest the kings of Spain and Portugal should come and take away his country; so he began to persecute the Christians. The end of it was that ALL the Christians were murdered. Many were thrown into the yawning mouth of a fiery mountain.

After this, some Portuguese were so bold as to go to Japan, but they were put to death, and this writing was placed on their tomb:—" So long as the sun shall warm the earth, let no Christian be so bold as to come to Japan, lest he pay for it with his head: not the KING of Spain himself, nor the Christian's God."

Thus Japan shut out her SAVIOUR and her GOD!

Yet one nation got leave to come to one place in Japan. It was the Dutch. Lately, other nations also have got the same leave. The British, the French, the Russians, and the Americans may all come to Japan; but only to three places in it.

The Japanese, like ourselves, are islanders; but they have more islands than we have. We live in two islands, but they live in three.

The largest of the Japan isles is called Niphon, and is much longer than Britain, but much narrower. The two islands beneath it are much smaller than Britain. All the three together contain about as many people as the British Isles.

The capital of Niphon is Yedo, or Jeddo, and is almost as large as London.

The Emperor lives at Yedo, but no stranger is permitted to come there.

One of the places to which our ships may go is Simoda. Sailors have walked about that town, and given an account of what they saw.

It is not a very large town, but it is very neat and clean. The houses are generally one story high. There is a good reason for this; for earthquakes are frequent in Japan, and therefore it is best to have low houses. The walls are very pretty, for they are covered with stucco in the shape of diamonds,—some blue, and some white. They have no chimneys, as the houses are heated by stoves, and therefore chimneys are not required; but there are parapets and wire-work over the roof, to prevent crows alighting on it, for the streets are filled with herds of crows walking about.

There are many cities which look beautiful at a distance, but which, when you enter them, are odious and loathsome. Such is Constantinople, and such is Lisbon. But the Japanese cities are not of this kind. There are other cities where the streets are clean, but where the inside of the houses is horrible. This is the case with Lassa, in Thibet. But this is *not* the case with Japanese cities; the inside of the houses is as clean as the outside.

The floors of the houses are covered with thick white mats, about three inches thick. These mats serve for cushions to sit upon, as well as for carpets to tread upon; for the Japanese do not sit on chairs like the Chinese, but on the floor, like Hindoos. The palace is called the

"Hall of the Thousand Mats." Instead of glass, the windows are covered with white oiled silk. They are adorned with flower-pots; sometimes with natural flowers, and sometimes with artificial. The rooms are warmed in winter by charcoal in copper pans; these rest on stands with gilt legs. The ceiling, the floor, and the walls of the rooms, are covered with paper, on which are paintings of birds, perched on trees, bearing gold and silver flowers. The rooms are divided, not like ours by walls, but by large paper screens, so that they can be made larger or smaller at pleasure. The chief ornaments are large chests, beautifully painted, and elegant porcelain jars.

It may be supposed that people who live in such fine *houses* wear fine *clothes*. A Japanese gentleman dresses in a loose tunic and trousers, a sash, and a jacket, all made of fine linen, wrought with various patterns. He wears stockings of white jean, and straw sandals. The top of his head is shorn, and the remaining hair is tied together so as to cover the shorn part, and to fall down in a little tail on the forehead.

You see the head-dress of a Japanese is very different from that of a Chinese; for though both have shorn heads, the one has a *long* pigtail *behind*, and the other a *short* pigtail *before*. So precious is his pigtail to a Japanese, that if a shipwrecked sailor escapes death, on his return home he offers up his pigtail to the god of the sea, because it is his greatest treasure. Rows of these pigtails may be seen in the temples of the sea-gods.

A Japanese Gentleman.

The Japanese generally wear nothing on their shorn heads, and protect them from the sun only by an umbrella; but when they go on a journey they wear large caps of oiled paper, or of plaited grass. How unlike both Japanese and Chinese are from the Turks and Arabs, —who always cover their heads with immense turbans.

The Japanese resemble the Chinese in their love of learning. They always carry about with them a memorandum-book and a small brush of camel's hair, and a brass ink-bottle. They often take this book out to write down English words which they wish to remember; for they are very anxious to learn English, and to increase their knowledge of everything. They have a college where many sciences and languages are taught. Yet they are very ignorant, compared with the nations of Europe.

It would be well if a Japanese gentleman carried nothing more about with him than his writing materials; but alas! he carries two swords. What are they for? One is to defend his country (and that is well);—the other to KILL HIMSELF. How awful! But the Japanese are told from their childhood that it will be their duty to kill themselves whenever they shall fall into disgrace with the Emperor. Therefore they are early taught how to kill themselves in an elegant manner. At five years old they begin to learn the dreadful art. They do not really cut themselves while learning, but they learn to hold the sword in the way that they mean to do whenever the dreadful moment shall arrive for putting an end to their own lives.

Every gentleman who serves the Emperor keeps a white dress in his chest, and carries it about with him wherever he goes, that he may have it ready whenever he may want it. This is his dying dress. He waits till he receives a letter from the Emperor condemning him to death. The Emperor thinks nothing of condemning a man to death. The least fault is punished in this way.

A common man would be put to death by the executioner; but a gentleman would think it mean to let himself be killed by another, so he determines to kill himself, and to die in a glorious manner. As soon as he receives the Emperor's letter he orders his servants to prepare a feast and he invites all his friends. He appears at it dressed in his white robe of death. When the feast is over, an officer of the Emperor reads aloud the sentence of death. Then the condemned gentleman takes his sword, opens his tunic, and makes a great gash across his body: at the same moment, a servant, who stands behind him, cuts off his head. The friends look on, and behold the scene with admiration, knowing all the time, that their own turn to suffer may soon come.

As a reward for dying thus, the son of the dead man is allowed to occupy his father's place at court. But what a place to occupy! with such an awful death at the last.

About four hundred gentlemen every year,

end their lives in this manner. It is called the Hari-Kari—or happy despatch.

What a cruel government it must be that thus hurries its servants out of the world! and what a horrible religion it must be that teaches men to think it fine to destroy themselves! The religion is that of Buddha, the God of Thibet. By how many names is that Buddha known? In China he is called Fo; in Burmah, Gaudama; in Siam, Codam; and in Japan, Budso.

There is another religion in Japan called the Sintoo. It was the religion before Buddha was heard of; but now all the people have left the ancient religion to follow Buddha. And why? One reason may be, that the Sintoo religion has no idol, but an unseen God, and unseen spirits; whereas the Buddhist religion is full of idols; and people naturally like to worship what they *see.* The Sintoos have a sacred bird—it is the crane; and brass images of it are found in the temples, but not to be worshipped. Looking-glasses also are there, to signify that unseen spirits are looking down upon the worshippers.

All the Japanese temples are beautifully situated in groves of high trees, with smooth lawns in front; while the voices of sweet-toned bells, or loud tom-toms, are made to sound in honour of the gods.

The ladies of Japan are shut up in the house,

their part being divided from the rest by a painted paper screen; but many *poor* women may be seen in the streets.

The married women may be known from the rest by having teeth blackened by iron, and by having their eyebrows shorn off.

The ladies take great pains in arranging their long black hair. They paste and grease their tresses, and then roll them round a wooden pillow at the top of their heads. With this wooden pillow they sleep at night, for they only dress their hair in the morning.

There are a great many hair-dressers in Japan; for all the ladies and gentlemen have a hair-dresser every morning. It is amusing, as you walk along the streets, to see so many people at the windows having their hair dressed.

The women wear a bundle at their backs; *rich* ladies wear a very handsome silk bundle, *poor* women wear a cheap cloth bundle.

People never walk arm in arm. To see two people walking together in that way, makes the Japanese burst out into a loud laugh.

One day some Japanese ladies came to see an English lady, who was staying in their land. They brought some cakes for the English lady's little girl. They liked her yellow hair, for they themselves have such dark hair, that a light colour seems strange and beautiful. The English lady offered them chairs. The Japanese ladies were so polite that they did not like to refuse to sit down; but they found themselves so uncomfortable perched up on chairs, that they soon sat down upon the floor. Then they took out their tiny pipes and filled them with tobacco, and smoked a whiff or two. When they were asked to drink a glass of wine they consented—but afterwards made faces, and stroked their throats to show how it had burned them. The little girl by accident knocked down a glass of red wine; the ladies took out their pocket handkerchiefs to wipe up the spilt wine—these handkerchiefs were of thin white *paper*. The ladies carried a dozen in their pockets, and threw them away after using them once.

Another time the English lady went to see some Japanese ladies in their own house. She was invited to dinner. The dinner-table surprized her much, for it was nearly as low and small as one of our foot-stools. Upon it—six little cups were placed, containing pickles and sauces. The family gathered round this little table, seated on the mat-carpet of the room. A strong active maid waited upon them; she carried in one hand a great pan of rice, smoking hot; in the other hand she held a great ladle, with which she filled some little cups. The children, who were sitting on the floor, were so rude as to put their little hands into the great rice-pan. They were in the habit of behaving in this naughty way, and were seldom reproved, but *this* time the maid was displeased. She put the lid on the great pan, and placed it again on the fire, and then took the little fellows by the hand, and led them up to their mamma. The mamma was sitting on the floor with a big baby tied by a scarf to her back. Mamma found great fault with her ill-bred children, and then permitted them to have their dinner. So the maid began again to serve the rice, and now the children behaved properly.

Several dishes were placed on little tables. One was minced meat, another was fish, another —scraped radish. No one had any spoons. There were nothing but chop-sticks, to eat with, and help with. These sticks are popped into every dish, and a nice little morsel fished up, just as each person may fancy.

The Japanese much resemble the Chinese, but they are much better looking. They are not so dark, for their country is not so hot as China, neither have they such curious eyes, nor such flat noses. They are much politer also. They are also very clean, being in the habit of bathing frequently. The shopkeepers take such care of their white matting, that they like no one to step upon the platform, where they sit by the

way-side, without first taking off his straw
sandals. The Japanese are an industrious
people, as may be seen by their lacquered ware.

What is lacquer? It is varnish; and the
varnish is the gum of a plant. This varnish
is mixed with some stuff to colour it, and then
it is spread upon the article that is to be lacquered; but one coat of lacquer will not do;
each coat must be suffered to dry, and must be
well rubbed in. After five coats have been put
on, the thing is lacquered, whether it be a cup,
or a tray, or a chest or a screen, or a stand. A
lacquered cup will hold *hot* tea, and a lacquered
plate *hot* soup, without any of the lacquer
coming off; even *boiling* water will not injure
Japanese lacquer.

When strangers come to Simoda, it is usual
for the natives to prepare a bazaar. By this
means the strangers can buy Japanese curiosities
to take home to their friends. The Japanese
think nothing of turning a temple into a bazaar,
for they do not feel that kind of respect for a
place of worship that we do.

At the bazaar crapes and silks are sold; for
there are silkworms and mulberry-trees in Japan.
Porcelain, also, of the more delicate kind, and
lacquered cabinets, trays, cups, and boxes, such
as can be made nowhere else, may be seen at a
Japanese bazaar.

The climate of Japan is charming, and almost everything will grow. Wheat and grapes will not grow in very *hot* countries, but they will grow in Japan. Rice and tea will not grow in *cold* countries, but they will grow in Japan.

The flowers and the birds are beautiful. The camellia grows wild in the hedges, and mingles with the tea-plant, as the wild roses in England entwine around the blackberry brambles. The most curious poultry run wild in the woods; some have feathers more like silken hair than feathers. There are peacocks in Japan more splendid than any in India.

The chief animals are almost the same as those in England. There are no camels nor elephants. There are a few horses, but they are used only by lords and princes, and their servants, when they travel.

Oxen are the most common animals. Men ride on them, and plough with them, but do not put them in carts; for a *hand*-cart is the only wheel carriage used. Neither do they kill the oxen for beef, as the Japanese do not care much for meat.

Once when some Englishmen wanted to buy beef, the Japanese refused to sell any, saying, "We cannot kill our oxen; they work hard, and are tired; they draw the plough, and bear burdens; they do their duty, and ought not to be eaten ; but the HOGS are lazy : you may have them to eat, if you wish it."

The cows in Japan are never milked, so that the calves have all their mothers' milk, and are the happiest calves in the world. The reason of their being so well treated is, that the Japanese do not care for milk, or butter, or cheese, but are content with their tea and their rice-wine, called *saki*. They eat their hot rice-cakes without butter, and their thin slices of fried meat without any sauce. How unlike the Thibetians, who delight so much in their buttered tea !

There are very few sheep and goats ; for mutton, milk, and wool, are not wanted in Japan ; but land is wanted for rice, and corn, and turnips, and potatoes. How unlike the Japanese are to the Persians, who value mutton, and milk, and wool so much, and who would not part with their flocks for all the tea in Japan !

But is Japan a good country to live in ? By no means,—pleasant as it is. The fiery volcanoes render it dangerous. Too often earthquakes and streams of burning lava turn the towns into heaps of ruins.

Of all the mountains, the most famous is Foojee Yama. It rises like a sugar-loaf, in the midst of the low hills, and it looks like sugar, for it is as white. A beautiful sight is Foojee at all times ; and it can be seen from a great distance, whether sparkling in the sun, or over-shadowed with clouds.

But there is another reason for not living in Japan, besides the fear of being suddenly destroyed : it is the government. The Emperor (as I said before) cuts off heads for the smallest faults, and in the most cruel manner. The laws are hard to be observed, yet everyone is afraid of breaking them, lest he should be boiled, roasted, or cut in pieces.

Once, in a storm at sea, a Japanese ship was wrecked. A Russian ship was lying close by. It would have been easy for the crew of the sinking ship to leave it and to swim to the Russian ship, but they stayed in it, and sunk with it. Only two of the Japanese left their ship and clung to the Russian ship; they were taken up and saved.

"Why did not your countrymen come with you?" said the Russians; "they might have been saved as well as you."

" But they were afraid of breaking the laws : the Emperor has forbidden his subjects to go to a foreign ship; and as for us, we do not know what will become of us, though we are saved, if the Emperor hears what we have done."

What a cruel government that must be which prevents men saving their own lives.

No people are fonder of travelling than the

Japanese. The princes, who live in their fine castles are often on the road with their train of servants, either going to see the Emperor or to worship at a temple.

But they must be content to travel in their own islands. No further may they go on pain of death.

Some think this a hard law.

Two American ships had come to Japan, and were at anchor in the harbour near Simoda. Two American gentlemen had left their ship, one morning, and were walking on the sea-shore near Simoda, when two young Japanese gentlemen approached. The young men saluted the strangers, saying,—"Eh!" and bowing and bending in the Japanese fashion.

They pointed to the ships in the harbour, inquired their names, and wrote them down in their memorandum-books. Then they began to examine the watch-chain of one of the Americans. While doing this, they secretly slipped a letter into his waistcoat. The American, knowing that letters were forbidden, wished to return it; but the Japanese looked at him in such an imploring manner, that he let it remain.

At this moment two Japanese policemen came up. Their coming induced the Japanese gentlemen soon to go away, for they feared lest the policemen should report them to the government, as persons fond of talking to strangers.

The American gentlemen did not read the letter till they returned to their ship. What did the letter contain? It was long, but the meaning was as follows :—

"Two scholars from Yedo, in Japan, present this letter to the high officers who manage affairs. We have desired to travel about in the five great continents, but the laws of our country forbid us to go. But since so many ships have come into these waters, and your officers are so kind, we have decided on a plan. It is to go *secretly* on board your ships, and to be carried out to sea. When a man on foot sees another riding, would he not be glad to ride too? How much more do we,—who for our whole lives could not leave our islands, when we see you riding in the high wind and over the vast waves, —long to ride as well as you. We entreat you not to let the matter be known, lest we suffer the most dreadful punishment."

Such was the letter; but the Americans knew that it was *impossible* to grant the request.

The very night after the letter had been re-received, an officer was watching on board the largest of the American ships—when suddenly he heard a low voice, saying,—

"America! America!"

He looked and saw two young Japanese coming on deck. They seemed tired; they showed their delicate hands covered with blisters from holding the ropes, and begged to be allowed to cut off the boat by which they had come, and let it float away. But the Americans were afraid of granting the request, lest the Japanese Emperor should forbid their ships ever coming again to his islands. So that very night the sailors took the two young Japanese back to the shore.

It was hoped that no one would discover what the Japanese had done.

A few days afterwards, some American officers were walking on shore. It so happened that they heard people talking of two young Japanese confined in a cage at the back of the town. The officers went to see who they were, and, behold,—they were those two wandering youths!

When the Japanese saw the American officers, they seemed pleased, and wrote a few sentences on a piece of board, and handed it to them through the bars of the cage. This is a part of what they wrote ;

" We have been seized, and shut up for many days. The chief men treat us with disdain ; but as we have done nothing wrong, it must now be seen whether we will act like heroes. Not being satisfied with travelling about Japan, we wanted to go over the five continents ; but we are disappointed, and we find ourselves in this little cramped-up place where we can hardly eat, sit, or sleep ; nor can we get out.

> "ISAGI KOODA.
> "KWANSUCHI MANJI."

As soon as the commander of the American ships heard what had befallen his midnight visitors, he sent to the chief men of Simoda to beg for them ; but the reply was,—

"They are gone to Yedo."

"What for?" inquired the Americans.

The Japanese who had given the answer replied by drawing his hand across his throat, and then the Americans understood that the poor youths were to be beheaded.

They were foolish youths for wandering at the risk of their lives. Yet who can but wish that they had escaped from their own heathen country, for then they might have heard the Gospel!

But as that Gospel has been brought to the Chinese, so it may reach the Japanese. Nor can any laws keep out the Saviour, when His time for getting in is come ; and we believe it is even NOW come—*just* come.*

---

* Chiefly extracted from Spalding's "Japan," Belcher's "Voyage in the Saramang," and "A lady's visit to Manilla and Japan."

www.ingramcontent.com/pod-product-compliance
Lightning Source LLC
Chambersburg PA
CBHW030823110726
47900CB00006B/1715

9 783337 279172